the
CRY

BOOKS BY S.D. ROBERTSON

S.D. ROBERTSON

the CRY

bookouture

Published by Bookouture in 2024

An imprint of Storyfire Ltd.
Carmelite House
50 Victoria Embankment
London EC4Y 0DZ

www.bookouture.com

Storyfire Ltd's authorised representative in the EEA is Hachette Ireland
8 Castlecourt Centre
Castleknock Road
Castleknock
Dublin 15 D15 YF6A
Ireland

ISBN: 978-1-83525-695-4
eBook ISBN: 978-1-83525-694-7

For Kirsten

PROLOGUE

She looks up at me through drowsy, unfocused eyes. Groans like she's trying to say something, still under the effect of the drugs I gave her, it seems.

On my guard, just in case, I remove the small rucksack from my back and kneel down a short distance away from her.

'Are you okay? Have you been eating and drinking?'

'Why?' she asks in a throaty gurgle.

'Because you'll die if you don't.'

'What do you care?'

'I wouldn't have left you anything if I didn't care. This is temporary.'

'Yeah, right.' Tears course down her grubby cheeks, already hollow from the ordeal of the past few days.

I desperately want to believe that this will all be over soon. That things will return to normal for both of us. But I'm not delusional. I understand the serious nature of what I've done. What I'm still doing.

I know deep down that there's no likely way back to normality for either of us. But equally, I pray that I can pull a rabbit out of the hat and – somehow, miraculously – find a route out of this that doesn't end in tragedy.

I'm not a killer.

Am I?

ONE

FOUR DAYS EARLIER

Kate

'Danny?' she calls through the open kitchen window, for the third time.

'Yes, love?' At last, he turns around from the barbecue to give his wife a big smile and a wave. 'Everything all right?'

'Could you come here for a minute, please?'

'Sorry?' he answers eventually, having looked away for a moment, distracted by something or someone else. 'What was that, darling?'

Kate takes a sip of her wine, wishing it was better chilled, before repeating the question.

'Sure,' he calls back. 'Will do. Let me find someone to man the food for me.'

Continuing to prep the potatoes and salad, she watches through the window as he taps up their son Lucas to take over from him at the monster new barbecue he insisted on buying last week to replace their perfectly good old one. A minute or two later, via a couple of brief conversations with their assembled guests, he trips on the step into the kitchen and narrowly avoids knocking over a collection of glasses on the counter.

'Oops.'

'Careful!' Kate says. 'How many beers have you had?'

'Only a couple.' He grins like someone who's had several more. 'Come on: it *is* Saturday evening. Don't worry. Everything is under control out there. The new barbecue is amazing. So much better than the old one. I feel like a proper chef. What's up, anyway? How can I be of assistance?'

What is it with men and their love of cooking meat outdoors? Kate wonders. If only he was so enthusiastic about cooking inside for the rest of the year. That would certainly make her life easier.

'Is everyone all right for drinks, Danny?'

'Um, hold on,' he says, bobbing straight back out into the garden, where he whistles loudly to get people's attention. Then he addresses the troops: 'My lovely wife has asked me to check how everyone is doing for drinks. But rather than asking that, I'd like to remind you all of my house rule number one: make yourselves at home. There's plenty of booze in and around the utility room fridge. Don't be shy. Help yourselves to whatever you like, whenever you like. All good?'

'As long as no one else touches my Guinness,' pipes up a chuckling male voice, which Kate recognises as Adrian, their neighbour and a doctor at the village GP surgery.

'Or my Chablis,' a female voice adds with a giggle: Adrian's wife, Sarah.

'Oh, here we go,' Danny says jovially. 'Bloody hell. I might have known you two poshos would make a fuss.' He gives a dramatic, exaggerated shrug. 'Whatever. I'm not getting involved.'

'That wasn't exactly what I had in mind,' Kate tells him when he comes back inside. 'We're supposed to be hosting.'

Danny throws her a blank look. 'Eh? What are you talking about? We *are* hosting.'

Lowering her voice, Kate reminds him that when the other neighbours present today, Scott and Becky, hosted last year's summer barbecue, they were the ones pouring all the drinks. It's become an annual tradition for the three families whose homes lie adjacent to one another on the same street, with Kate and Danny's in the middle, to take it in turns to do this every August. 'Remember, Danny? There was no helping yourself then. It was all very civilised.'

'And? That's not how we roll in our house. People prefer it this way, love. Trust me. There's no waiting around with an empty glass, trying to catch someone's eye. It's fine, relax. All sorted. Anything else, or am I all right to get back to the barbecue?'

'What about the vegetarian stuff for Paige: the halloumi and so on? Have you put any of that on yet?' She knows he hasn't, because she saw it in the fridge before she called him inside.

'Oops. I still haven't got used to that.' He heads across the kitchen to get the food for their daughter, who's fresh home just a few days ago from a year travelling abroad, during which she gave up eating meat. 'Do you think she'll stay veggie for good now, or is it just a fad?'

'Why don't you ask Paige? I'm sure she'd love to answer that question.'

'Hmm.' Danny gives his wife a peck on the cheek on his way back outside. 'Maybe not. Where is she, anyway? She wasn't in the garden last time I looked.'

Kate explains that she's upstairs with Jess and Amber, Scott and Becky's two kids, who are ten and seven respectively. 'I asked her to see if she could dig out some old toys or whatever to keep them amused. They've been up there a while. I'm sure they'll be down again soon. Certainly when the food is served. Roughly how long will that be, by the way?'

Danny looks at his watch. 'Um, twenty minutes? Actually, call it half an hour, bearing in mind this veggie stuff isn't on yet.'

'What? So long?'

'Maybe less. Some of it could be ready sooner. I'm managing expectations, that's all.'

'You're not at work now,' Kate replies. 'I don't need my expectations managed, thank you very much. A plain answer, please.'

'Twenty-five minutes, then. On the nose. How's that?'

'Better.'

Later, Kate is back in the kitchen, dropping off a pile of empty plates near the sink. Paige follows her inside with her own collection of dirty dishes.

'Ah, thanks, darling,' Kate says, wincing as the sound of a drunken Danny belly-laughing cuts through the general chatter outside. 'You're a star. Come here and give me a hug. It's so lovely to have you home at last. I missed you a lot while you were away, you know. I can't believe you left me outnumbered by boys.'

It feels great to hold her firstborn child in her arms again – still her baby girl, even at twenty-one years old. 'You definitely smell a lot better than your dad and brother,' she tells her.

'Thanks,' Paige replies. 'Although you might not have said that if you'd run into me at certain points during my travels. Backpacking can be a sweaty business.'

'I'm sure, although I'd rather not imagine that. It is good to be home, right?'

'Yeah, of course.'

'Not too boring?'

'Nope.'

'What a shame Jenna wasn't able to join us for the barbecue,' Kate says, referring to Paige's best friend, Becky's younger sister.

'Yeah, I know.'

'Why couldn't she come? I asked Becky earlier, and she wasn't sure.'

'Other plans, apparently. I don't know what. She didn't go into detail.'

'Was it nice to catch up with her this afternoon, at least?'

'Yeah, I guess. It was a bit... weird. Not how I expected. She, um, seemed really distracted.'

'She has been through an awful lot lately, love,' Kate adds. 'Her mum's death will still be weighing on her mind. And you've been away for a good while. Cut her some slack. I'm sure things will be back to normal between you two in no time.'

'I hope so.'

Kate kisses Paige on the forehead and gives her a squeeze. 'Trust me. Anyway, listen, we need to get back to the business of hosting this barbecue. I'll be serving dessert in a minute. I'd ask your dad to help, but I'm not sure how useful he'd be. Could you give me a hand?'

'Sure.'

'What about your brother? Where's he?'

'Dunno. But he's had a fair bit to drink as well, so let's just sort it ourselves. It's Eton mess or ice cream, yeah? I'll ask what people want.'

'Perfect. Thanks again. Maybe you could get Jess and Amber to help too. They were hanging off your every word earlier.'

'I'm not sure that's true... but good idea.'

As Kate watches Paige head back to the garden, Becky shows up to refill some glasses. 'Delicious food,' she says. 'You've done us proud.'

'Thanks. Hope you left some room for dessert.'

'Always.'

Kate glances at the clock – 8.51 p.m.

A sudden piercing cry from somewhere outside stops her and everyone else dead in their tracks. It must only last for a few seconds, but it's so loud it cuts through everything else, demanding her attention.

What the hell?

She and Becky race out of the back door to silence; a sea of stunned, bewildered faces.

Their minds both turn to Becky's young daughters, fearing they might have hurt themselves somehow. But Jess and Amber are sprawled there on the lawn, looking as dumbstruck as everyone else.

'What's going on?' Kate demands, eyes flicking from face to face, hunting for answers. 'What was that? Was it someone here?'

She's presented with various confused expressions, murmurs and shrugs.

'Beats me,' Danny says, scratching his head.

Kate watches as Becky first checks on her girls and then walks the perimeter of the garden, peering inquisitively over the fence in all directions, before shaking her head. 'Nothing to see. Weird. Everyone's here who should be, right? We're all accounted for?'

Becky glares at Scott, who puts down his beer and stands up to scan the gathering. 'Yes, we're all here.'

Soon everyone is on their feet, looking around, muttering theories to one another.

Kate sends her son, Lucas, to the front of the house to see if anything untoward is going on there. But the twenty-year-old, who's tall and brawny these days, with a fresh skin-fade haircut she can't wait to grow out, soon returns. 'Nothing to see,' he says. 'No one around. I reckon it was just kids messing about.'

'Do you think?' Kate says. 'It sounded so... urgent. Desperate even. What if—'

'Oh, Lucas is probably right,' Sarah chips in, rolling her eyes. 'I really wouldn't worry, Kate. You know what young ones can be like, especially the lads. We'll hear them again in a minute, I expect.'

But she's wrong about that. The cry isn't repeated after that one disturbing time.

It probably *was* kids messing around, Kate reflects. But a part of her remains unsure, on edge.

TWO

Adrian

'Bloody hell. That was a bit freaky, wasn't it, mate?' Danny says, walking over to him in the garden while opening a fresh can of beer. 'It gave me a proper fright. Enough to drive a man to drink.'

'Ah, it'll be something and nothing.' Adrian sips his stout. 'Probably what Lucas said... kids fooling about.'

'Yeah, I guess so.'

He nods. 'It doesn't seem five minutes ago that our own kids were young enough to do that kind of thing. They were a noisy lot when they wanted to be, playing in the garden or out in the street on their bikes, rollerblades, skateboards, etc. Now look at them, all grown up.'

Danny rolls his eyes. 'I know. Makes you feel old, doesn't it? Paige seems so mature after a year standing on her own two feet abroad. How's your Zack doing? Shame he couldn't make it this evening.'

'He's fine. Out with his girlfriend – sorry, fiancée – tonight.'

'Erin?'

'That's right.'

'When's the wedding? That could get expensive.' He nudges Adrian and winks. 'Not just down to the bride's parents these days, you know. At least Zack's an only child.'

Adrian gulps at the thought of this. Such a big expense is the absolute last thing he needs right now. Although, in truth, he's not convinced the wedding will ever actually happen. It was all very out of the blue when Zack announced the engagement in the first place. 'They've, um, not set a date yet.'

Paige appears, asking for their dessert orders, at which point Scott joins them too, leaving Becky and Sarah to continue some other discussion that Adrian's not close enough to overhear.

'So, two Eton mess, one ice cream?' Paige says.

'That's right,' Danny tells his daughter. 'Are you and your mum okay, or do you need a hand?'

'We're fine for now, thanks, Dad.' She heads for the kitchen before turning back and winking. 'We're saving all the washing-up for you and Lucas.'

The three men move on to other matters, like sport, drinking and eating dessert, while Jess and Amber have a handstand competition. The chilling sound that briefly interrupted everyone's fun is pushed to the backs of their minds, almost like it never happened.

But it did happen – and Adrian returns to thinking about it as Scott and Danny debate whether Japanese whisky is as good as or better than Scotch.

It got under his skin, that dreadful, spine-chilling sound, whatever it was. More than he lets on. It cut through him and his guilty conscience like a harbinger of something terrible to come.

THREE

From: Jen501
To: Mr888
Re: Yesterday

I can't stop thinking about yesterday. I barely slept last night.
I know you said not to mention it here, but my head will
explode if I don't. No one will see these emails apart from us.
That's why we communicate this way, right? Still, I know how
you worry. I appreciate you have a lot to lose. So I'll be
careful what I write, I promise.

Since getting home, I keep going over and over what
happened. I can't escape that image. I'm haunted by it.
Whenever I close my eyes, that's what I see. Don't you feel
the same? What we did was unspeakably bad. I can't believe
we just left like that. I still don't see why we couldn't have
made an anonymous phone call or something. I keep
wanting to check the news, but I daren't. I'm terrified I'll find
what I'm looking for.

We have to talk again in person. Soon. I know you said it
would be best if we didn't… for a while, at least. And I do get
why you said that. But I'm not sure I can live alone with the
guilt. I miss you. It was incredible having all that alone time.
Being able to act like a normal couple for once, away from
prying eyes, no need for secrecy. Spending two whole nights
in bed together. Waking up in each other's arms. It felt so
right.

And then this catastrophe struck its hammer blow, shattering
our happy interlude into rubble, like a punishment from
above.

I need you to hold me in your arms again and tell me everything's going to be okay. Please, please reply soon.

Sending all my love.

X

FOUR

Paige

I'm the first one up on Sunday morning, and although Mum and I did make a brief start on cleaning up the barbecue mess last night, the kitchen remains a tip.

'We're not doing all of this by ourselves now,' Mum said. 'We'll leave it till the morning and make sure your dad and Lucas pull their weight.'

I sigh before making myself a cuppa and heading through to the lounge. There's no point cracking on with the washing-up, although a part of me is tempted. The inevitable noise would only wake up the others and make them grumpy with me.

I've been back in the UK for almost five days and I'm still struggling with the jet lag. It's late afternoon in Sydney now. Weird. That was the city from which I flew out of Australia, having lived and worked in various temp roles there for the previous three months. I really miss it, although I'm not shouting about that to my family. Not just Sydney either: Australia as a whole, or at least the parts I visited in my twelve months travelling solo around the country. And the backpacker lifestyle, of course. I definitely miss that. It was so liberating. Living out of one bag. Standing on my own two feet without any of the usual support nets. Moving on whenever I got bored or unhappy. Meeting new people on a daily basis.

I did consider travelling further, rather than coming home once my working holiday visa expired. A dip into South East Asia on the way out, spending a few nights in Singapore and Malaysia, had tempted me to do something more adventurous on the way back. But in the end, I decided a year abroad was enough for the time being, not least because my funds were getting dangerously low. Which isn't to say I won't go travelling again in the near future. That's a definite possibility, once I've had a chance to work and save up some more cash while living at home. I'm keeping this plan to myself for the time being. It seems like the easiest option.

The one person I won't be able to keep it from for long is Jenna, my best friend. We stayed in pretty much daily contact while I was away, messaging and video calling far more than I did with anyone else. The original plan had been for the pair of us to go down under together. But then Jenna's mum had got sick again. Really sick. Even worse than the last time, leading to a diagnosis of terminal cancer. And that was the end of that.

I offered to delay the trip, but Jenna insisted on me continuing alone while I was in a position to do so. When her mum eventually died around five months ago, she also insisted that I shouldn't, under any circumstances, cut my trip short to fly home to support her at the funeral.

'Don't be stupid,' she told me. 'You can't come back now, midway through your adventure. Seriously, don't you dare. I'll be mad if you do. And it's not what Mum would have wanted. She loved hearing what you'd been up to. She'd want you to continue, like I do.'

'I could always come home and then fly back out,' I protested. 'You could possibly even join me... if you felt ready.'

'No. I'm not ready, and I won't be any time soon, seriously. There's too much to sort out here, and my head's all over the place. You and I both know that if you come home now, you won't return. It's too expensive; too far away. No, I'm not having that. I do not want you to come back, okay? I mean it.'

She's always been something of an old soul, Jenna, even before she had to start caring for her mum. Six months younger than me – not twenty-one until October – she was in the year below at school. But growing up together, it never felt that way. If anything, she was the wiser, more sensible one most of the time.

We were finally reunited in person yesterday. Not as soon as I'd hoped, but Jenna had been tied up with other stuff before that. She didn't seem at all like herself, which was odd. She came over to the house early afternoon, but when I asked if she was going to stay for the barbecue, she was weird about it.

'I can't,' she said.

'Really? Why not? Your sister and family are all coming. Hasn't Becky mentioned it?'

'Yes, she did, but I told her the same. Sorry, it's not possible.'

'Jess and Amber will be gutted not to see their favourite aunt. And I was really hoping you'd come too. I haven't seen you for ages; I've missed you so much. Is there seriously no way you can come? What else do you have on?'

'I have other plans. I can't make the barbecue. End of. Please don't give me a hard time, Paige. Just drop it now, yeah?'

'Fine.' I backed off for a bit. But later, when we were alone in my bedroom, I asked: 'What's going on? Is everything all right? You seem... I don't know, distracted or something. Upset. Is it to do with your mum?'

'No. I mean, of course I'm still not over that yet. Nowhere near. Grief is awful. Never-ending. I miss her more or less constantly.' She let out a long sigh. 'But this isn't about her. It's... nothing. Never mind.'

'Well, it's not nothing. That's obvious. I might not have been around for a while, but I can see that a mile off. Come on. What's up, Jenna? Spill. Maybe I can help.'

She sighed. 'Fine. I've had a bad break-up recently. Okay? That's the main thing.'

'What? You never said anything about seeing someone.' I was hurt she hadn't so much as mentioned this before, although I tried to hide it. 'Who's the guy? Has he cheated on you or something? Prick.'

'It's more complicated than that, which is *why* I haven't mentioned it.'

'You're not... pregnant, are you?'

She shook her head. 'No, definitely not.'

'Phew. So what is it, then? Is this guy someone I know?'

'No,' she said after a brief pause, which made me wonder whether that was the truth.

'Has he hurt you? Like been abusive, I mean. Because if so, you can't protect him. And he'll have me to deal with. I swear to God—'

'No, that's not the issue, Paige. Like I said, it's complicated. I don't want to go into it now.'

'Come on. You have to give me something.'

She ran a hand through her hair. 'Fine, but only because it's you. A really bad thing happened the other day, okay? But... I promised to keep it a secret. I'm sorry, I can't say any more.'

'Hold on,' I said. 'What? That's it? That's all you're going to tell me?'

'Sorry, it's all I *can* tell you right now, honestly.'

'You promise he hasn't attacked you in any way?'

'I swear. It's not what you're thinking. It's something else altogether. But I really don't want to talk about it now.' At this point Jenna plastered on a smile that didn't fool me for a second. 'So can we change the subject already? I haven't seen you in person for a whole year. Tell me all about the last part of your trip. How was the flight? What's it like to be home?'

I played ball, but I've been worried about my friend ever since. Plus, I still feel hurt that she's kept so much from me and isn't even giving me the full story now I'm home. I always thought we told each other everything. She's like a sister to me. She used to be round here daily, an extra member of the family; not least when she and Lucas were a thing.

There was this strange, tortured look in Jenna's eyes yesterday, like a part of her was absent, busy with other concerns.

Before she left, I asked: 'Are you sure you can't stay, or even just come back later for the barbecue? I'd love to see more of you.'

I reminded her again that her sister and family would be there. But my words made no difference. She was adamant she couldn't stay.

I messaged her before going to bed last night to check that she was okay, but so far she hasn't replied. She hasn't even read my message, which hopefully just means she was already in bed by the time it arrived.

Sitting on the sofa in the lounge, I stalk Jenna's socials. She's on all the usual ones, but she doesn't post any more. Not since her mum died. So it's no big surprise that there aren't any recent updates. She's not sharing her location on Snapchat either, which is annoying, but nothing new. She stopped doing that a while ago. Said she'd changed all her privacy settings after seeing some scary video about how we're all being spied on by our phones. Whatever. I'm pretty chilled about that kind of stuff.

After scrolling through TikTok for a bit, I reply to some messages from friends I met while travelling, knowing I'll probably never see them again. Then I send another one to Jenna. I can't stop myself.

You all right? I'm worried about you. You really didn't seem yourself yesterday. Can we meet up again today? You know you can tell me anything, right? I'm here for you. Whatever you need. Whenever x

My finger hovers over the send button.

What the hell. I go ahead and press it.

Then I proceed to stare at the message for several minutes, although it remains unread, like the previous one.

Chill, I think. It's still early on a Sunday morning. She'll be asleep in bed, like all the normal people whose body clocks aren't screwed up by different time zones.

But a bad feeling in my gut won't leave me alone. A sense that all is not well continues to bother me. It grows with every passing minute.

FIVE

Danny

He wakes from a nightmare in which he's about to take a flight somewhere, but while queuing to get on the plane, he suddenly can't find his passport or boarding pass. His eyelids flicker open after a long period of frantically searching his pockets and hand luggage; he breathes a sigh of relief as his mind acclimatises to reality and the anxiety fades.

Danny enjoys a brief moment of contentment before the ongoing stresses of his actual life flutter back into his thoughts like unwanted homing pigeons, accompanied by a throbbing headache and a sandpaper throat. God, why did he let himself drink so much at last night's barbecue? Hangovers at forty-nine are dreadful. His body can't deal with them like it used to back in the day.

He looks over at Kate, next to him in the double bed, on her side and facing the opposite direction. Still fast asleep, apparently. Lucky her. He'd love another hour of shut-eye, but that's never going to happen now. Once he's awake, he's awake. And boy, is he thirsty. Why didn't he think to grab a glass of water before hitting the hay? Because he was too pissed, that's why. He barely even remembers going to bed. He'll probably be in trouble today. Kate never likes him getting so drunk, not least when they're hosting. He'll be treading on eggshells all day, particularly if he kept her awake snoring last night, which is entirely possible. Best not do anything to wake her now. He'll quietly get up in a minute and leave her to sleep as long as she needs. That might gain him a brownie point.

First things first. He reaches across to the bedside table, grabs his mobile and turns off airplane mode. He's planning to have a quick flick through the morning's news and social media updates, but before he gets the chance, a message jumps to the fore.

Hi Danny! Soz for the late notice, but I'm not going to be able to work tomorrow or for the rest of the week. Something important has come up, and I need to go away for a bit. Will explain when I'm back.

Oh for God's sake, Jenna. Not again.

He puts his phone back down in exasperation. It's all he can do not to swear out loud, but he manages it for the sake of not rousing Kate.

Bloody hell. That girl is a liability as an employee. He'd have fired her ages ago if it wasn't for their personal relationship. She's his daughter's best friend and his son's ex-girlfriend. There was a time when she was round at their house nearly every day, often staying for tea. Plus, she recently lost her mum. And she's actually a pretty good cleaner when she bothers to turn up. Way better than that last girl, who he fired for being useless, only for her to start making accusations that he'd bullied her. Bloody chancer. He stared her down when she talked about solicitors and employment tribunals; thankfully, she eventually disappeared. At least there's never likely to be any of that nonsense with Jenna.

But who the hell is he going to get to fill in for her now, in mid-August, when loads of people are away on their holidays? Dammit.

He resists the urge to fire an angry message back, opting instead to get up and see if Paige is already awake. Jenna *is* her best friend, after all, and she saw her yesterday before the barbecue. Perhaps she might be able to shed some light on Jenna's sudden disappearing act.

He slips out of bed, shrugs on his dressing gown and heads downstairs, via the bathroom, where he uses the loo and pops two paracetamol tablets. He finds Paige in the lounge, already dressed and on her mobile.

'Morning, love,' he croaks, rubbing a hand across his greying stubble. 'You're up early again. Still not used to the time zone?'

'Hi, Dad. Something like that. How's the head?'

'Fine,' he lies. 'Just you up, or your brother too?'

'Lucas is still in bed, as far as I know. What about Mum?'

'Zonked out. I thought it best not to wake her. Hey, can I ask you something, love?'

'You just did.'

'Very good. Um, you saw Jenna yesterday, right?'

'You know I did.'

'Okay, well... Did she say anything about going away?'

'No, why? Going away where? When?'

Danny shrugs. 'I've no idea where, but in terms of when: now, I guess. I'm not entirely sure.'

'Dad, where's this coming from? She didn't say anything to me about it yesterday.'

'She just messaged me to say that she couldn't clean at the business centre this week because something important had come up and she needed to go away for a bit.'

Paige bites her lip. 'Really? That's weird. *When* did she message you?'

'I dunno. Sometime between me going to bed and getting up this morning. It came through when I turned my phone on. Have you had any contact with her since she was here yesterday?'

Paige shakes her head.

'Right,' Danny says. 'Brilliant. Well, do me a favour: if you do hear from her, tell her I'm not a happy bunny, and I need her back as soon as possible. It's not the first time she's done this, you know. If it was anyone else, I wouldn't stand for it. But... well, your old dad's a soft touch, apparently, especially when it comes to Jenna. I think of her like family, but she's really pushing her luck this time. God knows who I'll get to fill in for her at this late notice. You don't fancy—'

'No thanks, Dad. You're all right. I can barely keep my own room clean, remember, as you and Mum used to love telling me before I went away.'

SIX

Paige

I don't let on to Dad, but what he's just told me about Jenna really bothers me, especially after how she was behaving yesterday.

Once he disappears into the kitchen to make a drink, I slip upstairs to my room and shut the door behind me.

Sitting down on my bed, I take a deep breath and then dial her number. It takes ages to connect, and when it finally does, instead of the ringing sound I'm hoping for, my call goes straight through to voicemail. Crap. I almost hang up, but I manage to keep my composure and speak after the tone.

'Jenna, it's me, Paige. What's going on? I know everything's not okay, so please don't try to fob me off again. Dad's just told me about the message you sent him. What's that all about? Where are you going? Not somewhere with this mystery boyfriend of yours, I hope. Are you back together already? Whoever he is, I got bad vibes from what you said yesterday. Please call me back, or at least message me. Love you. Bye.'

After hanging up, I hold my mobile in front of me, scowling

at it and willing it to spring to life with an incoming call. It doesn't. A watched phone never rings, so they say. I check it's not on silent and then shove it into the back pocket of the denim shorts I'm wearing.

I walk across the landing to my brother's bedroom. The door is ajar, so I peek inside to see if he's awake yet. 'Lucas?' I say in a loud whisper, directed at his bed.

'What?' he groans from under the covers, which I take as permission to enter.

The room is stuffy and smells like stale sweat and alcohol. It brings back memories of dorm rooms I stayed in while backpacking; the first thing I do is open a window.

'What's going on?' Lucas asks, still buried under his duvet.

'I let some fresh air in so I don't pass out.'

'Why are you here? I'm sleeping.'

If I'd done this before I went away, he'd have shouted at me to get lost, as I would at him in the same circumstances. But the novelty of me being home again hasn't worn off yet. So I might as well push it while I can.

I perch on the end of the bed. 'I need to speak to you about something.'

'Can't it wait?'

'No. It's about Jenna. Something strange is going on with her. I'm really worried.'

This gets his attention, as I thought it might. Lucas was in Jenna's year at school, and they went out for a while in their mid-teens. Jenna was the one to end it, which I was glad about at the time, because I found it a bit awkward. Lucas was gutted, though. He's carried a torch for her ever since, if you ask me, although I'm sure he'd deny it, especially since he's been with his current girlfriend, Sylvia, for more than a year now. I saw how he looked at Jenna when she was over at the house yesterday, like an adoring puppy eyeing its owner.

'Jenna?' he says, face finally emerging from the covers. 'What about her? She seemed fine yesterday.'

'Did she? How much did you speak to her?'

'Not much. Just to say hello.'

'Well, when the two of us were alone in my room, she was on edge and upset about something, plus she wouldn't come to the barbecue. Now she's messaged Dad to say she can't work because she has to go away for a bit. And she's not answering her phone.'

Lucas rubs his eyes and shakes his head as if to kick it into gear. 'Shit. Um, that does sound a bit weird. You could maybe try heading over to her house; see if she's still there. Or what about Becky? She might know something. And what about her socials? Have you checked them?'

I resist telling him that all these suggestions have, obviously, already occurred to me. Instead, I ask: 'Have you seen much of Jenna these last few months, since her mum died?'

'How do you mean?' he replies, suddenly defensive.

'It's a straightforward question. I'm not trying to catch you out.'

'Not a lot. I went to the funeral. We all did.'

'Yeah, I know that, Lucas,' I say, probably sounding a bit defensive myself now, because I still feel bad that I wasn't there.

'But I didn't really speak to her then,' he continues, 'other than to offer condolences or whatever. She was busy and, um... well, really upset, as you'd imagine. I've bumped into her a few times since, out and about. Had a quick word. But she's not been round here or anything. Not while you were away. You're the one she's close to, right? I'm just an ex, your little brother. I reckon I'm barely even on her radar these days.'

'Little brother? She's the same age as you.'

'You know what I mean.'

'She mentioned splitting up from a boyfriend recently. Do you know anything about that: who it was, for instance?'

'She didn't tell *you* that?'

'Um, no. I've been away, remember.'

'But I thought you two stayed in touch while you were travelling.'

I roll my eyes. 'We did, Lucas, but she didn't mention the fact she was in a relationship. Okay? How are these comments helping? Do you know who she's been dating or not?'

He shakes his head. 'No, I had no idea she was seeing anyone. But there's no reason I would, considering how little our paths have crossed lately. Have you asked Dad? Maybe it was someone from the business centre.'

'Not yet. I will do.' I stand up to leave. 'Thanks anyway. I'll let you get back to sleep.'

He laughs. 'Yeah, right. I'm wide awake now.'

As I reach the bedroom door, something occurs to me for the first time. 'Shit. You don't think...'

'What?'

'Nothing. Never mind. I'm probably just being stupid.'

'Oh, come on.' Lucas finds a used sock from somewhere and throws it at me. 'Don't do that, sis. Tell me.'

'Fine. As long as you stop throwing smelly socks at me.'

He giggles, making me smile for a moment too, like we're kids again. 'I'll do my best.'

I take a deep breath and turn back towards the bed, serious again. 'Remember that noise last night, during the barbecue: the cry, scream or whatever that freaked everyone out?'

'Yeah.'

'What if that was Jenna? What if she was in trouble, came looking for help, and we all just ignored her? She could have been kidnapped. Maybe this ex-boyfriend of hers is a psycho who dragged her into his car and then drove her off somewhere to hurt her.'

Lucas pulls a face at me like I've lost the plot, which, to be fair, I possibly have.

'Based on what?' he says. 'That's one hell of a leap to make. She didn't even *come* to the barbecue, so what makes you think it was her? And she's messaged Dad since then.'

'What did you see when Mum sent you round to the front of the house to check out the noise?'

'Nothing. Like I said at the time. There was no one around. The street was dead. It will have been kids, Paige. Seriously. Remember when we used to ring people's doorbells and run off before they answered?'

'Hmm. Maybe.'

I turn to leave the room again. 'One more thing,' Lucas adds.

'What?'

'Are you brewing up?'

'No.'

'Oh, come on. It's the least you can do after waking your favourite brother when he's hung-over.'

'No, I don't have time. I'm busy.'

'Doing what?' I hear him ask, but I'm already out of the door.

SEVEN

Becky

> *Thanks so much for last night, Danny and Kate. Great hosting skills. We all really enjoyed ourselves! X*

Becky sends the message to the neighbours' group chat, which, for the time being, is still titled *Summer BBQ*. Then her toast pops up, so she grabs it and spreads it with butter. Is it weird to thank them this way when they're right next door and she could easily say so over the fence or by dropping round? Maybe, but this is easy, and it's what everyone does nowadays.

With perfect timing, as if to validate her choice, her phone pings a second later with a reply from Sarah.

> *Yes, absolutely. Huge thanks from us too. What a lovely night! Great job x*

Becky and family usually have a proper breakfast on a Sunday, sitting together around the kitchen table with eggs, fresh bread and croissants or similar. Not today. They all went to bed late last night so agreed in advance to keep things casual.

The girls, who've been up for a bit, are together in the lounge, quiet rather than arguing for once, watching a film. Scott is still in bed, reading the paper on his tablet and sipping on the cup of filter coffee she took up to him.

Carrying her own cup of coffee and her toast, Becky walks through the hallway to join Jess and Amber.

'What film is it?' she asks, taking a seat.

'*The Princess Diaries,*' Amber replies. 'Jess has seen it before, but I haven't. It's really good. It's about a normal girl who finds out she's a princess, and guess what: she has a cat called Fat Louie. He's so cute.'

'You've both had breakfast already, right?' Becky checks.

The pair of them nod.

'Can I get you anything else?'

'No, I'm fine,' Amber says.

'What about you, Jess? You're very quiet.'

'I'm fine too. I'm concentrating on the film.'

'Okay, sorry. I'll keep quiet.'

Becky can't help feeling a bit bad about the girls getting their own food, even though that's what they agreed last night. The booze was talking then. Today, in the cold light of morning, she wishes they'd had the usual family breakfast. These things are important, especially for a mum who's a family law solicitor and works long hours during the week. She's usually gone before they're up in the morning, Monday to Friday, and is rarely home before six o'clock in the evening.

Scott is the one who takes care of them most of the time. He's a stay-at-home dad, who hopes one day to fulfil his dream of becoming a full-time novelist. Not that he's had much luck so far. Publishing is a tough industry to break into. He's written two novels since quitting his former job as a corporate lawyer, which paid well yet made him miserable, but he hasn't managed to get anywhere in terms of securing an agent or publisher. His manuscripts are really good, in Becky's opinion: laugh-out-loud comedies that she was convinced would snare him that elusive deal. But apparently, comedy is a particularly difficult genre to break into, based on the encouraging but ultimately negative content of his most recent rejection letters. He's currently licking his wounds and considering whether to throw in the towel or to attempt a different kind of book, hopefully with more success.

'Give it one more go while you have the opportunity.' That was her advice when they last spoke about it. 'We're managing okay for now on one salary, and it's great that the girls have someone at home before and after school. You're a brilliant writer, and I believe in you. If you give up now, it'll all have been for nothing.'

'Thanks,' he said. 'You're amazing. What would I do without you?'

Is she jealous sometimes of the freedom Scott's current position affords him? Of all the time he gets to spend with their daughters, unlike her? Of course. Who wouldn't be? But she also remembers how stressed he was before he ditched his job. He was a shell of the happy-go-lucky man she met at university all those years ago, and that wasn't good for any of them. Plus, Becky enjoys her job. She'd be lost without the focus it gives her. As much as she loves her girls, she wouldn't want to be a stay-at-home mum. It's not her. Scott's more suited to it than she is; he does a great job of ensuring Jess and Amber are where they need to be, at the right time, with all the right gear. The arrangement works. And if it ain't broke, why fix it?

That said, she could really have done with some more spare time when her mother was first fighting and then dying from cancer. Her work commitments meant that much of the weight of caring for their mum ended up falling on Jenna's shoulders, which she still feels bad about. Mind you, that wasn't the only reason. Becky and her mum were always arguing, whereas Jenna was very close to her, and lived with her on the other side of the village. Scott's theory was that Becky and her mum clashed a lot because they were so similar. Now that she's gone, Becky really misses her.

As for her and Jenna, they've never been that close. There's a sixteen-year age gap between them, for a start, so it's not like they grew up together. Becky, now thirty-six, left for university when Jenna was a toddler, and apart from the odd return visit during holidays, she never really lived at home again. She and Scott, who are the same age, moved in together after graduating, and stayed up in Newcastle for several years before eventually returning to her home village, here in North West England, when they wanted to settle down and start a family.

During her time away, their parents split up, which was also very divisive. Becky now realises that, subconsciously and unfairly, she probably held her mum and Jenna to account for this. In reality, the true villain was her father, who immediately shacked up with a much younger woman and started another family, more or less disappearing from all of their lives. However, by the time she was old and wise enough to realise the truth, the damage had been done. What had brought her mum and Jenna closer together had pushed Becky apart from them. Even moving back to a house just a short walk away from theirs was never enough to truly fix that, although things did gradually improve. It was more a case of supergluing the cracks, so they held together but remained visible.

That said, Mum was always brilliant with Jess and Amber, and they loved her to bits, sobbing their poor little hearts out at her funeral earlier this year. Jenna's great with them too. They pretty much worship her, treating her more like an older cousin than an aunt.

Jenna was supposed to be babysitting this evening. Scott had convinced Becky to go to the cinema with him for the first time in ages, to see some new spy thriller. However, Becky got a message from her sister overnight, following her no-show at yesterday's barbecue, saying that something important had come up and she needed to go away for a bit. She said she'd explain when she was back.

Becky responded:

Guess that means you can't babysit tonight?

So far, though, she hasn't had a reply, which she's taking to mean it's not happening. They'd have to find someone else to do it at the last minute, which isn't likely. Unless... What about Paige? She was great with Jess and Amber at yesterday's barbecue, and considering she's recently returned from travelling, there's a decent chance she's short of cash and has no plans. Plus, she's right next door.

Becky drains the last of her coffee and is about to go and get a refill when there's a ring on the doorbell. Once she's found the key and unlocked the front door, she swings it open. 'Oh, hello there, Paige. I was just thinking about you. How weird.'

Paige tilts her head, so her dead-straight long brown hair shifts neatly to one side. 'Nothing bad, I hope.'

'No, of course not. What can I do for you? Would you like to come in?'

'Yes please, if that's all right. I'm not interrupting, am I?'

'No, not at all.' Becky gestures for her to step inside.

EIGHT

Paige

It's ages since I've been in Becky and Scott's house. A good while longer than my year abroad. I've never spent much time inside any of the neighbours' homes, mainly speaking to them outside.

The layout is comparable to our house. Not surprising considering they're both detached properties built in the mid-1970s. But theirs is a mirror image of ours, which, combined with the different fixtures and fittings, furniture, and so on, gives it an oddly different yet familiar vibe.

'Would you like a coffee?' Becky runs a hand through her short, wavy dark hair.

'Yes, that would be lovely.' I follow her into the kitchen, where she pours us each a mug from a half-full pot of filter coffee. She doesn't look especially like Jenna – she never has – although they do share the same smoky grey eyes. Watching her as she puts on another pot, which Scott 'definitely needs', apparently, I pick out mannerisms that remind me of my best friend, such as the way she wrinkles her nose when she asks a question and uses lots of hand gestures in general conversation. You can definitely tell they're sisters if you look hard enough. And they're equally sharp and quick-witted.

Jenna might be working as a cleaner for my dad at the moment, but that's out of convenience; a stopgap to help pay the bills. No one expects her to stay in the role long-term, although she has been there a while now. She was always a high-flyer at school, and if her mum hadn't got sick with her first bout of cancer when she did, she'd have probably got straight A's at A-level rather than the lukewarm results she actually achieved. She'd have almost certainly gone to uni. Not that this would necessarily have been the best path for her. It wasn't for me, as I learned the hard way.

'Sorry about that,' Becky says once she's done preparing the coffee. As the machine starts up with its distinctive brewing sound, she sits down opposite me at the kitchen table. 'How are you? I didn't get much of a chance to speak to you last night. Are you settling back into home life? It must feel strange. Your mum kept me up to date on where you were and what you were doing while you were in Australia. It sounded like you had an amazing time.'

'I did. It was perfect... other than Jenna not being able to come with me, of course. I really wanted to fly back for your mum's funeral, you know, but she was adamant I shouldn't.'

'Oh, I totally agree with her about that.'

'As for being home, it's lovely, but I am still getting used to it. I think it'll take a while to get fully settled back in. My body clock is all over the place.'

Becky nods. 'I bet.'

'How are things with you after, um, everything?' I want to ask about her grief, but I can't seem to find the right words; I hope she realises that's what I mean.

'Oh, you know. It's hard, but you have to get on with your life. Put one foot in front of the other. Keep busy at work. That

kind of thing. Anyway, was there something specific you wanted?' She shakes her head. 'Sorry, Paige, that came out wrong:
too blunt, like I'm trying to get rid of you, which I'm really not. I
think I slipped into solicitor mode for a moment. Blame the
hangover. Blame your parents for having such a boozy
barbecue.'

I laugh, because she's right. I *am* here for a particular
purpose.

'I wanted to speak to you about Jenna,' I say, bringing her up
to speed about the message Dad received and the subsequent
lack of communication.

'She's not answering her phone at all this morning,' I say.
'Have you heard from her? I just want to know that she's okay.
Yesterday was the first time I'd seen her since being home, and...
she wasn't herself. Not how I know her, anyway. I mean, yes,
I've been away, but we kept in contact the whole time, so...'

Becky clears her throat. 'Ah, right, okay. Yes, I did get a
message from her when I woke up today. It sounds more or less
the same as what she told your dad. I wouldn't worry, though.
She's been like this a bit lately. It's not the first time she's taken
herself off somewhere without warning. She did exactly the
same a short while back. When she returned, she said she'd
taken the train to Edinburgh for a little break "to clear her
head".'

'By herself?'

'As far as I know.'

'Did she stop answering her phone then too?'

'Honestly, Paige, I've no idea. We don't have the kind of
relationship where we call or message each other frequently,
even since Mum died. If we do, it's because we have something
specific to ask. You've always been much closer to her than
I am.'

After peering over at the coffee pot to see if it's done, she
offers me a top-up, which I politely decline, then refills her own

mug. 'Bear with me a minute,' she says before nipping upstairs with the coffee pot to give Scott his share.

While I'm alone, I wonder whether I should mention what Jenna told me about having a recent bad break-up. I'm afraid of betraying a confidence, as I have a feeling she might not have told Becky. Since neither Lucas nor my parents knew about the relationship – I checked with Mum and Dad before coming here – I get the feeling it wasn't exactly public knowledge. However, when Becky returns, I put my concerns for Jenna's safety first and tell her.

'Really?' She looks bewildered. 'That's news to me. She's never mentioned anything about seeing someone, but like I said, we're not that close. Mum's illness and then her death brought us together for a bit. But since then, we've slipped back into old habits. I wouldn't even have a clue who this bloke might be.'

Hearing this makes me sad and even more anxious for my friend. I imagine Jenna alone, rattling around the family house she grew up in, with only memories to keep her company. Driven into the arms of an unsavoury, violent man who didn't deserve her. Someone she couldn't tell anyone about, perhaps because he was married.

'You look pensive,' Becky says. 'What are you thinking?'

'Oh, nothing,' I lie, telling myself to stop being overdramatic. I've no real evidence to think of Jenna's life having gone this way. I certainly never got those vibes from speaking to her while I was away.

'I wouldn't blame you for thinking I'm a bad sister and daughter,' Becky says, lowering her voice, unexpectedly candid. 'I know very well it was Jenna who carried the weight of Mum's illness while I was busy burying my head in work. I appreciate the heavy toll it took on her at a young age; not least how it affected her A-levels. And I won't insult you by trying to make excuses for myself.' She shrugs. 'I screwed up.'

'That wasn't what I was thinking,' I tell her, truthfully,

although I have had such thoughts in the past. 'That's not why I'm here. Do you remember that chilling cry or scream or whatever that shocked everyone at the barbecue last night?'

'Of course.'

'What if that was her?'

'Jenna?'

'Yes.'

'Why would you say that?'

'It's a gut feeling. A thought I keep having that won't leave me alone.'

Becky looks unconvinced. 'Right. But it was much later than that when she messaged me. I put my phone on airplane mode when I went to bed at one o'clock; her text only came through when I reconnected this morning. It's great that you're looking out for her, Paige, but honestly, I don't think there's anything to worry about. Mark my words, she'll be back in a few days, perfectly fine, like she never disappeared in the first place.'

'I hope you're right.'

I make my excuses and leave soon after that. At the door, Becky asks: 'You're, um, not free tonight by any chance, are you? I need a babysitter for the girls. No pressure, but I'd make it worth your while.'

NINE

From: Jen501
To: Mr888
Re: First email

It feels strange contacting you like this, but I'm rolling with it.
My first email to you... a relationship milestone. I know we
have to be careful, and I will, I promise. The last thing I want
is to make things difficult. For anyone to find out. At least we
have a safe way to keep in touch now. Not being able to chat
to you whenever I want is so hard. You're all I can think about
sometimes.

You will email me back, right? I get that the stakes are higher
for you than for me. I'll bear that in mind while I'm refreshing
my inbox over and over, but please find a moment when you
safely can.

I've never felt like this before. Being with you has opened up
parts of me that I didn't know existed. I actually think... I
might be falling for you.

Wow. I can't believe I just typed that. I wouldn't dare say it in person yet, but it feels easier to be bold here. Hopefully it'll make you smile.

I can't wait until we're next alone together. I won't be able to keep my hands off you! I look forward to hearing back from you in the meantime. Haha. That sounds so formal. Like a job application. It's the whole email thing. I'm way more used to messaging, but I'll get used to it. I'll find my voice here.

Lots of love.

X

TEN

Paige

I agreed to babysit Jess and Amber tonight. Apparently, Jenna was supposed to be doing it. Becky put me on the spot, and I couldn't think of a good excuse to say no. It will at least give me a chance to find out if the girls know anything about what their aunt has been up to lately. Sometimes children get wind of things you wouldn't expect.

They're nice kids, so it shouldn't be much of a chore. Plus Becky said she'd pay me for my time, which will mean some welcome extra cash. It has to be an easier option than Dad's earlier suggestion that I could cover Jenna's cleaning shifts at the business centre.

I will need to get a proper job at some point, but I'm not in too much of a rush just yet. I have no idea what I want to do for a start, although office work would be my preference over anything physical. I took whatever jobs I could get my hands on in Australia, from fruit picking and packing to waiting at various bars, restaurants, cafés and events. I even served in a souvenir shop at Sydney Airport for a couple of weeks. But that was different. It was super temporary, and if I didn't earn enough dollars, I wouldn't have been able to afford to eat or pay for accommodation.

Now I'm safely back under Mum and Dad's roof, I have more breathing space to be picky. I probably have a month's grace before they start talking about me paying my way, looking to the future, finding a career, etc. There was already a fair bit of that after I unexpectedly dropped out of uni halfway through the second year of my history degree. But deciding to go travelling allowed me to kick the can down the road until, well, now. I genuinely thought I'd return home refreshed, reinvigorated and with a good idea of what I *did* want to do with my life. Hmm. I never quite got around to working that out. I was too busy enjoying myself and doing my utmost to forget about the spectacular failure of Paige Plan A.

I push these thoughts to the back of my mind as I press the doorbell of my parents' other next-door neighbours, Adrian and Sarah. It's one of those posh ones with a video camera, which has given me an idea.

'Oh,' I say, thrown when their son, Zack, a little older than me at twenty-three, unexpectedly answers the front door. He didn't come to the barbecue yesterday due to being out with his fiancée. Mum told me he spends most of his time at her flat these days, so I wrongly assumed he wouldn't be home.

'Paige,' he replies, nodding but not smiling. 'I heard you were back.'

'Hi, Zack. How are you?'

'Great.'

I pause for a moment, expecting him to at least ask me the same, if not to enquire about my travels. But then I remember that this is Zack. Not really his speciality, being polite or putting people at ease. He stares at me with a blank look on his face, neither inviting me in nor asking about the reason for my house call.

'Is, er, your mum or dad around?' I ask.

'Dad's at the surgery, but Mum's home.'

'Could I have a word with her, please?'

He turns around as I wait outside. 'Mum?'

'Yes.' I hear her faint reply from inside.

'Paige from next door is here.'

'Right.'

'She wants to speak to you.'

'Okay. Could you show her through, please?'

'Where are you?'

'In the conservatory.'

He turns back towards me. 'She's in the conservatory.'

'Right.'

'Are you coming in, then?'

'Sure, thanks.'

I step inside. He shuts the door behind me, points in the right direction and disappears up the stairs.

I guess I'm showing myself through.

Why am I here? Purely because of their fancy doorbell. I noticed it out of the corner of my eye as I was walking back from Becky's, and it made me think: what if the camera happened to record whoever let out the cry during the barbecue yesterday? It's probably a long shot. I'm not sure how these devices work, but I suspect they're only triggered when someone stands in front of them. Still. You never know. It's worth a try.

Sarah beams at me as I approach. She's sitting in one of four wicker seats looking out on the immaculate back garden. She's always been so much more welcoming than her glum son. Both her and her husband. I'm not sure what happened when it came to Zack.

'Hi, Paige. Great barbecue last night, although I'm feeling it today, I must admit.' She nods at the coffee table in front of her, which holds a glass half full of a thick, bright red liquid on ice. 'Bloody Mary,' she explains. 'Hair of the dog. I wouldn't usually, but what the hell. It's summer, right? Even us health-conscious yoga instructors need to let ourselves go sometimes. Can I get you anything? Tea, coffee, water; something stronger?'

'No thanks. It's a flying visit.'

'Have a seat, at least. You're making me uncomfortable standing there.'

'Thanks.' I take the chair next to hers.

'I hope Zack was polite.' She rolls her eyes. 'Being well-mannered still isn't his forte.'

I shrug. 'He was... fine.'

She looks unconvinced. 'Tell me, Paige, have you ever tried yoga?'

I shake my head. 'I haven't, actually.'

'Really? I bet you'd enjoy it. You should come along to one of my beginners' classes. It's a good time to start because it's quiet at the moment. It always is in the summer. Everyone's busy with family stuff or away on holiday.'

'Thanks.' I smile politely. 'I'll bear that in mind.'

'Anyway, to what do I owe the pleasure of your company?' She tucks an errant lock of her loosely tied-back long blonde hair behind one ear and throws me an expectant look.

'Do you remember that weird scream-type thing we all heard last night?'

'Sure.'

'Do you think it was kids messing about, like everyone else seems to agree?'

'Most likely. They've all got plenty of time on their hands, what with school being out. And doing silly things to wind up adults, or even just for the hell of it, is pretty standard. I know it's what I used to do as a kid. Didn't you? Why do you ask?'

'Um, I have a bad feeling about it, that's all. It's got under my skin.'

Sarah tips her head to one side. 'I see. Any particular reason?'

'Not really,' I lie.

Obviously, I could tell her about my specific concerns regarding Jenna. In fact, I probably should. But she's looking bemused, and I don't want to sound like a paranoid weirdo. So all that comes out of my mouth is: 'I noticed your camera doorbell thingy and... well, I, er, wondered if it might have recorded whatever did happen.'

'Ah,' she says, nodding. 'Now that makes sense. And it would actually be a decent idea to check. But there won't be any footage, I'm afraid.'

'Really?' I say. 'How come?'

'Because the camera doesn't work. It did for about five minutes, ages ago, and then it conked out, dead as a doornail. It's a knock-off Adrian picked up cheap online. No subscription, but as good as the real deal, supposedly. Yeah, right. You get what you pay for. Goodness knows why he bought it at all. I was never bothered. We should have returned it, of course, but... you know how it goes when everyone's busy. Anyway, it does ring at least, and it looks real enough to fool a savvy young woman like yourself, so that's something.'

ELEVEN

Zack

He's listening from the hallway as Paige talks to his mum.

Why is she here, asking about their doorbell camera?

For fuck's sake. What does she know? What does she suspect?

Zack feels a wave of panic rising in his chest. He could almost puke. But he reminds himself that there is no video footage. Like Mum said, the camera's a knockoff, a dud. Thank God for Dad being cheap. If it did work, he'd have had to delete yesterday evening's recording, that's for sure.

After several minutes of eavesdropping, he senses the conversation is drawing to a close, and Paige will be leaving soon, which is a relief. He pulls away and creeps upstairs to his bedroom, barely making a sound.

She might be sexy, but he doesn't want her here. She's being a nosy bitch right now about stuff that doesn't concern her.

At least she doesn't seem interested in what *he* was up to last night, thankfully. So far no one seems to have twigged that he was still around at the time of the ear-piercing scream that apparently got everyone's attention at the barbecue.

He's not surprised by that. It was one hell of a loud cry. The kind that hurts your ears, gets right under your skin and makes you wince. Especially close up, when it's directed into your face.

From the safety of his room, he listens to Mum show Paige out through the front door. Letting out a long, heavy breath, he feels himself unwind. He stands in a discreet position by the window and watches her return next door, admiring the curve of her hips as she walks. It's almost like old times, before she went away. What he'd do to grab hold of that pert little arse with both hands and give it a hard squeeze.

She glances back towards his window at one point, but he doesn't move, confident she won't be able to spot him. He's an old hand when it comes to watching the hot girl next door. Letting his imagination run wild. If only she wasn't so bloody annoying.

Once she's disappeared inside her own house, he crosses the room to his bedside table and pulls out something he shouldn't have. That doesn't belong to him. He holds it in one hand and then drops it into the other, squeezing it between his palm and fingers.

The trouble this could cause him, especially if someone like Paige were to discover he had it. He should probably ditch it somewhere far from the village. He could take it to work tomorrow, slip it into a public bin or into a street gutter, and that would be that. But he can't bring himself to do so. He likes the way it feels against his skin too much, knowing where it's been. So he'll keep it, at least for now.

Mum calls his name from downstairs.

'Yes,' he replies, stashing the item away in the pocket of his shorts, where he can still run his hand over it whenever he likes.

'Could you come here a minute, please?'

'What now?' he mutters to himself, letting out a loud sigh.

Walking to the landing, he leans over the banister and peers down at his mother, who's standing at the foot of the staircase.

'Don't do that,' she says.

'What?'

'Lean on the banister. How many times—'

'Right,' he says, taking a step back. 'What's up?'

'Why were you rude to Paige when you answered the door?'

'I wasn't.'

'Well, you weren't very welcoming.'

'I showed her in, didn't I?'

'Barely. Would it kill you to be nice to our neighbours?'

He shrugs. 'Can I go now?'

'What are you doing up there? Why don't you come and join your old mum for a bit in the conservatory?'

'Maybe later. I'm busy at the moment.'

'Doing what?'

'Stuff.'

'Of course.' She rolls her eyes before turning and walking away.

TWELVE

Adrian

He told Sarah he was going to the surgery to catch up on paperwork, which she bought without question, but that was a lie. He needed some time alone to think, so he jumped in the car and started driving.

Now he's in a small car park in the middle of nowhere, near a walking trail that leads to a local reservoir, hopefully far enough from home not to bump into anyone he knows.

Should he be driving yet after the number of drinks he had at the barbecue last night? Possibly not. But it is mid-afternoon already. He didn't have as much as some of the others, and he stuck to Guinness rather than getting into any wine or spirits; it's not like he was trolleyed. He felt fine when he got up, more or less. Not bad for a man of fifty-three, anyway, still able to keep up with his younger wife of forty-six... most of the time.

As the day progressed, he felt increasingly stifled. Eventually, he had to get out of the house. So he made his fake excuses and left, just as Sarah was mixing herself a Bloody Mary, of all things.

'What?' she said to him. 'Don't give me that disapproving look. It's a Sunday. It's August. I might as well behave like I'm on holiday, because it's not like we're actually going anywhere this summer.'

Adrian sighed. 'Not this again. If I could have taken the time off, I would. It's a one-off glitch. You know that. We've got our week in Greece to look forward to in October; we'll get some winter sun around Christmas too, I promise.'

'Yeah. Great.'

'I told you to go ahead and book a summer trip with your sister or one of your friends, if it helps.'

'They're all busy going away with their families.'

'Well, I'm sorry about that, but what else can I do?'

'Never mind. I thought you were going to the surgery?'

'I am.'

'See you later, then.'

Sitting behind the steering wheel of his parked car, he picks up his mobile and stares at the blank, dark screen; his own weary eyes, brimming with secrets, are reflected back at him. It would be so easy right now to flick it into action and... No, that's not why he came here.

He shoves the device firmly into the pocket of his jeans and, heavy of heart, steps out of the vehicle. Locking it with his key fob, he puts one tired foot in front of the other and trudges into the distance.

THIRTEEN

Scott

'How come Paige was round earlier?' he asks Becky while making himself a cheese, tomato and pickle sandwich.

'She's worried about Jenna.'

'Oh. Why's that?'

Becky explains about Danny getting a similar message to the one she received from her sister.

'Well, it's not the first time she's disappeared like this, is it?'

'I know. That's what I said. But Paige claimed Jenna was weird with her yesterday afternoon. And something about her having a bad break-up recently.'

'Who, Paige?'

'No, Jenna.'

'Eh? Who's she been seeing?'

'No idea. She kept that one quiet. So you didn't have an inkling either?'

'Me, no. Why would I?'

'I don't know... Sometimes I think you're closer to my sister than I am.'

'What? I've helped her fix a couple of things around the house. And we have similar taste in music and TV shows. She might tell me about a new indie band she's heard or a sci-fi series that's just launched, but it doesn't go much deeper than that, love. She certainly never mentioned having a boyfriend.'

'Okay. If you say so.'

'I do.' He cuts his sandwich in half and puts it on a plate.

'That looks nice,' Becky says. 'Did you ask the girls if they wanted one?'

'Seriously? It's gone three o'clock. This is the first thing I've eaten all day. They've already had breakfast and lunch, right?'

'They made themselves breakfast and I made them lunch.'

'Exactly. I make their packed lunches every weekday, Becky. And I cook tea for us all nearly every night. Now you're having a go because I took a minute to make myself a sandwich in between meals. You're in a good mood today.'

Becky flashes him a mardy scowl.

'Girls, would you like some fruit?' Scott calls into the lounge.

'No thanks,' they both call back.

'See, my gorgeous, hung-over wife,' he says, grinning. 'Not hungry.'

'You only offered something healthy.' Becky cracks a smile. 'That's cheating.'

'I assume the cinema is off tonight,' he says, in between mouthfuls of sandwich. 'Seeing as our babysitter has gone AWOL.'

'You should never assume anything,' Becky replies. 'I took the opportunity to ask Paige to fill in when she was here; luckily, she agreed.'

'Really? Good thinking. Nice one.'

Later, Scott shuts himself away in the study on the pretext of doing some writing.

He switches on his trusty, if somewhat ancient, desktop

computer and opens a new word processing document, which he saves with the title *Book Three*. Then he minimises it and clicks open the web browser. It's no coincidence that when he rearranged the furniture in the study a few months back, he ended up with both monitors facing away from the door. Privacy is hard to come by in a household with two inquisitive young children.

He closes his eyes for a long moment and takes several slow, deep breaths. Calm down, he tells himself.

Then he gets to it.

FOURTEEN

Paige

It's almost time to head next door to babysit while Becky and Scott go out. I wish I hadn't agreed to it now. It's the last thing I feel like doing, but it would be shady to let them down at this late stage. Plus, I want to keep them on side – especially Becky. I need to ask her a favour.

I'm brushing my hair when my brother walks into my bedroom unannounced. 'What are you up to?'

'Babysitting next door in a minute. You? Seeing Sylvia tonight?'

'Nah. She's not about. I'm knackered anyway. Tomorrow will be busy.' Lucas is an apprentice heating engineer. 'We're starting a big job at this crappy ancient mansion some guy thinks is worth renovating. Personally, I'd knock it down and start again. It's gonna be a pain in the arse. And I'll be lumped with all the biggest ball aches, no doubt, as usual.'

He pulls his vape out of his pocket to have a puff.

'Um, not in my room, please,' I snap. 'I thought you weren't supposed to do that in the house.'

He chuckles, putting it back in his pocket. 'What Mum and Dad don't know won't hurt them. Why are you bothered?'

'I don't want to breathe in that crap. You wouldn't come in here and smoke a cigarette.'

He shakes his head. 'It's not the same, is it? Vapes aren't bad for you like cigs.'

'Hmm. They definitely aren't *good* for you. People used to think smoking wasn't harmful, back in the day. Look how that worked out.'

'Whatever. When did you get so boring?'

'Sensible, you mean. It's probably something to do with spending a year looking after myself, being an adult, rather than relying on Mum and Dad.'

'Okay. Well, I'll be the one going out to work tomorrow, sis.'

It didn't take long for us to slip back into competitive, argumentative old habits. I get up to leave the room. 'Well, this has been fun, but I need to head next door.'

Minutes later, I'm in Becky and Scott's kitchen, for the second time that day. Becky shows me where everything is, with instructions to help myself to drinks and snacks.

'Thanks so much for stepping in at the last minute,' Scott says before they leave.

Once I'm alone with the girls, sitting together in the lounge, they chat at me with such animated energy you'd think having me as their babysitter was the most exciting thing they'd experienced in ages. Other than the height difference you'd expect, considering the three years between them, they look rather alike, with hazel eyes and light brown hair, long, straight and – this evening at least – worn down without any clips or bobbles. They both have a look of Jenna, especially the way their eyes crinkle when they smile.

I get all the usual questions about Australia.

Was it really hot?

Did I see any kangaroos or koalas?

Did everyone say 'g'day, mate'?

Did I stay in the jungle or visit 'that big famous rock' (Uluru)? And so on.

It particularly amuses me when Amber asks: 'You know how Australia is on the other side of the world: did it feel like you were standing upside down the whole time?'

Jess gives me a knowing look and shakes her head before I explain that it didn't, somehow keeping a straight face.

'Are you two going on holiday anywhere nice this summer?' I ask.

'We've already been,' Jess explains. 'To Portugal last month.'

'Oh, right. I didn't realise. Was it good?'

'Yes, it was amazing,' Amber chips in. 'I made seven friends, and I swam in the pool and the sea every day. There was a kids' club, and the woman who ran it was called Monique.'

'That sounds perfect. Did you enjoy it too, Jess?'

She nods. 'I liked it more when we went to Spain the year before, though.'

'Really? Why was that?'

She shrugs. 'The food was nicer at the hotel.'

'It was not,' Amber argues.

'Whatever,' Jess says, reminding me of the conversation I had with Lucas earlier.

I bring up Jenna by asking if she's their regular babysitter, even though I already know the answer.

'She was supposed to be here tonight,' Jess confirms, 'but Mummy said she's gone away. Do you know where, and when she'll be back?'

'I don't, I'm afraid.'

'Are you still best friends?' she asks.

'Of course. I haven't seen much of her lately, what with being away, but we did meet up before the barbecue yesterday. She seemed a bit... sad, I thought.'

'It's probably because of Grandma,' Jess says in a solemn voice. 'We all miss her so much, and because Aunt Jenna lived with her, I think she feels lonely sometimes.'

'Has she been seeing any other friends while I've been away?'

She shrugs.

'What about a boyfriend? Do you know if she's got one at the moment?'

The girls share a look with each other, but neither says anything.

'Come on,' I say. 'What do you know? You can tell me.'

It's Jess who breaks the silence. She looks at Amber. 'I know Aunt Jenna told us not to say anything, but Paige *is* her best friend. Shall we tell her?'

'Okay.' Amber turns to me, eyes deadly serious. 'But you *can't* tell anyone else. It's top secret.'

'I won't,' I say, matching their sincerity. 'Promise.'

'Well,' Jess says, 'we don't know much, but she did tell us a few weeks ago, when she was babysitting for us, that she was in love.'

Bingo. 'Really?' I reply. 'Oh, that's cute. Who's the lucky boy?'

'She didn't tell us that,' Amber pipes up, 'even though we asked her loads of times. She said she couldn't.'

'Did the girls behave themselves?' Scott asks me after he and Becky get home, having enjoyed their film.

'They were as good as gold.'

'No playing up when it was time for bed?'

'Nope. You've clearly got them well trained.'

'Here's your money,' Becky says, appearing with a couple of notes. 'Thanks again for helping us out. You're a star.'

When she leads me to the front door, I seize the opportunity to ask her for that favour I've had in mind. 'Heard any more from Jenna?'

'No, not so far. Not since her message this morning. I haven't tried to contact her since, though, I must admit. I wanted to earlier, but I got tied up with other stuff and… Look, honestly, I really don't think there's anything to worry about. Have you, um, tried her again?' She wrinkles her nose.

'Yes, several times throughout the day,' I say. 'She's still not answering. I popped around to her house too and knocked on the door a few times, but there was no sign of anyone there.'

'Well, no, there wouldn't be if she's gone away, would there?'

'I suppose not. Still, I was wondering… Do you by any chance have a spare key?'

'Yes, I do.'

'I thought so. Listen, if we still haven't heard from her by tomorrow, could I possibly swing by to borrow it for an hour? I'm probably fussing about nothing, but it would make me feel much better if I could have a quick look inside to check there's no sign of anything untoward.'

Becky puts a hand on her hip. 'What exactly are you expecting to find, Paige?'

I give her my best pleading look. 'Hopefully nothing. Peace of mind, maybe, if I'm lucky. She wouldn't have a problem with me being there, you know that. She and I have been best friends for ever. It would mean a lot.'

She relents. 'Fine, but let's wait and see what tomorrow brings first. I wouldn't be at all surprised if you hear from her by the morning.'

'Thank you. Let's hope so. Oh, one more thing. The girls seemed to know something about Jenna having a secret boyfriend. I didn't get much more out of them than that, but it might be worth you asking. See if you can find out anything else.'

'Really?' Becky says. 'They told you that?'

I nod. 'You didn't hear it from me, though.'

'Little tykes. I can't believe they kept that secret. They do love their Aunt Jenna, that's for sure. Thanks, Paige.'

'No probs. I'll get out of your hair. See you later.'

FIFTEEN

Adrian

He calls his wife from his office at the surgery. It's 16:58 according to the clock in the corner of his computer screen.

Sarah answers on the third ring. 'Hi, love,' she says. 'How's it going?'

'Oh, you know. Usual Monday. Busy as hell. You?'

'Fine. Pretty quiet this end. Only had one class today. What time do you think you'll be back for tea?'

'It could be pretty late,' he says. 'I've got appointments through till six, and then I need to catch up on some admin stuff. You and Zack should go ahead and eat whenever you're hungry. Just leave something covered on a plate for me, if that's okay, and I'll heat it up when I get in.'

'Are you sure? I don't mind waiting. I had a late lunch.'

She's in a good mood today, he notes. He hadn't expected this phone call to be quite so easy.

'No, no. You go ahead. What's on the menu?'

'Quiche, new potatoes and salad.'

'Lovely,' Adrian says, even as he rolls his eyes, thinking: not again.

Once he's hung up, he calls through to reception. 'I'm going to head off in a minute. Thanks for clearing my final hour. You're a lifesaver.'

'You're welcome, Doctor. I hope everything is okay at home.'

'Thank you. I appreciate that. I'm sure it'll all be fine. Sometimes you just have to be there for your loved ones, don't you? Family first. That's the important thing.'

'Absolutely.'

'I'll see you in the morning.'

He invented a family emergency earlier this afternoon as a way of getting out of here ahead of time for once on a Monday. Not something he's done before, and all the more believable for that. He's kept the whole thing vague; tomorrow he'll say it's sorted but just as well he was there. And that will be the end of that.

People don't question you much when you're a respected local GP. Especially the staff working under you. It comes in handy sometimes.

A few minutes later, he walks out of the back door into the surgery car park and heads towards his reserved parking space. He gets behind the wheel and starts the engine.

But he doesn't drive home. Not yet. He has other things to do first.

SIXTEEN

Paige

I watch the neighbours' drive from my bedroom window as Monday afternoon turns to evening, waiting for Becky's car to pull up. Finally, just after 6.30, she arrives home, right as Mum announces that our tea is ready. Dammit.

'Have I got five minutes?' I ask, trying my luck.

'No,' Mum says. 'It's ready now.'

'What are we having?' my brother asks, drifting into the kitchen. 'I'm ravenous.'

'Good,' Mum replies. 'Lasagne.'

'Really? With meat?'

'No, a new vegetarian recipe. It's supposed to be delicious.'

'Of course. Thanks, Paige. Any garlic bread?'

'No,' Mum says. 'I've made a big salad, which is far healthier.'

'Brilliant.'

'Less of the sarcasm, please.'

'Who says I was being sarcastic?'

'Your mother,' Dad chips in, having walked in from the back

garden. 'So less of it, please, or you'll be on cooking duty tomorrow.'

The meal seems to last for ever. Dad and Lucas both talk about work; I barely hear what they're saying.

It's only when I notice Mum looking at me with expectant eyes that I realise she must have asked me something. 'Sorry, what was that?'

'I was asking after Jenna. Have you heard anything from her yet?'

'No.'

'Oh well. I wouldn't worry.'

Why does everyone keep telling me that? It makes me want to scream. But on this occasion, I bite my tongue and nod, focusing on the remaining food on my plate.

'It's very tasty, this lasagne,' I say.

'Not as tasty as the meaty version,' Lucas snipes. 'How's it fair that we all have to eat veggie because of Paige?'

'You ate half a cow at the barbecue on Saturday,' I reply.

'Whatever.'

'It's delicious,' Dad butts in, throwing evils at my brother. 'And I'm sure a bit less meat will do us all some good.'

When dessert is finally mentioned, I can't restrain myself any longer. 'Sorry, I'm really full. Please could I be excused? I, er, have somewhere I need to be. It's to do with Jenna.'

'Really?' Dad asks. 'Well, if you do manage to get hold of her, tell her I need her back at work asap. Otherwise, there might not be a job waiting for her.'

'Danny!' Mum scolds him. 'Remember everything that poor girl has been through. Cut her some slack, for goodness' sake.'

'What?' He holds his hands aloft. 'She couldn't ask for a more understanding boss than me. I—'

'So is that a yes?' I ask Mum. 'Am I excused?'

'Of course.'

Lucas rolls his eyes. 'Seriously? When do you ever let me leave before dessert?'

I don't get involved. I thank Mum for the lovely food and head straight out of the front door to Becky's.

She ushers me through to the kitchen, where I can see that they have also recently finished eating. 'Scott mentioned that you called round earlier, before I was home. You're after the key, I guess?'

I nod.

'Okay, well, I will lend it to you, as promised, but first I want to try calling her.'

'Go ahead. She won't answer. You'll get voicemail.'

She presses the screen of her phone, selects her sister's number, then holds it up to her ear. She soon lowers it to hang up.

Told you so.

'You were right,' she says. 'But it doesn't necessarily mean anything, other than the fact she doesn't want to be contacted.'

Don't say she's done this before. Please don't say that. Not again.

Thankfully, she doesn't, although I don't give her much of a chance. 'Have you had any thoughts about where she could have gone?' I ask. 'Is there someone other than this mystery boyfriend she might have gone to visit? What about your father? I guess that's pretty unlikely, right, considering the history?'

'Dad? I doubt it. She wasn't exactly glad to see him when he showed up at Mum's funeral. Neither of us were, but she could barely look at him.'

'Maybe she felt bad afterwards,' I suggest. 'I don't know... perhaps she decided it was time to build bridges; to connect with her one remaining parent. Or could she have gone to him looking for support – financial help or whatever?'

Becky frowns. 'I really wouldn't think so, but I suppose I could give him a call to check. It'll have to be later, though, after the girls have gone to bed. I haven't seen them all day. Plus, I'll need to build up to it. Speaking to that man is rarely a pleasure, usually a chore.'

'Can I take the key in the meantime? I'd really like to go to the house this evening.'

She nods. 'Seeing as it's you. I doubt you'll find anything, though. Make sure you lock up afterwards, and do bring the key back, please.'

'Of course.'

She opens a jar on the kitchen counter and pulls out a single key attached to a tiny replica tennis ball.

'Have you checked her social media?' she asks before handing it over.

'Yeah, several times. Nothing. No recent updates at all.'

'Is that, er, unusual for Jenna? I ought to know this, but it's not really my thing. I don't have time. I'm on Facebook and LinkedIn, but I can't remember when I last checked them. Would she even use either of those?'

'Probably not. She's not really one for posting stuff anywhere these days.'

'Right. Here's the key.'

'Perfect. Thanks so much, Becky. I'll be back with it later. If I find anything, I'll let you know.'

Before I leave, she closes the kitchen door and lowers her voice. 'One more thing. It might sound a bit weird, but how was Scott when you spoke to him earlier?'

Her question throws me. 'Um, how do you mean?'

'Was he offhand with you or anything?'

'No, not really. I didn't mention the key, because I thought it best to speak to you directly. Was that wrong? Have I—'

'No, no, it's nothing to do with that. He just seems a bit... distracted this evening. I wondered if something had happened earlier, that's all. Never mind. It's probably writing-related. He's gone out for a walk now to clear his head. Forget I said anything.'

That's not hard, as once I've said goodbye, the only thing on my mind is Jenna. I hit the pavement and race without further ado to her house.

What am I going to find inside? Please, please let there be some answers.

SEVENTEEN

From: Mr888
To: Jen501
Re: First email

Thanks for your email. Sorry, that sounds overly formal. I'm not used to communicating with you like this. Are we writing the modern version of love letters to each other here? I like the sound of that. How romantic.

I apologise for not replying sooner. I wanted to, but I couldn't get a minute to myself, never mind enough time to log in and construct something meaningful.

I really appreciate the careful way you're going about every-thing. I know it's not ideal, but it won't be like this for long, I promise. We'll find our way through the obstacles in our paths. We have to, because I feel the same way you do. I'm mad about you. You're constantly on my mind.

Let's meet up soon, somewhere we can be alone. I'm sure I

can make an excuse to get out for a few hours one evening. How are you fixed Wednesday/Thursday?

I miss you every moment we're apart.

Love always.

X

EIGHTEEN

Kate

She's alone in the lounge. Danny's doing the washing-up, Lucas is upstairs in his room, and Paige is out – something to do with Jenna.

Kate's on her phone, scrolling through the usual mind-numbing nonsense. Why does she do it to herself? It's like a drug she can't wean herself off.

As a classroom assistant at the local primary school, she gets so much free time over the summer – and this is how she chooses to spend it.

She could be doing far better things, like reading a book, walking in the countryside or visiting somewhere cultural. So why the hell doesn't she?

She switches off the screen and tosses her mobile into the empty space next to her on the sofa. Then the bloody thing vibrates with a notification. What now? She tries to ignore it, only for it to vibrate again. Sighing, she reaches over and picks it back up. There's a new message from a contact saved in her phone as Helen Work.

Hi. Can you chat?

She does actually work with someone called Helen, who lives outside the area and keeps herself to herself. However, they've never exchanged phone numbers.

Her heart races. After first looking towards the doorway to check that neither husband nor son are lurking, she shifts her position so her screen is facing away from it.

Her hands are clammy, and she's breathing faster than usual. Calm down, she tells herself. Take a beat. She closes her eyes and inhales a series of deep, mindful breaths. Then she checks the coast is clear one more time before replying.

Yeah, but not for long. D & L both home. You good?

The response is almost instant.

Not bad. Better if I was with you.

Kate smiles, feeling her face flush as another message follows hot on its heels.

When can we meet... in private? I want you.

NINETEEN

Paige

Jenna's house is on the other side of the village, less than ten minutes by foot if you take the direct route, as I do today.

It's a traditional mid-terrace property built from locally quarried stone. The small patch of grass in the front garden could do with a mow. Weeds are running riot in the gaps in the flagged entry path, which Jenna's mum would never have stood for. The grimy, green-tinged uPVC front door needs a wipe. Otherwise, from the outside at least, the house looks much as I remember it from before my year abroad.

I slide the key into the lock and let myself in. The hallway light is on. Weird. I'm sure it wasn't when I called round before.

'Hello?' I call out, closing the door behind me. 'Jenna? Is that you? Are you here? It's me, Paige.'

There's no reply. Hmm. I turn off the light, as it's plenty bright enough without it and sunset is still some time off.

I walk past the stairway, on my right, and step into the small front lounge on the left. A large cheese plant hugs one corner. There are two sofas, a coffee table between them, a TV on the wall above the fireplace and a circular mirror opposite. An open can of cola stands on the small table, no coaster. This was here when I peered through the window yesterday. I lift it up and give it a shake. Barely any left.

I see movement in my peripheral vision and almost have a panic attack, only to realise it's my own reflection – blue eyes, pale skin despite my travels – caught in the mirror.

Next, I walk through to the kitchen diner at the rear of the house. This is where I first sense that something might be wrong. The place is a mess. There are dirty dishes, used cutlery, cups and pans stacked all around the sink. The hob is filthy; the table is covered in crumbs; the floor hasn't seen a vacuum in a good while. I can smell the bin from the moment I walk into the room. It's like a student house – a particularly grimy one.

Gross. It was always neat and tidy as I remember it, even after her mum got sick. And it's not like Jenna doesn't know how to clean. She gets paid for doing exactly that. From what Dad says, she's pretty good at it too.

Who am I to judge? I've never lived alone like she does. More to the point, I've never lost a parent and had to deal with that kind of intense grief. Her mental state must have been all over the place since the funeral; before that even, watching her beloved mum slowly fade away, knowing there was nothing she could do to stop it.

However, what strikes me as really strange about the filthy scene before me is the unpreparedness of it. Who would go away for a few days leaving their kitchen in this gross state? Not the Jenna I know. Surely she'd tidy up a bit first; at least take out the bin.

I need to see more. I need to go upstairs – to her bedroom in particular. That could well be the best place to find some clues.

As I turn to do so, I jump out of my skin at the sound of a loud bang overhead, like something falling over, or perhaps a door slamming.

What the hell?

Is someone else in the house?

'Who's there?' I shout, heart thumping in my chest. 'Jenna, is that you?'

I force myself to the bottom of the stairs. A large part of me wants to leg it out of the front door, but somehow I stand my ground.

'Jenna?' I repeat. 'My phone's in my hand. I've already dialled the number. All I have to do is press call and I'll be through to the emergency services. I'll say there's a burglar in the house, and they'll be here in no time. Tell me if it's you up there, Jenna. Tell me right this minute.'

My phone's not actually in my hand. It's in my pocket. And I'm not convinced they would be here that quickly either. But what else am I supposed to say?

'Hello?' I shout. 'Last chance. Three... two... one... Okay, that's it. I'm doing it. Don't say I didn't warn you.'

I stand there in silence and listen hard for even the slightest of sounds from upstairs. But there's nothing. Not a peep.

I wait for what feels like ages, not moving a muscle, eyes locked on the top of the stairs. Still nothing.

Shit.

What do I do now?

TWENTY

Danny

He's supposed to be washing up, but he hasn't even started that yet. He's at the kitchen table, on his phone, secretly looking at last-minute holidays. He wants to surprise Kate for their twenty-third wedding anniversary at the end of the month.

Twenty-three years. Wow. Where has the time gone? It feels like only yesterday he was watching her walk towards him down the aisle, resplendent in that gorgeous ivory dress. Happy tears coursing down her smiling cheeks as they made their vows. Holding her tight for their first dance, never wanting to let go.

God, they were so in love back then: him twenty-six, her twenty-four. Babies, really, only a bit older than Paige. That mad, passionate love where they could barely stand to be out of each other's sight for more than a few hours at a time. When arguments were few and far between, and always followed up with profound apologies and intense make-up sex.

Ah, the sex. They couldn't keep their hands off each other at that point. They were always at it. Not just in the bedroom either.

Now. Well, things change over the years, inevitably, especially when children come on the scene. People change, grow
older, with less energy and not quite the same sense of adventure. Far more things to do, each clamouring for a piece of your
precious time. Family takes priority. And the original spark
behind it all becomes part of the furniture.

Recently, this has been bothering Danny more and more.
The spark is still there – certainly from his perspective – but
it feels like it needs nurturing. Over the last few months,
Kate's been increasingly niggly with him about all sorts, and
their love life has slowed right down. Having a twenty-year-
old still living at home, now rejoined by his elder sister,
doesn't exactly help with this. At least toddlers go to bed at a
reasonable hour! It's hard to get in the mood for sexy time
when your adult children are metres away, wide awake,
hanging out in their bedrooms; liable to burst in at any
moment because they can't find the right socks to wear the
next morning and assume you stopped having sex the moment
they were conceived.

Anyway, Danny hopes that a surprise anniversary getaway
– just the two of them – will be exactly what they need to
reboot their relationship. He just has to find the right deal, in
the perfect location, on dates that include their anniversary but
get them back in time for when Kate has to return to work in
September.

Apparently easier said than done. He's been at this for a
while now and still hasn't managed to settle on anything suit-
able. He switches off his phone screen, rubs his eyes and gets up
to put the kettle on.

'Anyone want a brew?' he calls, sticking his head out of the
kitchen door.

'I do,' Lucas replies from upstairs.

'No thanks,' Kate says.

'Are you sure, love?' he asks, bobbing into the lounge, where she's on the sofa with her phone. She places it face-down on her lap and looks up, flustered.

'Sorry? What was that?'

'Are you sure you don't want a brew? That's not like you.'

'Right. Yes, I'm sure.'

'Anything else: water, squash, wine?'

'No, I'm fine.'

'Everything okay? You seem—'

'Could I just get a few minutes to myself, please?'

'Of course. Sorry, love.'

Danny plods back to the kitchen, more convinced than ever that he needs to surprise his wife with this holiday. The ideal location, of course, would be Lake Como, in Italy, where they went on their honeymoon. Surely that would inject some magic back into their relationship. But he's not having much luck finding a good deal for such a popular, picture-perfect location. Any holiday would be better than a silver plate, though. That's what the Internet told him was the perfect present for this anniversary. Yeah, right. What would she want with one of those? Bloody Internet.

TWENTY-ONE

Paige

I've been standing in silence at the bottom of Jenna's staircase for ages now, frozen to the spot. I still haven't heard a thing since that initial crash from upstairs, and I'm starting to calm down. Thinking something must have fallen over by itself. Like the shelf in the shower at home, for instance, that's held in place by suction cups and occasionally works its way loose. Perhaps a vibration from a passing lorry was to blame. I didn't hear or feel anything, but I was at the back of the house at the time.

It'll be nothing. Calm down.

If I think that enough, will I start to believe it?

Cautiously I edge forward towards the bottom step. I place one foot on it and then the other, squeezing the banister with my hand.

Come on. You can do it.

Slowly but surely, I make my way upstairs, eyes like searchlights, scouring every fresh section of the upstairs landing as it gradually comes into view.

There are three bedrooms, but it's the bathroom I tiptoe

into first. I guess I'm hoping to see something along the lines of that shelf in our shower, hopefully lying on the ground and thus offering an easy explanation for what I heard. But Jenna's house doesn't have a stand-alone shower like ours. It's an over-the-bath one with a curtain. And that's currently drawn. Oh my God, like that iconic horror film, *Psycho*.

I step towards the bath, knowing I have no choice but to do the obvious and whip the plain white shower curtain to one side. And yet that's the very last thing I want to do. Because what if there actually is someone on the other side, waiting to pounce?

Don't be stupid. Of course there isn't. Remember why you're here. Who you're here for.

Okay, okay. I'm going to do it. But first a moment to pull myself together. I take a deep breath and let out a noisy exhale. Raise my right arm so the tips of my fingers are almost touching the curtain.

Slam!

Shit.

I spin around, terrified, and see that the bathroom door has banged shut behind me.

What?

I freeze, crouched.

Then I hear the *thump, thump, thump* of someone racing down the stairs.

Escaping.

This sudden realisation kick-starts me into action. They'll be gone without a trace if I don't react.

I yank the door open and spill out onto the landing, straight down the now empty stairs into the hallway. The front door is wide open. I run down the path, onto the street, panting from fear and sudden exertion.

Look one way.

Then the other.

But there's no one in sight.

'Aaaah!' I let rip at the top of my lungs.

I pace up and down the pavement for several minutes, peering into nearby gardens and alleyways, watched from their windows by several concerned neighbours, but I find nothing. No one.

Dammit. If only I hadn't frozen. If only I'd reacted that bit quicker.

In my exasperation, I knock on the front doors of a couple of the curtain-twitchers.

The first is a scrawny grey-haired man, who I'd guess to be in his late sixties. 'Hello,' he says, eyeing me warily from inside his hallway. 'Is everything all right? Can I help you?'

'I'm a good friend of your neighbour Jenna,' I say. 'Strange question, but did you happen to catch sight of anyone leaving the house just now, other than me?'

He frowns and slowly shakes his head. 'No, I'm afraid not. Is that what you were shouting about? Is everything all right?'

'Yes, sorry. I didn't mean to alarm you, but... Never mind. What about Jenna? When did you last see her?'

'Oh, um, I'm not really sure. At the weekend, perhaps. Why? Is she all right? Poor girl. She recently lost her mother to cancer. Cared for her right until the end.'

'I know. She's, er, fine, as far as I'm aware. She's had to go away for a few days. I'm just, um, checking up on things.'

The next neighbour I speak to – a mum in her early thirties, who comes to the door with her young baby in her arms – didn't see anything either.

'Sorry, love,' she says. 'I only came to the window after I heard you shout. So do you think it was a burglar you interrupted? Did they take anything? How did they get in?'

'I'm not sure. I'd better go back and have a look.'

'Well, you be careful,' she says. 'Would you like me to call the police?'

'No, that's okay. I've got it covered.'

'If you need anything, give me a shout,' she adds. 'I'll be in all day. She's a lovely girl, Jenna. Always has a big smile on her face, despite everything she's been through.'

I thank her and head back to Jenna's house.

The last thing I want to do is call the police. Just thinking about that freaks me out with bad memories. But if there is any sign of forced entry, what choice will I have?

The weird thing is, I can't find any evidence whatsoever of a break-in. I check every door and window, upstairs and down, and they're all as they should be. Which can only mean one thing: the intruder had a key. Okay, I guess they could be some kind of experienced master lock-picker, but is that realistic? I've had a close look at the locks on the front and back doors, and there's nothing I can see to suggest any tampering. Plus the front door was locked when I arrived. They *must* have had a key. It's the only sensible explanation.

Unless...

What if it was Jenna herself?

Hmm. I can't imagine that being the case. Why would she run away from me, of all people? Ignoring my calls and messages is one thing, but pretending not to be home and then scarpering without identifying herself, giving me one hell of a fright in the process... No, that makes no sense. My best friend would never do that.

There is another option.

What if I imagined the whole thing?

No, not this again.

But what if the bathroom door slammed shut due to a gust of wind?

Wind from where? There were no external doors or windows open at the time. And what about the front door being left open at the bottom of the stairs after the intruder ran out?

Exactly. Maybe I didn't close the front door properly when

I came inside, and that blowing open was what led to the bathroom door slamming shut.

But I did close it. I'm sure I did. Well, fairly sure.

And the noise I heard upstairs prior to that?

Plus the sound of someone running down the stairs afterwards.

I did definitely hear that... didn't I?

Oh God. I'm going round in circles, arguing with myself.

I thought I was well past all this indecision and self-doubt. It didn't rear its head at all while I was travelling.

Now, back home, the first sign of stress and I'm at it afresh. Questioning what I've seen and heard with my own eyes and ears.

Well, I'm definitely not calling the police. That's for sure. Not while there's any room for doubt about what happened here. I'm not being led down that rabbit hole again. They were the ones that started this.

I lock the front door from the inside and walk back through to the kitchen. Fill the sink with hot water and washing-up liquid. Start the lengthy process of cleaning the place up.

Why? Because this I can control.

This is tangible. This makes sense.

TWENTY-TWO

Becky

She's been feeling bad ever since Paige left for Jenna's house. Like she should have gone with her to check things out and not been so quick to dismiss her concerns. She doubts there's anything to worry about, but still... Jenna is her sister. Also, Paige has been gone nearly two hours now and hasn't yet returned with the key, although maybe she's already back next door and plans to return it tomorrow.

Either way, it'll be good to show Paige that she cares and isn't a heartless bitch, which is how she fears coming across sometimes, especially at work.

Scott's shut himself in his study since returning from his walk and the girls are upstairs. She sits down in the lounge and dials Paige's number.

'Hi, it's Becky. Sorry to bother you. I thought I'd give you a quick call to see how you got on. Are you still at Jenna's, or...'

'Um, yeah. I'm still here.' Paige hesitates. 'Sorry. I was about to leave, actually. I, er...'

'No need to explain. I'm not checking up on you. Have you

found anything, though? Any sign of my sister at all, or where she might have gone?'

'Um, no, not really. Sorry.'

'Oh, that's a shame. I was hoping you might have had some luck.'

'There is one thing that seems a bit weird.'

'Go on.'

'She left the kitchen in a right mess. Dirty plates and all that. She hadn't even taken the bin out. Don't you think that's odd if she knew she was going away?'

Becky laughs. 'I have to say it really doesn't surprise me. She's kept it that way ever since Mum died. It's disgusting, I know. I probably should have warned you in advance. I've told her it'll attract ants or even vermin if she's not careful, but my words seem to go in one ear and out of the other. She's the one who has to live there, and she's a fully grown adult. What can you do? And yes, I know she works as a cleaner. The irony is definitely not lost on me. Honestly, I wouldn't read anything into the mess. That's my sister for you. Is the rest of the place a tip too?'

'Not really.'

'Well, that's something.'

'I, er...' Paige hesitates again, her voice falling away. 'This is embarrassing, but the reason I'm still here is actually because I've been tidying up the kitchen.'

Becky pulls a face in disbelief. 'What? You haven't. Seriously?'

'I guess it made me feel like I was doing something useful. You must think I'm a right idiot.'

'Hey, no judgement here. All I'm thinking is that you're a great friend to my sister. I hope she appreciates it when she gets back. Are you nearly done?'

'Almost.'

'Good. You really didn't need to do that, but nonetheless, let me say thank you on her behalf. And please, wherever you're up to with it, you've already done more than enough. Get yourself home now and put your feet up.'

'I will. Is it okay if I drop the key back tomorrow?'

'Sure.'

'One more thing,' Paige adds. 'Does anyone else have a spare key – a neighbour, for instance – or is it just you?'

'Only me, as far as I know. Why?'

'No particular reason. I'm curious, that's all.'

Becky squints into the distance, not buying that explanation, but she lets it go for now and says goodbye.

She quizzed her elder daughter in her bedroom earlier regarding Jenna having a secret boyfriend.

'How do you know that?' Jess asked. 'Did Paige say something, or Amber?'

'No,' Becky lied. 'Jenna told me a while ago, but she wouldn't say who it was. I wondered if you might know more, seeing as you're close to her.'

Jess hesitated. 'She, um, said she was in love. That's all.'

'Did she tell you who with?'

'No, never. She said she couldn't.'

'Hmm. Anything else?'

Jess scratched her head and fidgeted. 'Um. Why? Is Aunt Jenna okay?'

'Yes, I'm sure she's fine. But I would like to know, love. Come on, you can tell me. I'm Jenna's big sister. Like you are to Amber. I ought to know.'

'They, er...'

'They what? Come on, spit it out.'

'She got really upset when I was with her last week. She was crying, and when I asked her why, she said they'd had a fight.'

'A fight? What kind? What about?'

Jess shrugs. 'Like an argument. Not an actual fight. I don't know why. Honest. She wouldn't say. But I think they might have split up.'

While mulling over the details of this conversation, Becky remembers her earlier promise to call her father to see if Jenna has gone to visit him, as unlikely as that might be.

It's the last thing she feels like doing, but she probably owes it to Paige.

Fine. But first she needs to pour herself a glass of wine.

TWENTY-THREE

Zack

He's watching from his bedroom window when Paige returns home, carrying something in a plastic bag in her right hand. He's angled the blinds so he can see out without anyone being able to see in. Hence he's comfortable standing there staring at his neighbour, eyes freely wandering up and down her body.

She's gorgeous. Always has been. The things he'd like to do to her, given half a chance. He missed watching her while she was away. Is that the reason she looks so incredibly hot right now? Or has she blossomed? Either way, he's not complaining. He's simply enjoying the view.

Zack's never admitted this to anyone, but one of the reasons he first got with Erin, his now fiancée, was because something about her smile reminded him of Paige. Erin's nowhere near as sexy, not least because of her low self-esteem – he'd never have dared to talk to her otherwise – but she's nice enough for the time being. Will he ever actually marry her? Unlikely. He only proposed after she caught him watching porn on his phone and was ready to end things. She was brought up in a religious household, and while she's not too strict about following rules like no sex before marriage, luckily, she's definitely very vanilla and firmly opposed to sleazy things like one-night stands, strippers and, naturally, porn. He's well practised at keeping his seedier desires hidden away. This was a rare slip-up.

His mind flashes back to that thorny scene, here in his bedroom a few months ago, when his parents, Adrian and Sarah, were away for the night.

There he was, lying on top of the covers, pants around his ankles, while she was supposed to be having a shower.

She burst in without warning to get something she'd forgotten. 'Oh my God! What the hell are you doing?'

'Shit,' he replied, dropping his phone and scrabbling around to cover himself up. 'Sorry. I, er... You said you weren't in the mood, that's all, and I was horny. I thought I'd sort myself out.'

'Gross.' Erin pulled a disgusted face. 'I thought you said you didn't do that.'

'I don't usually,' he lied. 'It was a one-off thing. A mate mentioned this website the other day and, well, curiosity got the better of me.'

'What exactly were you watching?'

Thankfully he'd had the volume muted, and when he'd dropped the phone, it had landed face-down.

'I'll show you if you like,' he said, reaching for it as part of his bluff. 'You might be into it.'

'Yuck. You're disgusting. No, keep it away. I don't want to see. I'm going for my shower.'

Phew. He quickly cleared all evidence from his browser.

When she returned, though, after initially pretending not to be bothered, she launched into a diatribe against the 'normalisation of pornography'. Tired, grumpy and unsated, Zack made the mistake of arguing. Next thing, she was ready to go home and call quits on their entire relationship, because they had 'totally different mindsets' and it was 'clearly going nowhere'.

Zack, who'd never enjoyed a long-term relationship or frequent sex of any kind before, panicked. Foolishly, with hindsight, he said he knew exactly where they were going, before getting down on one knee and popping the question.

Anyway, it did the trick, together with a fib that he'd not look at porn again. Now he keeps kicking the matter of a wedding date into the long grass whenever she brings it up, blaming money or whatever he can think of at the time, while frequently using the word 'fiancée' to keep her reassured.

Now, watching Paige and her pert behind disappear into the house next door, he imagines himself casually asking her out.

Yeah, right. Like he'd ever have the balls to approach her in real life, expecting to have a chance. When she called at the house yesterday, he was every bit as awkward as he always used to be around her. Later that night, when he was having sex with Erin, he imagined it was Paige; that they'd just met in an Australian youth hostel, and she'd climbed into his bunk bed in the middle of the night, going at it regardless of the people all around them.

How many guys did she sleep with over there? Zack wonders, not for the first time. The idea of it being a lot fills him with a heady cocktail of lust and disgust.

She and Jenna are the same, he thinks, shutting his bedroom door and walking towards the bed, a kinky sneer folded into his face. What a pair of dirty little slags. Utterly filthy. And there's only one way to deal with sluts like that: by teaching them a lesson. Yeah, by disciplining them.

TWENTY-FOUR

Paige

As soon as I get home, I go to my bedroom. Before I do anything else, I need to stash away what I found in Jenna's kitchen.

Having finally finished the washing-up, I was opening drawers and cupboards, trying to work out where things went, when I struck gold. In an unassuming bottom drawer, next to some neatly folded napkins, I came across a pink case that I remembered Jenna using to protect her laptop. And sure enough, when I unzipped the padded sleeve, it contained exactly that. So I brought it home with me.

I hide the laptop under some clothes in my cupboard. I already tried switching it on at Jenna's, only to get a low battery warning. There was no charging cable in the case or anywhere I could find, but I'm sure we must have something compatible here. There's a desk drawer in Lucas's bedroom full of all kinds of old cables. I'll have a rummage when he's out at work tomorrow. For now, I don't plan on telling him or anyone else, particularly Becky, that I have the laptop.

Should I have taken it? Probably not. But this is Jenna we're talking about. And if she is in trouble, she's only going to thank me in the end for doing everything I can to help. Right? That's what I keep telling myself.

Also, if there was someone in her house, maybe this was exactly what they were looking for. That would make taking it away – keeping it out of their grasp – a good thing.

I found nothing else of note, despite rooting around all three bedrooms. There was no sign of Jenna's phone, keys, wallet or ID; no information to suggest she'd gone away on a planned trip. Her bedroom was messy, but nothing out of the ordinary. Her mum's room looked untouched from when she was alive. A half-read romance novel on the bedside table, never to be finished, brought a lump to my throat, as did the stack of sympathy cards on the bed in the spare room.

Maybe I'll return the laptop tomorrow before I give back the key. Becky will be out at work in the day, so plenty of time.

We'll see. It depends what I find on there, assuming I can access it. I know what the password used to be, from using it occasionally when we were hanging out. Fingers crossed she hasn't changed it.

Lucas appears at my door. 'All right, sis? You were gone for ages. Did you find anything out?'

'Not really.' For a moment I consider telling him about the person I thought I heard in Jenna's house. But the words won't come out. I'm terrified even he, my brother, will insist on me reporting it to the police. And I can't go through that again. Not after last time. That's what sparked this doubting and questioning myself in the first place. And then I was starting from a point of clarity. I was a hundred per cent sure what had happened until they made me rethink it. Now there's no clarity at all.

'She left the place in a right mess. Well, the kitchen, anyhow. It was full of dirty dishes and stuff. I, um, tidied up a bit. A lot, actually. That's what took so long.'

Lucas throws me a look like I've lost the plot. 'You did her washing-up? Seriously? Bloody hell, sis, you really *are* a good friend.'

I smile at this last comment. 'I know, right?'

'But there was no useful info there?'

'Not that I could find.'

'This might be of interest to you, then. I meant to tell you earlier, but I forgot.'

'What?'

'You know John and Lucy opposite.'

'Yeah.' He's referring to a retired couple in their seventies who live over the road.

'They got CCTV fitted about six months ago,' he says. 'The cameras aren't obvious, which is weird if you ask me. Where's the deterrent in that? Anyway, this mansion I'm working at, there was a CCTV guy on site today and it reminded me. I was thinking about that loud cry we heard at the barbecue. Maybe one of their cameras caught what happened. If you ask to see the footage, you might be able to find out whether it was Jenna or not.'

I run over to him and give him a tight squeeze and a kiss on the cheek. 'That's brilliant. Lucas, you're a star. I love you.'

'Easy, tiger. No need to get carried away.'

'I mean, you could have thought of this sooner.' I wink. 'But better late than never.'

TWENTY-FIVE

Paige

'Hello, stranger,' John says in a booming voice, answering the front door. 'This is a nice surprise on a Tuesday morning. Home from your travels, I see.'

'Hi. That's right. How are you, Mr Brown?'

'I'll be better when you stop calling me by my father's name.' He chuckles, scratching one ear, which draws my attention to his hearing aids. 'It's John, please.'

'Sorry.' I try to speak nice and clearly without being too obvious about it. 'How are you, John?'

'Great, thank you. And please, don't be sorry. I appreciate the courtesy. It's rare these days, especially among youngsters like yourself. That Zack from next door to you, Adrian and Sarah's lad, he barely even makes eye contact if I see him out and about. You're not pals or anything, are you?'

'Um, no. I don't really know him very well, to be honest.'

'Probably better that way. He's a strange one all right. Always staring at people from his bedroom window, like one of those stalkers.'

I can't disagree, but I have more important things to talk about than Zack, so I roll my eyes and nod rather than say anything specific.

'How are *you* keeping, Paige?' John asks. Your parents told me bits and bobs about your trip. Sounds like you had a whale of a time. Is it nice to be back?'

'Oh yes. I loved it over there, but it's always good to come home, right?'

'I think so. Anyway, what can I do for you? Would you like to come in?'

'I will, if that's okay. Thank you. I was hoping to ask you a favour.'

'Of course.' He stands back and swings the door wide, gesturing for me to enter, before leading the way to the kitchen. 'I was about to make some tea. Lucy is upstairs. I'll give her a shout. Please, have a seat. Make yourself comfortable.'

He goes to the foot of the stairs. 'We have a visitor, love,' he calls. 'Paige from opposite. I'm putting some tea on.'

Back in the kitchen, he fills the kettle and gets out three cups. 'Tea okay? Or would you prefer coffee?'

'Tea, please.'

'Coming right up.'

He doesn't hear what I say next. 'Sorry, what was that?'

'She asked if we did anything nice at the weekend,' Lucy replies, entering the kitchen at the perfect moment. She turns to me, placing a hand on my shoulder. 'How nice to see you. We heard you were back.'

John leaves us to chat while he makes the drinks, which he then carries to the table on a small tray with a plate of chocolate digestives.

'Here we are.' He sits down opposite me.

'Did you catch any of what we were just talking about, love?' Lucy asks.

'Not really. The kettle was drowning everything out.' He looks at me and shrugs. 'My ears aren't what they used to be.'

I smile. 'Yes, don't worry. Mrs... sorry, Lucy was just explaining.'

She places a hand on her husband's knee. 'Do you remember that dreadful blood-curdling scream I heard when I was in the garden on Saturday evening? You missed it because you were inside watching television. I told you and you said not to worry about it.'

John nods unconvincingly. 'Right.'

'Well, Paige and her family all heard it too. They were in the back garden having a barbecue, and it was so loud it gave them quite the scare.'

'I see.'

Lucy gives him a look that says: *I told you so*. Then she adds: 'Paige is concerned it might have been something to do with her friend Jenna. She wondered if we could check our security cameras to see if they caught anything. We can do that, can't we?'

'Um, yes. I don't see why not, as long as we know roughly when it happened. It should all be recorded on the computer. Whether or not there's anything to see, though... that depends if it took place in view of a camera. I can certainly have a look for you, Paige.'

He heads upstairs to his office while Lucy asks all about my year abroad.

A few minutes later, John calls: 'Lucy? Paige? You'll want to come up here and have a look at this. I might have found something.'

TWENTY-SIX

Scott

Jess walks into the kitchen, a sheepish look on her face, as he's making a pot of coffee. 'Daddy?'

'Yes,' he replies, waiting for it.

'I have to tell you something.'

'Right. Go on then.'

'I, er, think I might have blocked the toilet.'

Running a hand through his hair, he resists letting out a frustrated sigh. 'Okay. Thanks for letting me know. It's fine, love. I'll sort it.'

'Sorry.'

'You didn't try to flush anything weird, did you?'

She shakes her head vigorously. 'No, I promise. Just normal toilet paper.'

'Don't worry, then. It's not your fault. It happens.'

Shit happens, more like. And far too often with that bloody loo. He's given the girls strict instructions to tell him if it blocks rather than try to fix it themselves, so he can hardly be annoyed at Jess for doing what she's been told.

Leaving the coffee to brew, he goes upstairs to sort it, armed with rubber gloves, a watering can, an empty bucket and an ancient wooden spoon. He's an old hand at fixing this particular problem. And one if not all of these devices should do the trick.

It takes a couple of attempts, but he soon manages to shift the smelly blockage and returns downstairs feeling pleased with himself.

He cleans and puts away his makeshift plumbing tools, then pours himself a much-deserved mug of coffee.

'The toilet is all fixed now, girls,' he calls out.

'Thanks, Daddy,' Jess replies, her voice coming from his study, where the door he deliberately left closed is now ajar.

He storms in to find her, to his horror, sitting at his desk, hand on the mouse, looking at the screen like it's the most normal thing in the world.

'Get off there now!' he shouts. 'What on earth do you think you're doing, using my computer without asking? How dare you. You know you're not even supposed to be in here without permission.'

'But Daddy, I—'

'I don't want to hear it. I said off. Now.'

Her eyes well up and her lower lip begins to quiver, but Scott is unaffected. He's still seeing red. 'What are you waiting for? Now means now. Right this minute. Up to your room, young lady. And stay there until I tell you otherwise.'

In one sudden move, she gets up from his office chair and runs around the desk, past him and out of the room. He hears her thump up the stairs behind him before slamming shut her bedroom door.

Bloody hell. What did he even leave up on the screen? Nothing bad, he doesn't think. Thank fuck. But that's not the point. On another occasion, it could have been. Both girls know not to touch his computer, iPad or mobile unless he specifically grants them permission to do so. Or at least he thought they did,

Jess especially. But apparently not. She shouldn't even have been in this room without supervision. Thank the stars his phone wasn't on the desk. That was safely tucked away in his pocket. Plus, it's locked with a strong pin and biometrics.

It's probably time to start locking the computer down too, with a passworded screen saver.

He managed to avoid swearing at Jess, anyway, which is something. He doesn't like raising his voice at either of the girls. However, it does feel warranted on this occasion, like a kind of shot across the bows.

When he gets in front of the computer screen and sees what Jess was doing, he immediately softens. It's an educational game from school called *Marvellous Maths*. So he just laid into his ten-year-old daughter for voluntarily doing homework during the summer holidays. Brilliant.

Amber appears at the study door. 'Why were you shouting, Daddy? Jess is in her bedroom crying.'

'Your sister came in here and used the computer without asking. You know you must never do that, right? Otherwise, Daddy will get cross. Like I just did with Jess.'

Amber nods vigorously. 'I won't, Daddy, I promise. Is Jess in big trouble now?'

'Never you mind about your sister. That's a matter for me and Jess. You run and play, okay? Leave your sister alone for now, please. Would you like a drink or a snack?'

She shakes her head. 'I'm fine.'

Once she's gone, Scott gulps down his cooling mug of coffee before heading back to the kitchen, leaving the study door firmly shut, to pour another. He'll go up and speak to Jess in a few minutes to try to calm the waters. First he needs to work out how to do so while still conveying the message that what she did was wrong.

He takes a seat at the kitchen table and puts the radio on in a bid to drown out the voices screaming in his head.

TWENTY-SEVEN

Kate

She's busy rearranging the coat rack when Paige bursts through the front door.

'Oh, you startled me,' Kate says, letting out a breath. 'I thought you were upstairs in your room.'

'I think it could have been her, Mum.'

'Sorry? What do you mean?'

'Jenna,' Paige says, panting like she's been running.

Kate throws her daughter a blank look. 'I'm not with you.'

'I think she may have been the one who let out that horrible cry we all got freaked out by at the barbecue. What if it wasn't kids messing about? What if it was Jenna?'

'Based on?'

'The fact she was definitely on our street that evening at around the right time.'

Kate frowns. 'How do you know this?'

'Because I've seen proof.'

'What proof? What do you mean?'

'John and Lucy opposite have CCTV. I got John to look at

the footage from that evening, and there she was, walking past their front garden before crossing over to our side.'

'Really?'

'Yeah, I reckon she changed her mind and was coming to the barbecue after all, but then something bad happened to stop her. Something serious enough to make her cry out in fear, agony or whatever. You were there. You heard that scream, Mum. It was ear-splitting. You must remember how it cut through all our noise. Everyone literally froze.'

'Of course I remember. But what did you see on this CCTV footage? What actually happened?'

'I don't know. The camera didn't catch any of that. It only covers as far as the pavement on John and Lucy's side. So once Jenna crossed the road, she was out of sight.'

'But you heard the scream on the video?'

'No. It's just a camera. There's no microphone, so you can't hear anything.'

'Right. And could you see anyone else walking with her or following her?'

Paige shakes her head, a deflated look starting to spread across her face.

'What about any vehicles passing by?'

'No, you couldn't see as far as the road.'

'When exactly was it that Jenna walked past the camera?' Kate asks next. Having looked at the kitchen clock right before hearing that chilling scream on Saturday, the time – 8.51 p.m. – is burned into her memory.

'Eight twenty-five.' Paige sounds confident.

'The cry wasn't until quite a bit later than that, love. Nearly half an hour. And I bet several other people passed the camera in that time, right?'

'Yeah, but... Jenna was nearby, then there was that scream, then she disappeared. It can't be coincidence.'

Kate scratches her head. 'She hasn't disappeared, though,

has she? She's gone away, that's all. And she took the time to tell your dad and Becky exactly that. If she'd told you too, would you still be so concerned?'

Paige looks down at her feet.

'Come on, darling,' Kate says. 'We all love Jenna, you know we do. She used to be round here all the time, especially when she and Lucas were a thing. She's almost part of the family. And I get that you're bothered about the fact she's gone off somewhere without telling you. No warning or explanation. But don't forget that you've been gone for a year. She's got used to doing things without you. You can't expect everything to go back to how it was straight away.'

'But Mum, I—'

'No, Paige. I really think you ought to listen to your dad. Jenna's worked for him for some time now and she's done this before. More or less exactly the same. She'll be back soon enough, I'm sure of it. You mustn't get hung up on this. You've talked about little else for the last couple of days, and, well, it's starting to worry me.'

'*I'm* really worried about Jenna, Mum, but apparently I'm on my own. No one else seems to give a crap.'

'That's not fair. If I thought there was a reason to worry about her, I would, of course. But I genuinely don't. Sorry. We even sent Lucas round the front to have a look after we heard that cry, remember. If it was Jenna, why didn't he see her?'

Paige stamps her foot like she used to when she was little. 'But Mum... Aargh! I know something is wrong. I can feel it in my gut. I can't stop thinking about it.'

'Relax. There's no need to get worked up. I'll make us a cup of tea, and we can talk this through in a sensible, reasoned fashion. Okay?'

'Fine.'

TWENTY-EIGHT

Paige

I join Mum in the lounge and thank her for my cuppa. It's weird how much people here still rely on tea as the solution for everything. Feeling rough or had some bad news? Stick the kettle on. Need to solve a gnarly problem? Stew over a brew.

Australians drink plenty of tea too, but not with quite the same fervour as here, in my experience. Coffee was more popular among backpackers.

'What are you thinking?' Mum asks, locking her eyes on mine from where she's perched facing me.

I felt like I'd made a real breakthrough when I saw Jenna on that CCTV video. Now, having spoken to Mum, not so much.

'Dunno,' I tell her. 'That I'm still really anxious about Jenna, I guess. That I'm sure something bad has happened to her.'

'Okay,' she replies in a calm voice. 'I understand that. But do you think it's a rational concern? Do you actually have any solid evidence of that being the case?'

'Um...' My mind flashes back to the door shutting behind

me in Jenna's bathroom. Followed by the sound of someone running down her stairs.

That was what I heard, right?

Wasn't it?

No, there's no way I'm telling Mum about that. Not while I'm so uncertain.

She would either think I was losing it again, like last time, during the nightmare period that ended with me crashing out of university. Or she'd insist on me reporting a break-in.

Nope. Definitely not happening. I'm not saying a word about any of that, or the laptop. So what else is there?

'Well?' Mum says after a long silence. 'What did you find at the house?'

'Nothing much,' I tell her. 'But it was a right mess. Loads of unwashed stuff in the kitchen, bin full and so on. It didn't feel like how you'd leave a house if you were going away.'

She rubs her chin. 'Anything else?'

I reel off the obvious again: Jenna's recent bad break-up, the anxious state she was in when I last saw her, plus the fact she's not answering her phone or responding to messages. 'And she looked upset on the CCTV footage.'

'You could tell that without any sound, just by her walking past?'

I ignore this question. I manage to bite my tongue and stay silent, eyes burrowing into the floor.

Mum clears her throat before continuing. 'My advice is to be patient and concentrate on something else. Now your travels are over, it probably feels like you have nothing to focus on, so you're fixating on this. Why not start to have a think about your future instead. What's next for you? Do you have any ideas? You're a clever girl, Paige, and you still have your whole life ahead of you. There are so many exciting things you could do with it.'

Oh my God. I can't believe this has turned into *that* conversation. I knew it was coming, but now? Really? What she's basically asking, in a roundabout way, is when I'm going to go out and find myself a proper job. Time to grow up and settle down. Wow. There was me thinking she really wanted to help track down Jenna. Instead, she serves me a thinly veiled reality check. In her mind, I'm bored and delusional. I need to pull myself together and find some genuine purpose. Brilliant.

I'm about to lash out when my phone vibrates.

I glance at the screen and my mind whirls.

No frigging way.

It's a message from Jenna.

TWENTY-NINE

Adrian

He puts the phone on airplane mode and, with a heavy sigh, slips it into the top drawer of his desk at work.

He needs to stop.

This isn't going to end well.

If anyone was to find out, particularly Sarah... God, he doesn't even want to think about that.

He'd be finished.

If only stopping was that easy.

He's let things go too far. He's dug himself into a hole. What was once pretty easy to keep under wraps is getting harder to control by the day.

Adrian wiggles the mouse on his desktop computer and the screen comes to life. Who's next? Oh, great: Deirdre Fisher, one of the biggest hypochondriacs among his patients. Fifty-five and fighting fit, but firmly convinced she'll be dead by sixty. So she's managed to get past triage. Super. What does she think is wrong with her this time? No doubt she'll have been trawling the

Internet again, convincing herself that whatever minor ailment she happens to be suffering from, if she's actually suffering at all, is a sign of some serious illness.

He tries not to think like this. He does his best to go into every appointment with an open mind, not wanting to miss something significant due to a presumption. But it's hard when you get someone like Deirdre, who's cried wolf more times than he cares to recall and refuses to address the underlying problem of her hypochondria. He's spoken to her about anxiety, prescribed self-help books and even referred her for counselling. However, there's a long wait for the latter, and in the meantime, she continues taking up precious appointment slots that other people usually need far more than she does.

Honestly, sometimes he wants to throttle the woman; give her an actual reason to be concerned about her health. He's imagined himself doing this, or worse, on various occasions.

To the untrained eye, Deirdre would probably come across as happy and relaxed. Anxiety sufferers often have an inherent ability – a kind of self-protection mechanism – to hide their true nature from those who don't know them very well.

Mind you, plenty of people are good at hiding things they don't want other folk to know, even from those closest to them. Sometimes the ones you live with are actually the easiest to keep secrets from. Familiarity has a weird tendency to make people blind to what's right in front of them. He should know.

Anyway, time to get this over with. Adrian buzzes her through and waits for the imminent rap on his door. It usually takes patients around twenty to thirty seconds to walk from the waiting room once their name appears on the LED display.

Knock, knock.

Adrian sighs. 'Come in.'

'Hello, Doctor. Sorry, me again.'

He beams his friendliest smile, effortlessly slipping into the jolly GP persona he hides his true self behind. 'Deirdre! Not at all. How lovely to see you. Have a seat. What seems to be the problem today?'

THIRTY

Scott

There's a quiet knock on his study door.

'Hang on,' he says. 'Don't come in. Wait a minute, please.'

'What are you doing, Daddy?' Amber's voice asks from the other side. 'Why can't I come in?'

'Top secret,' he replies, on his feet. He winces at the clinking sound he makes while tidying away what he doesn't want her to see. 'I could tell you, but then I'd have to tickle your feet.'

His younger daughter giggles. 'You know I don't like feet tickles. They make me wriggle like a fish.'

'Really? That sounds fun to watch. Maybe I'll have to try it.'

'No way. I'm not letting you.'

He sits back down now the coast is clear. 'Okay, you can come in.'

The door swings open and Amber glides into the room, sliding her socks across the laminate floor rather than walking normally.

'Where are your slippers?' he asks. 'You know you're not supposed to wear socks on their own. It's too easy to slip.'

'I like slipping.'

'You won't when it happens unexpectedly. I want you to go and put them on, okay?'

'Okay.'

'Do you know where they are?'

The seven-year-old shrugs dramatically. 'Maybe in my bedroom.'

'What can I do for you anyway?'

'I'm hungry.'

'Really?'

She nods.

'It's a bit early for lunch. Why don't you have a piece of fruit?'

Amber pulls a sad face and bats her eyes at him. 'Likkle bickie?'

'Okay, you can have one out of the tin. But only one, yeah? And ask your sister if she would like one too, please.'

'Thank you, Daddy.' She runs unexpectedly around his desk, into view of what he's just taken pains to hide from her, causing him to jump to his feet in alarm.

'What do you think you're doing?' he snaps.

'Coming to give you a hug,' she replies defensively, looking at him wide-eyed, like she's about to burst into tears.

Calm the fuck down, man, he tells himself, using his left foot to carefully slide the bottle of Scotch under his desk without knocking it over. His glass, thankfully, is already tucked away in a drawer.

'Right. Of course.' He lifts her onto his knee and kisses her head. 'Your hair smells nice. Like freshly cut apples.'

'I washed it last night,' she replies, 'with Mummy.'

'I can tell.'

'Your breath smells funny.'

'Oh? That's probably because I, um, had some cough medicine a minute ago. It tasted yucky.'

'Are you sick, Daddy?'

'No, I'm fine.' He feigns a brief coughing fit. 'Apart from this little tickle in my throat.'

'Why couldn't I come in at first?' she asks, squinting at him.

'Never you mind, nosy.'

She flashes him a cheeky grin. 'Was it something to do with my birthday?'

'Birthday? That's not coming up any time soon, is it?'

'Daddy! Of course it is.' She rolls her eyes. 'It's next month. You know that.'

'Do I? Hmm. We'll see. Now run along and let me get on with my work, please.'

She reaches forward for his mouse. 'Can I see what you're doing?'

Scott bristles, but he reminds himself that he turned the monitor off before inviting her in. 'No. And don't touch that.'

'Why not?'

'You know why not. We've been through this. On your way now. And don't forget to shut the door again.'

She does as he asks, for once, and as soon as she's gone, he feels bad.

If only he *had* been doing something for her birthday. He's barely even thought about that yet, other than the odd rushed discussion with Becky about presents and a party. It's not until the end of September, which still feels ages off, but it'll be here in no time.

He has to get his mind back in the game of being a good dad. He should be doing more with the girls while they're on holiday, taking them out on day trips and so on. He certainly shouldn't be shutting himself away in here all the time and leaving them to their own devices, while numbing his pain with covert daytime boozing.

He needs to sort his mess of a life out. It feels like he's juggling hand grenades right now. He has to fix things sharpish, or soon enough he'll get found out.

THIRTY-ONE

Paige

'Earth to Paige. Hello? Can you hear me? What's going on? I've asked you several questions and now you're staring at that bloody phone like you got a message from God.'

'Um, sorry, Mum. I really need to read this.'

'Do you know how rude you're being? Maybe this kind of thing was okay when you were with your backpacker friends, but—'

'No, Mum. You don't understand. She's messaged me at last. I have to—'

'Sorry, who messaged you?'

'Jenna. Please let me read it.'

Hi Paige. Sorry, I'm not avoiding you. Honest. Just need some time away alone. Crap phone signal here! Don't worry, I'm fine. Will explain when I'm back x

'And?' Mum asks after a lengthy silence. 'What does she have to say? Is everything all right?'

I put my phone down. 'She says she's fine. The mobile signal is bad, apparently.'

'There you go. I told you so. Where is she?'

'She didn't say.'

'Presumably somewhere remote if the signal is so poor. Anyway, you can stop worrying about her now and relax.'

I nod without saying anything in reply. Because I'm still concerned. Sure, it's great that I've finally heard back from her, but... I don't know. I have a bad feeling. *Is* it even her? How do I know for sure? Is the tone of the message off somehow, like someone else wrote it? Or am I so paranoid I'm seeing things that aren't there?

John's silent CCTV video of her walking along the pavement alone on Saturday evening haunts me. The lack of sound made it feel really eerie. And then, of course, there's what happened at her house yesterday.

'Do you think I should try and call her?' I ask Mum.

'No, love. Leave her be. If she wanted to chat, she'd have called you. You already left her several messages, right? So she knows you're here for her. Sometimes the best thing you can do as a friend is to give a person space when they need it.'

'I guess so.'

That evening, I go to return Jenna's spare key to Becky. She invites me in and, chatting alone in the kitchen, I tell her about the message I received earlier from her sister.

'Oh good. I'm so glad she got in touch at last. She said everything was okay, right?'

'Yes. She mentioned having a bad mobile signal. Does that sound like your dad's place?'

Becky shakes her head. 'No, she's not there. I rang him yesterday evening; he said he hadn't heard a peep from her.'

'And you believed him?'

'Yes. He's a terrible liar. I'd have known if he wasn't telling me the truth.'

'Right, I see. Where do you think she might be, then?'

'Your guess is as good as mine. At least she's been in contact now. I was getting worried after everything you said. I thought I was maybe being too complacent about the whole thing. Jenna and I might not be close like you two are, but she'll always be my baby sister. I couldn't bear for anything bad to happen to her.'

When I return home, Mum and Dad are watching TV in the lounge.

Upstairs, I find Lucas lying on his bed, scrolling through TikTok on his phone.

'Hey, sis,' he says, chuckling. 'Have you seen this cat singing blues music? It's hilarious.'

He angles his phone screen in my direction, but I wave a dismissive hand in the air. 'Not now. I'm not in the mood.'

'How come you're still sulking? I thought you'd be happy now you've heard from Jenna.'

'I'm not sulking. I'm knackered, that's all.'

'Whatever.'

I continue to my own room, shut the door behind me, and perching on the edge of my bed, pull Jenna's laptop out from underneath and onto my knee. I swivel into a more comfortable position on top of the duvet, open the screen and power it on.

To my relief, it finally loads up. I managed to find a charging cable in Lucas's desk drawer, as hoped, earlier today. But as soon as I plugged it in, the damn thing started a major software update, which took for ever.

At the login screen, I take a deep breath and enter the password I remember Jenna used to use. Please work.

Yes! It's accepted. The old machine chugs its way through the procedure of opening up the operating system.

Okay. Now we're getting somewhere. Do I feel like an

intruder? Yep, one hundred per cent. Even more so than when I was snooping around inside Jenna's house – probably because I got permission first from Becky to do that.

I'm doing this for my best friend, I remind myself.

I find bits of old schoolwork, loads of random documents and a web-browsing history featuring online clothes shopping, hair and make-up tutorials, plus – eww – videos of people squeezing spots. Typical Jenna.

But when I open her email app – which is already logged in, luckily for me; no further password required – I find something that feels significant. There are two separate email accounts set up: her usual one, which I recognise, and another that I don't, in the name of Jen501. The inbox for this account contains several messages, all from the same sender: a Mr888.

My jaw drops as soon as I start to read.

THIRTY-TWO

From: Mr888
To: Jen501
Re: Last warning

Okay, you really need to stop sending me emails now. I'm not going to check the account again after I send this, so you'd be wasting your time anyway.

We're done. I've told you that plenty already, but apparently not enough for it to sink in. Our relationship is over. Have you got that? It was fun while it lasted, but now it's finished – for good. Please accept this and move on.

Don't think this means you can approach me in person or try to contact me via any other means. If you do, you'll regret it, trust me. I won't stand for it. I've had enough.

And the same applies to you-know-what. I don't want to hear any more about how bad you feel. Get over it and move on.

Don't even think about trying to clear your conscience by telling someone. Not if you know what's good for you.

If you dare say a word to anyone about any of this, from start to finish, I'll find out. You DO NOT want me as your enemy, trust me. Last warning.

THIRTY-THREE

Zack

He bumps into his mum as he's putting his trainers on by the front door.

'Oh, hi,' she says, walking in from the kitchen and looking briefly startled. 'I didn't know you were home. I thought you were still at Erin's place, or at work.'

'Day off,' he says. 'I got back from Erin's a few minutes ago. I didn't know you were home either.'

'Right. I was doing some gardening out the back. I'm off to a yoga class in a minute at the sports hall. Are you going for a run?'

'Yeah.'

'Nice day for it. Heading up on the moors?'

'That's the plan.'

'How come you're off work on a Wednesday?'

'I had a lieu day to use up.'

'I see.'

No you don't, Zack thinks, because I've just told you a big fat lie. He should be in the office today, slogging away doing grunt work in his role as a trainee chartered accountant. But he phoned in sick because he didn't feel like it. One of the few advantages of living in the sticks is that no one around here has anything to do with his job. So he can easily get away with going out and about when he's supposed to be stuck on the loo with chronic diarrhoea and vomiting.

'It's coming out both ends,' he told his pushover boss at the city-based accountancy firm earlier, using his well-rehearsed pathetic ill voice. 'I've been backwards and forwards from the loo all night. I could try to bung myself up and head in, but I'm afraid of having a messy accident. And I wouldn't want to spread this about the office. My girlfriend had it the other day. You should have seen the state she left the bathroom in...'

'No, no. You stay home. Get yourself better.'

No one likes hearing people talk about crapping and puking, which is exactly what he was going for. Worked a treat.

Now he could probably get away with being off for the rest of the week. He'll aim to return on Friday, though, staying at Erin's tomorrow so his parents don't catch wind of it. That way, he'll look like a trouper to his colleagues, especially if he plays it up and acts like he's dragged himself in too soon.

'I'll see you later,' he says to Sarah, swinging his small ruck-sack onto his back and heading out of the front door.

'Okay. Have fun. You've got your key, right, in case you're back before me?'

'Yep. Bye.'

He pops in his Bluetooth earbuds, turns on some music and starts jogging as soon as he's outside on the drive. When he emerges onto the pavement, mind elsewhere, he almost bumps into a figure walking past.

'Hey!'

'Mind where you're...' he says, only stopping himself from blurting out something rude when he looks up and sees Paige frowning at him, mouth agape. He removes one earbud. 'Oh, it's you.'

'You nearly took me out there, Zack!' she replies. 'Bloody hell. Don't you think you ought to be the one watching where you're going, shooting out of nowhere like that?'

'Right,' he says, wanting to meet her eye but fixing on his trainers. 'Oops, I guess.'

'Seriously? Is that your idea of an apology?'

'What's up with you?' he snaps. 'Jeez. It's not like I actually ran into you. Chill.'

'*You* chill. What the hell's your problem?'

Before he can reply further, his mum's voice cuts in. 'Morning, Paige. How are you?'

'Hi,' she says, face softening. 'I'm fine, thank you for asking. Just doing my best not to get mowed down by Zack.'

Brilliant.

'Oh dear. Watch where you're going, Zack. Neither of you are injured, are you?'

'No, Mum. We're both fine. I didn't actually run into her. It was a near miss.'

To his dismay, rather than getting in the car, she approaches the pair of them with her yoga mat in one hand and gym bag in the other. 'Come on, you two. Play nice.'

He wants to roll his eyes, although he knows better than to do this in front of her.

She squeezes his arm. 'Zack, have you said sorry for nearly knocking Paige over?'

Great. She's taking her side.

'Sorry, Paige,' he says, realising it's his only way out of this excruciating exchange.

'And?' Parental death stare.

'My fault. I, er, should have been looking where I was going.'

'That's better. Are you happy with that, Paige?'

She nods.

'Good. Let's all get on, then, shall we? I'll be late if I don't hurry up. See you both later.'

All three say goodbye, and Zack continues on his way, earbud back in place, music pumping as he curses under his breath. He pulls out his vape and has several long puffs to calm himself down.

THIRTY-FOUR

Kate

Paige has gone out for a walk. Kate's not sure where to or for how long. She didn't ask. But safe in the knowledge that she has the house to herself, for a little while at least, she can't resist picking up her phone and pinging a message to the contact saved as Helen Work.

Hi. How's it going?

As ever, she feels a rush of excitement surge through her body when she sends it. It's nice to be able to do so without looking over her shoulder for once.

The reply arrives in less than a minute, making her smile.

All the better for hearing from you. What are you up to?

She sits back on the sofa and gets comfy, digging in for the kind of flirty chat that she knows will get her pulse racing and make her feel alive again.

What they're doing is dangerous. She knows that. That's a big part of the reason it's so exciting. She's tried to stop, but the adrenaline rush it gives her is like a drug. She keeps coming back for more.

It started innocuously enough. A brief exchange about day-to-day stuff. But then it continued, and gradually developed into the kind of racy conversation that required precautions: frequent deletions and, eventually, the disguising of contact names.

So far, it hasn't moved beyond messaging.

It's still in the territory of fantasy.

But for how long?

If they are both truly as into each other as it seems, it's inevitably going to spill over into real life at some point, right? If they were alone in a private room at this very minute, with no chance of getting caught, she doubts she'd be able to stop herself doing what she's imagined so many times.

Because of this, she knows she should bring it to a halt. Now. Before it escalates out of all control.

But she doesn't.

She can't.

K: *Not much. Thinking about you.*

HW: *Oh yeah? Thinking about me doing what?*

K: *I think you know what.*

HW: *Ripping off your clothes?*

K: *Maybe.*

HW: *With my teeth...*

K: *Now I like the sound of that.*

HW: *What are you wearing?*

K: *What do you want me to be wearing?*

HW: *As little as possible. God, do you know what you're doing to me with these messages?*

K: *Sounds like you need some relief.*

HW: *That's an understatement.*

K: *Maybe you should help yourself.*

HW: *I'd rather you helped me.*

K: *Slow or fast?*

HW: *Maybe both? I could help you too.*

K: *Like how?*

HW: *With my tongue.*

K: *Now we're talking. You'd have to lick me all over first, tease me until I'm ready to burst.*

HW: *Minx. I'm throbbing.*

K: *Oh yeah?*

HW: *Would you like to see?*

Kate gasps. Bites her lip. Pauses. Puts the phone down.

This would be a significant escalation. Even though they've frequently chatted about meeting up and so on – doing all sorts of things to each other – they've never moved beyond words before.

If she says yes, there will be no going back.

She takes a deep breath.

And then, heart pounding like a lusty teenager, unable to stop herself stepping into the void, she snatches the phone back up and starts typing.

Okay, do it. Let's see what I'm missing.

THIRTY-FIVE

Paige

Oh my God. Zack. What a total bellend. First he nearly runs straight into me, and then he tries to make out it's my fault. If Sarah hadn't shown up when she did, we'd have had a full-blown row in the street.

How can someone so nice have such a dickhead as a son? It's not like his dad's a weirdo either. Adrian's always been lovely to me, as both a caring GP and a friendly neighbour. What the hell happened with Zack to make him such a nasty piece of work? And why does he so obviously hate me? Goodness only knows what this fiancée of his sees in him. She must either be weird too or the exact opposite: an angel with a heart of gold who's somehow able to see past his many flaws.

He picked the wrong morning to be a prick. He's lucky his mum stepped in. I'm in a terrible mood, because Jenna's laptop is screwed. Right after I read the most recent email in her inbox last night – a damning collection of warnings and threats from the so-called Mr888 – it had a meltdown. Frozen screen, no cursor movement, nothing at all.

Then it went from bad to worse as the screen changed to blue with a sad face and a message about the PC needing to restart. And has it? Not a chance. Not even overnight. This morning it remains stuck on zero per cent progress.

I'm once again firmly convinced that Jenna is in trouble, regardless of the message she appeared to send me yesterday. Something is wrong – badly wrong. I can feel it in my bones. And it's driving me mad knowing there are various other emails to and from this Mr888, which I'm desperate to read but can't bloody access.

Last night I even tried logging into the Jen501 email account using the web browser on my phone, but it wanted a different password. I made a few incorrect guesses. Then a warning popped up about the account being locked if I got it wrong another time. So I gave up and phoned Jenna again – but of course she didn't answer.

And yes, I've tried turning her laptop off and on. Loads of times. Same stupid blue screen.

I'm at my wits' end. That's why I've come outside for a walk. To try to clear my head. Calm myself down. Fat chance with Zack around.

So what next?

Well, I messaged an old friend of mine earlier: a girl I lived with during my time at uni, who recently graduated with a first-class honours degree in computer science. Carmen's parents only live a short drive away, and I reckon there's a good chance she's probably living with them again at the moment while she sorts out what she's doing next with her life.

It's ages since we've seen each other, largely thanks to me being abroad, but she was a massive support to me when things went wrong during my disastrous second year at uni, and I'll never forget that. She's a friend for life. We've kept in touch online, and I can't think of a better person to ask about this. It's not like I'd be happy taking the laptop anywhere official to get it looked at. How could I when it's not even mine?

I feel my mobile vibrate in my pocket. I pull it out and see, as I hoped, that it's Carmen calling. 'Hey!' I answer. 'Long time no speak. How's it going?'

'I'm great. You're back at last!'

After catching up, we get on to the reason I contacted her. 'So you're in need of my IT super skills, are you?'

'Yeah, I really am. Quite urgently. I need the laptop for something important and it's lost the plot. It won't budge past that bloody blue screen.'

'The blue screen of death.'

'Is that what they call it?'

Carmen laughs. 'Yeah, I'm afraid so.'

'Does that mean I'm screwed?'

'Not necessarily. Not when you have me in your corner.'

'So you'll look at it?'

'Sure, if you can get it to me at my parents' house. I have some spare time. No promises on a fix, though. There is a reason this kind of system crash has such a dramatic name, but I'll do my best.'

'You're a legend.'

'You know it.'

'When would be a good time for me to pop over?'

'Whenever you like. We could go for a coffee or something to have a proper gossip. I'm thinking of going travelling myself, so I'd love to pick your brains about Australia.'

'Perfect. I could possibly get over sometime today, if that works. Assuming Mum isn't using her car and she's happy for me to borrow it.'

'I've no plans today, so yeah.'

'Amazing. Leave it with me.'

THIRTY-SIX

Carmen

'My friend's probably coming round later,' she tells her mum after getting off the phone.

'Oh, that's nice, love. Someone from school?'

'No, from uni. Remember that girl Paige I lived with who dropped out during second year?'

'Um, the one who had a breakdown?'

Carmen frowns at her mother, who's busy gardening. 'That's not a very nice way of putting it.'

'Sorry, I didn't—'

'She had a really tough time of it, Mum. I'd have probably dropped out too in the same circumstances. The university let her down big-time. They closed ranks and sided with one of their own; threw her to the dogs. It was disgusting.'

'Poor girl. Is she all right now? I didn't realise the two of you were still in touch.'

'Yes, she seems good. She recently got back from a year travelling around Australia.'

'Are you looking to get some tips?'

'Exactly. Can I invite her to stay for tea?'

'Sure.'

'She went alone, by the way. Like I told you, loads of people do it.'

'It's not that I don't believe you, Carmen. I worry, that's all. Your father and I both do. It's not you we don't trust. It's other people. Whatever you say, you are vulnerable as a young woman travelling alone. There are lots of predators out there.'

'Yeah, I'm not stupid, Mum.'

'Of course you're not. But you're not invulnerable either. If you really want to go by yourself, that's your choice. You're a fully grown adult. We simply want you to be aware of all the risks and take the necessary precautions. Plus, we'll miss you. We've only just got you back.'

She puts down her trowel and, arms open wide, gestures for Carmen to come into a hug, which she does, despite rolling her eyes. 'Cut us some slack, love. You're our only child and we love you dearly.'

THIRTY-SEVEN

I let myself into the disused property, having walked most of the way with a baggy hoodie on to disguise my identity from any passing motorists. Luckily, I didn't see anyone else on foot. There were a couple of cyclists, but I made sure to look away when they passed. I'm as certain as I can be that no one would be able to identify me if it came to it.

Not that I expect any such thing to happen. This place is in the middle of nowhere in the countryside, far off the road I walked along, down a muddy track, nowhere near anything or anyone else. That's why I picked it. There's not even a rambling trail in the vicinity.

An abandoned, ramshackle old cottage hidden away by overgrown trees and bushes. The slate roof is moss-covered and bowed in disrepair. Thick ivy coats the stone exterior walls, its tendrils enveloping the grimy window panes and rotting wooden frames with their flaking, blistered remnants of ancient white paint.

An ideal place to hide away from the world – or, more to the point, to keep someone problematic hidden away while you decide what to do with them.

I follow the overgrown path past the long-abandoned Citroën 2CV with its flat, perished tyres and frayed, mouldy soft-top hood. The once light blue paint is now more of a greenish yellow, flecked with rust spots and years of accumulated grime.

I go to the back door, which remains surprisingly solid, despite the peeling black paint, and use my key to slide open the shiny, heavy-duty padlock I've put in place to secure it.

Inside, the old cottage is cool, bare and eerily quiet, other than the sound of the heavy timber door closing and then the echo of my shoes crossing the hard stone floor.

I make my way up the creaky staircase, covered by the threadbare remains of a blood-red carpet, and stop outside the bedroom door, which is held shut by another padlock. It will open with the same key I used to get inside the property. I should know – I installed this one too, with a little help from the Internet. But before I do this, I pause and listen for any sign of potential trouble. I know she's securely tied up in there, but still... better safe than sorry.

Gingerly I slide the key into place, open the chunky padlock, remove it and hold it in my right hand so I can use it as a weapon if required. I take a deep breath.

How the hell did we end up here? Not long ago, the main thing I wanted to do to her with my hands was caress her soft skin. If only she'd listened. If only she hadn't been so bloody stupid. She brought this on herself, foolish girl. She pushed me to the edge and turned me into this person I barely recognise. Capable of doing things I didn't know were buried within me. Self-preservation is a far more powerful thing than I ever realised until now.

I swing open the door, fists clenched.

She's lying on the mattress on the bare floorboards, ankles bound with thick cable ties, attached to the big low beam above by two heavy-duty security chains. I fixed them so she can only move a small distance. Not as far as the window or door, but *enough to reach the two buckets I've provided as makeshift toilets.*

I've also left plenty of water within reach, and several packs of plain biscuits to stave off her hunger in between my visits. I'm not an animal.

She looks up at me through drowsy, unfocused eyes. Groans like she's trying to say something, still under the effect of the drugs I gave her, it seems.

On my guard, just in case, I remove the small rucksack from my back and kneel down a short distance away from her.

'Are you okay? Have you been eating and drinking?'

'Why?' she asks in a throaty gurgle.

'Because you'll die if you don't.'

'What do you care?'

'I wouldn't have left you anything if I didn't care. This is temporary.'

'Yeah, right.' Tears course down her grubby cheeks, already hollow from the ordeal of the past few days.

I desperately want to believe that this will all be over soon. That things will return to normal for both of us. But I'm not delusional. I understand the serious nature of what I've done. What I'm still doing.

I know deep down that there's no likely way back to normality for either of us. But equally, I pray that I can pull a rabbit out of the hat and – somehow, miraculously – find a route out of this that doesn't end in tragedy.

I'm not a killer.

Am I?

I don't think I am.

The last time doesn't count, because that was an accident. There was no clear intention on my part. It was a case of wrong place, wrong time. Right?

But this is different. If I...

No. I mustn't think that way.

I pray it'll never come to that.

I'm sure I'm not a killer.

But what if I can't trust myself?

I didn't think I was a kidnapper either. I wouldn't be in different circumstances. If that accident hadn't happened, or if she'd responded to it in a more reasonable way, none of this would have come to pass.

And yet here we are.

THIRTY-EIGHT

Paige

I'm nearly at Carmen's parents' house, according to the satnav in Mum's car.

It feels weird, driving in the UK again. I did it a few times in Australia, where they thankfully also drive on the left, but not for long, so I'm definitely out of practice. I've already stalled the car a couple of times, and I had one hairy moment on a busy roundabout. But I'm getting the hang of it again now, I think.

Towards the end of the short journey, as my confidence grows, my mind starts to wander. I find myself thinking about the day I left university for good, basically running home with my tail between my legs.

Carmen was the last person I spoke to before I got into this very car, in which both my parents were already waiting, with the last of my things filling every available space in the boot and on the back seat.

'So I guess this is goodbye,' I said to her at the front door. She was the only one of my housemates around; she should have been in lectures, but she'd made a point of being home to wave me off.

'I'm really going to miss you, Paige.'

'Me too,' I said, tears pricking my eyes. 'You've been such a good friend these past few weeks. I don't know how I'd have survived without you. Thanks so much.'

'You're welcome. I still can't believe everything you've had to go through. You deserve so much better. The whole thing is a pile of bloody shit. I totally get why you're leaving, but it shouldn't have come to this.'

I nodded, words escaping me.

'Who am I going to hang out with now?' she added, a catch in her throat.

'You'll be fine. You have loads of friends here.'

'Not like you.' She took my hand in hers and squeezed it. 'At least you've got lovely Jenna to look out for you at home. She's a superstar, that one.'

'I know. You too, Carmen. I'm so lucky to have the pair of you in my life.'

'Let's meet up when I'm next back home, yeah?'

'I'd like that.'

'And if you ever need to chat, I'm always here for you.'

I nodded again, my emotions threatening to get the better of me. 'Thanks,' I croaked.

We hugged goodbye for ages, neither of us saying anything. I was sobbing, and when we finally pulled apart, I saw she'd been crying too.

The mere memory of that moment – vibrant, compassionate Carmen, a rose among the thorns of such a devastating time in my life – is powerful enough to bring tears back to my eyes now. I gulp, shake my head and blink them away.

'Come on, Paige,' I say out loud, like my own personal life coach. 'Pull yourself together. You're nearly there now, and you don't want to arrive all emotional. This needs to be a happy reunion. You need to show Carmen how much you've rebuilt yourself since that day. How you're so much stronger and full of self-confidence now.'

THIRTY-NINE

Carmen

'Girl, you look amazing,' she says as they embrace on the pavement. 'It's so great to see you.'

'You too,' Paige replies. 'You look fantastic. The blue hair is such a slay.'

'Ah, thanks.' Carmen throws her head back and laughs. 'Please tell that to my mum. She's not feeling it at all. She says it looks like I've joined the blue-rinse brigade, whatever that means. Definitely not a compliment.'

It's fantastic to see Paige looking so much better than when she left uni. She was broken then. A shell of her normal self, shattered by the very system that should have protected her.

It was heartbreaking to witness. And such a wrench on Carmen's conscience at the time. She'd been ready to drop out of uni herself in solidarity at one point, when things had first turned to shit for her friend. She'd been all for roping in the students' union and getting militant. But that wasn't what Paige had wanted. She'd already had enough and was purely focused on getting out of there.

'But it's not right,' Carmen recalls saying to her washed-out, barely functional friend, still in bed late one weekday afternoon. 'It's not fair. They should be protecting you, not him. Justice needs to be served.'

'But it's not that straightforward, is it? No one believes me, Carmen.'

'I do – and others will too if we tell them. We can stop this being brushed under the carpet. It's not like the old days any more. Victims get heard now. MeToo has made a difference.'

'Has it? Maybe in some cases. That's not been my experience, though.'

'I know. And that's exactly why we need to act. If we get the right people involved – make a fuss, get press coverage – we can bring the truth to light.'

'Tell that to the police. They think I'm a liar. I don't have the strength for it, Carmen. I'm done. I'm not the kind of person who can spearhead a campaign like that. I'm already beaten.'

'Who's going to stop this happening again?'

'Someone tougher than me, hopefully. I wish I could, believe me. I wish I was strong enough. But I can barely leave my room. I've taken this as far as I can. I can't go on. I need to get away from here. Start again.'

'I can do it for you. I can be the strong one.'

'No, we've been through this before, Carmen. I don't want you to get drawn into my mess. I'm not letting you put your own future at risk for me. Steer clear, please. You're an amazing friend, but this isn't your fight.'

Looking at Paige now, eighteen months on, she seems so much better. Almost back to how she was before... and yet different. She'll always be scarred by what happened to her, no doubt. But hopefully she'll be stronger as a result, like a broken bone that's been allowed to properly heal.

She's smiling again, like she used to. And yet, after a few minutes of chatting in person, Carmen also gets the sense that something's weighing on her friend's mind. Not like before. Different. As if she's concerned about something or someone other than herself. It's hard to say exactly how Carmen comes to this conclusion. It's a hunch more than anything, but she's always been good at reading people. Could it be something to do with this laptop Paige wants her to look at, which is presumably in the rucksack she's carrying? There must be some reason she's so keen to get it fixed, although she hasn't even mentioned it yet.

As Carmen puts the kettle on, her mum walks into the kitchen.

'Hello, Paige.' She shakes her hand, weirdly formal. 'I'm not sure if you remember me. I'm Angela, Carmen's mother.'

'Yes, of course, hi,' Paige replies with a big smile.

Mum probes her about her travels before disappearing into the garden.

'Thanks for that,' Carmen says.

'For what?'

'Everything you said about travelling alone. Mum's stressing big-time, so hopefully what you told her will put her mind at ease.'

'Are you definitely going? Australia?'

'Well, now's my chance, isn't it? I also fancy South East Asia and India, but Mum doesn't know that yet. Did you meet any nice boys in Oz?'

Paige cracks a cheeky grin. 'Oh, you know. There were a few hook-ups. Nothing serious.'

'Oh yeah? Get you. Hopefully I'll come across a few hot surfer girls along the way.'

'Still a single Pringle, then?'

'Yep. I was kind of seeing a girl for a while during my final year at uni, but I ended it a couple of months ago.'

'How come?'

Carmen giggles. 'Well, it was never really heading

anywhere beyond the bedroom. She was pretty dull to chat to. Zero banter. Very closeted. I'm enjoying playing the field again now.'

They agree to head out for a walk and some cake at a nice café on the high street. But first, Carmen asks to see the laptop.

'Pretty much as expected,' she says, closing the lid after a quick look. 'How soon do you need it?'

'Asap.' Paige pulls a face. 'It's, um... There's a story behind it. Confession: it's not actually my laptop. It belongs to my friend Jenna. You remember her, right?'

'Of course.'

'Well, it's complicated, but I'll do my best to explain. Shall we walk and talk?'

As they make their way to the café, Paige brings Carmen up to speed.

'So that's it,' she says, wrapping up. 'That's everything. The whole story. I've told you more than anyone else, even Lucas and my parents.'

'Wow,' Carmen replies. 'That is a lot to take in.'

'What do you think?'

'Um. It does all sound really sus. If Jenna was my best mate, I'd be worried too, even if she has taken herself off somewhere.'

'Do you reckon that's likely?'

'I've no idea. But even if it is, that doesn't mean she's fine. The break-up obviously left her fragile. And this mystery man of hers sounds like a scumbag. Do you reckon it was him in her house when you were there? Because that's seriously creepy. Proper sinister.'

'I know, right?'

'Basic question, but she's not posted anything on her Insta or whatever since she disappeared?'

'Nope. I've been checking all her socials every day. Her Snapchat location's off too.'

'That sucks.'

'So you'll help me with the laptop?'

'I'll do my best. I can't promise to fix it, though. It might be beyond saving.'

'Thanks, Carmen.'

'No worries. How are you, um, dealing with it all?'

'It's really hard that no one else seems worried about Jenna. It makes me question whether I might be imagining the whole thing. What if she *has* just gone away for a bit?'

'I get that,' Carmen says. 'It's not... too much, is it? You're not...'

'Losing the plot again?'

'Those aren't the words I'd choose. But you are dealing with it all okay, right? You're not letting it get on top of you?'

Paige stops walking and takes her hand, squeezing it tight. 'Yeah, I'm okay. I'm much stronger now than I used to be. The travelling was a big help. But I still have my moments from time to time. I can't help but think back to what went on at uni. If enough people tell you something didn't happen, it's hard not to question yourself. You know how badly it affected me back then. I was starting to doubt my own memories. If I hadn't had you, Jenna and my family to support me, believe me, I'd have gone to pieces even more than I did. My mind was playing all sorts of tricks on me. For a while I was in danger of losing all sense of what was real and what wasn't. I can't go through that ever again.'

'Oh, Paige. Come here.' Carmen pulls her into a tight hug.

FORTY

THEN

Paige

I approached him at the end of the lecture, having waited until most of the other students had drifted out. He shuffled his papers into order on the lectern, following a brief conversation with a lad from the front row. By the time I was standing in front of him, he was shutting his leather briefcase.

'Hi,' I said, trying to keep my voice steady despite the nerves. 'I wondered if I could, um, have a quick word about my essay, sir.'

He peered at me over his reading glasses before removing them from his heavily wrinkled face and sliding them into the top pocket of his tweed jacket.

'Sir?' He scratched the side of his short grey hair before offering me a tight smile. 'Is that what you used to call your teachers at school?'

'Um, yes. The male ones.'

'Right. Well, we're not at school now, are we? Please just call me Jeff. I feel old enough as it is, surrounded by all you bright young things. Sir makes me sound like a relic, which I probably am, but I'd rather not be reminded of that.'

I chewed the inside of my cheek and told myself not to be fazed. But I couldn't help feeling like a stupid, naïve kid in that moment, rather than the confident second-year university student I wanted to project to one of the most senior, well-respected members of the history department. 'Sorry... Jeff.'

'That's better. So you want to discuss an essay?'

'Please.'

'No problem. Now please don't be offended by this, but I'm afraid you'll have to remind me of your name. I'd love to be able to remember every student in the department, but I've learned to accept that this is not within my capabilities.'

Of course, I was a little bit offended. No one wants to be forgettable, but at least once I informed him of my name and the essay in question, he seemed to remember me.

'Ah, yes, Paige,' he said. 'So what would you like to discuss? Is it something quick, or would you rather walk back with me to my office and talk about it there?'

I opted for the latter – and how I wish I hadn't. If I'd known the rabbit hole of misery it would lead me down, I'd never have done it.

FORTY-ONE

NOW

Danny

He gets in late from work, just after 6.45 p.m., to find Kate in the kitchen making a curry for tea.

'Oh, hi. I thought you were out,' he says, giving her a peck. He was aiming for her lips, but she turned her head at the last minute so he got a cheek. 'Good day?'

'Why did you think I was out?'

'Because your car isn't on the drive.'

'Oh, right, yeah. Paige has gone to see an old uni friend. She's staying there for food, so it's just the three of us eating tonight.'

'So there's meat in it?'

'Yes, chicken.'

'Excellent. Uni friend? Who?'

'That nice girl Carmen she used to live with. The one who was really supportive before she left. She's finished her course now and is back with her parents.'

Danny tells Kate the food smells lovely and asks how long he has until it will be ready.

'At least another half an hour,' she snaps, frowning, like she's annoyed by the question.

'Chill out. I was only wondering whether I had time to have a shower first, which apparently I do.'

'I'm glad my meal time meets your requirements, sir.'

'Bloody hell, Kate. What's got your goat today?'

'I'm tired. And I've already had enough of Lucas asking me when it will be ready. He's ravenous, so he keeps saying. And he still hasn't emptied the dishwasher, although I've reminded him numerous times.'

'Where is he? In his room?'

She nods.

'I'll have a word.'

Before leaving, he tries to put his arms around his wife from behind as she tends to the stove, but she shrugs him off. 'Not now. Can't you see I'm busy?'

God, she's so cold with him these days. She didn't even ask if he had a nice day at work. He needs to get this surprise last-minute getaway booked sharpish. Tonight, preferably. Surely that will cheer her up and get him back into her good books. He's still aiming for Lake Como, even though he's not yet found a good deal. It might have to be for four or five nights, rather than a full week, to make everything work: cost, timings, etc. But that'll put a smile on her face, won't it? A nice romantic gesture and a well-earned break for them both from the stresses of day-to-day life. Like always having to remind your twenty-year-old son to empty the dishwasher, despite it having been one of his regular chores for as long as Danny can remember.

He bobs into Lucas's room. 'All right, son?'

Lucas is lying on his bed, watching something on his phone. 'Hi, Dad.'

'Good day at work?'

'Yeah, fine. You?'

'Busy. Could you empty the dishwasher, please?'

'Yeah.' Lucas remains glued to his mobile.

'Before we have tea. Your mum says she's already asked you loads of times. Come on. This isn't a hotel.'

'Right.'

'I'm going for a shower. If it's not done by the time I'm out, there'll be trouble.'

Lucas sighs and puts his phone down. 'Chill your boots. I'll do it now.'

Before heading into the bathroom, Danny tries to phone Jenna. Arranging further cover for her was one of the reasons he was late home this evening. Her absence is a hassle, and it's starting to do his head in.

Her number goes straight to voicemail. Again. Bloody hell. This is ridiculous.

He messages her instead.

Are you coming back soon, Jenna? I need you at work. It's not on, disappearing like this without warning. You need to get back to me and let me know what's going on asap. My patience is running thin.

He leaves his phone on the bedside table while he goes for his shower: a much-needed soothing few minutes of warm relaxation.

Afterwards, sitting on the bed as he slides on comfortable shorts and a T-shirt, his mind returns to his AWOL employee. He checks his mobile for a reply. Nothing. Goddammit. If she was anyone else – rather than his daughter's best mate, Lucas's ex and a generally lovely girl who recently lost her mother to cancer – he'd have canned her already, poor phone signal or not.

He's too damn soft for his own good.

And yet... He thinks back to that awful cry that sliced through the air during Saturday night's barbecue. So loud and shocking that it instantly silenced everyone. Paige convinced herself at one point, according to Kate, that it was somehow linked to Jenna. At least until her friend finally messaged her back.

What if Paige's suspicions were right?

What about this secret ex-boyfriend of Jenna's? Could he have done something to her?

Hmm. It sounds far-fetched. More like a TV drama than reality. He can't imagine that kind of thing happening somewhere so quiet, so ordinary as round here.

'Tea's ready,' Kate calls from downstairs.

'Coming.'

FORTY-TWO

Adrian

'Who wants a brew?' he calls from the kitchen after he finishes doing the dishes.

Both Sarah and Zack shout back that they do, from their respective locations elsewhere in the house, so he fills the kettle and sticks it on.

A moment later, someone rings the doorbell.

'I'll get it, shall I?' Adrian says after no one else reacts.

He swings open the front door to reveal Lucas from next door.

'Good evening, young man,' he says. 'How are you?'

'Good, thanks. Is Zack home?' So much for small talk.

'Yes, I think he's in his bedroom if you want to head up.'

'Thanks.'

'I've just put the kettle on,' he adds as Lucas steps inside the hallway. 'Would you like a tea or coffee?'

'I'm fine, thanks. I won't be long. Flying visit.'

Adrian watches Lucas sprint up the staircase, like he

himself used to before his knees started to complain. Then he returns to the kitchen.

He pushes the door to, pulls out his phone and opens the app he's been itching to use ever since he got in from work. The home page appears, his eyes soaking up its familiar colours and branding. He's instantly engrossed, filled with the usual mixed emotions of excitement, anticipation, hope, dread and, of course, guilt.

'Adrian?' Sarah's voice calls from the conservatory, breaking the spell.

Dammit. Can't he ever get a moment's peace?

He swipes the app shut, pockets his mobile and closes his eyes for a second or two before replying in the calmest voice he can muster: 'Yes, love?'

'Could you come here, please? I need to speak to you about something.'

'I'm just finishing off your cuppa. I'll be through in a minute.'

His mind starts to race. What does she want to speak to him about?

Could this be it: the conversation he's been dreading for ever?

Could Sarah finally have got wind of what he's been up to?

Could this be the big showdown, the moment when his house of cards is brought tumbling down?

God, please no.

He thinks back to how Sarah behaved towards him over the dinner table while they were eating this evening. Any hints of an impending face-off? No, not that he can think of.

It'll be fine, he tells himself. It'll be something and nothing. Like all the other times he's got himself needlessly worked up.

'Zack, your coffee's in the kitchen,' he calls to his son.

'Can't you bring it up, Dad?' Zack calls back, bold as brass, probably trying to show off in front of Lucas.

'No. What did your last slave die of? You can come and get it yourself.'

Taking a deep breath, he walks through to the conservatory carrying mugs for himself and his wife.

'Here we are,' he says, painting on a smile, hoping his voice gives away nothing of the anxiety gnawing away at his stomach. He puts the drinks down on coasters on the glass-topped coffee table and takes a seat next to Sarah.

'So, what did you want to talk about, love?' he asks, holding his breath and feigning calmness.

'That son of ours,' she replies, to his infinite relief. 'Did you know he had a random day off work today? Seems suspicious to me. He was also very rude to Paige next door this morning, after nearly knocking her over when he went out for a run. Plus, he's still at that vaping, which can't be good for his health. We need to have a word with him.'

'Right,' Adrian says, breathing normally again. 'Oh dear. Yes, it sounds like we do.'

FORTY-THREE

Becky

She pulls onto the drive at 8.48 p.m. Moments later, as she's removing her work stuff from the boot, Kate's car arrives next door, and Paige gets out from behind the wheel.

'Hi there,' Becky calls across the small stretch of front lawn that separates them. 'How's it going?'

'Hiya, Becky,' Paige replies. 'Just home from the office?'

'I'm afraid so. Busy day. At least it's still light, though. Getting home at this time in winter is like arriving in the middle of the night. Have you been up to anything nice?'

'Visiting a friend I used to live with at uni.'

This surprises Becky, considering the cruel way in which Paige crashed out of her second year at university. She'd almost expect her to have cut off all ties from that time. 'Did you have a nice catch-up?'

'We did.'

'Right, well, I'd better get in. I've not eaten yet and I'm ravenous. Hopefully Scott has a plate of something delicious waiting for me inside.'

'Sure,' Paige replies. 'Er, Becky, I was actually going to pop round to ask you something. So rather than bothering you later...'

Becky's heart sinks, but she tries not to sound impatient. 'Yes? Go on.'

'It's just that...' Paige pauses to clear her throat. 'You know when I was over at Jenna's house?'

Becky takes a slow, deep breath. 'Yes.'

'I've, er, not been able to find my favourite summer cardigan since then. I know I was wearing it when I went there. I remember removing it when I was, um, cleaning the kitchen...' Her voice peters off, like she's embarrassed. Then she adds: 'I must have forgotten to pick it up when I left. I've looked everywhere else for it, high and low, so I'm convinced it's still there. You or Scott haven't been round since and noticed it, have you?'

'No, sorry. Are you sure that's where you left it?'

Paige nods.

'Could it wait until Jenna gets back?'

Chewing her lip, Paige looks down at her feet. 'Um, I guess so... although I was hoping to wear it for this thing tomorrow. Is there any chance you or Scott could possibly swing by there for me in the morning? Or, if it's easier, I'd happily go back myself.'

'Why don't you just do that?' Becky says. 'That'll be the easiest option. Give me a second and I'll grab the key for you.'

She bobs into the house, calling hello to Scott and the girls, gets Jenna's key and takes it out to Paige. 'Here you go. Drop it back when you're done. You can give it to Scott if I'm not around.'

'Thanks, Becky. Sorry to be a pain.'

'It's fine. Anyway, I need to eat. I'll see you later.'

'Yes, you go and have your tea. Thanks again.'

Scott's standing in the hallway, looking confused, when she returns inside. 'Oh, there you are,' he says. 'I thought I heard you come in and then I couldn't see you.'

A little later, he joins her at the kitchen table, both with a glass of cold white wine, as she wolfs down the spaghetti bolognese he prepared earlier.

'Good day?' he asks.

'Busy. You? Did you get a decent amount done while the girls were out?'

'Not bad.'

Jess and Amber, who are both already upstairs in bed but not yet asleep, spent the day with Scott's parents, who drove over to take them to the zoo. By the sound of things, and based on their haul of tat from the gift shop, the girls were spoiled rotten and had lots of fun.

'How were your mum and dad?'

'Fine, yeah.'

'You're chatty today. Everything all right?'

'Hmm. I'm tired, that's all.'

Really? Becky can't help but think. From what: being home alone, seeking creative inspiration, while she was busting a gut on a particularly trying day at the office, earning enough cash to keep a roof over their heads? More like because he was up until all hours last night, doing whatever it is he does when everyone else is fast asleep.

She doesn't say this out loud, of course; she feels bad simply for thinking it. But it's hard not to have such thoughts from time to time, especially on days like today, when Scott's had it easy compared to her. Does he appreciate how lucky he is to be getting the chance to follow his dream? She wonders sometimes. Yes, it must be hard, having received the various rejections he has so far, but as she understands it, that's all part and parcel of the process. Scott's said so himself on countless occasions.

'Almost every successful writer has to surf various waves of rejections before they make it,' she recalls him telling her some time ago. 'The important thing is to hold on tight and never give up.'

'So have you landed on a new idea yet?' Becky asks him in between mouthfuls of spaghetti, partly to make amends for her uncharitable thoughts.

'What's with all the questions?' Scott snaps.

Startled, she puts down her fork. 'All what questions? I'm asking about your day, that's all. It's what couples do. I wasn't exactly giving you the third degree.'

'It feels like everyone's always asking about my next idea.'

'Like who?'

'Well, you and my parents, for a start. And that's only today.'

'Right. Pardon me for showing an interest.'

'If only it was as easy as coming up with a bestselling plot and churning it out. My last two attempts at novels have got me nowhere – and that's haunting me the whole time. Maybe I don't have any good ideas. What about that for a possibility?'

She places her hand on top of his, where it's resting on the kitchen table. 'You'll get there, and whatever you do decide to write this time, I'm confident it will be your breakthrough book. You can do this, Scott. I believe in you.'

To Becky's surprise, she sees tears forming in the corners of his eyes, although he quickly turns his head away in a bid to hide the fact. 'Do you want to talk about it?' she asks, wincing.

'Not really.' He wipes his cheeks, downs his half-full glass of wine in one and immediately pours himself another. Then, hand gripping the stem like he's about to crush it, he stares into the distance, eyes glazed over.

Becky raises an eyebrow but keeps calm. 'Well, it seems like maybe you need to. What's going on, Scott? You're worrying me. Talk to me, please.'

FORTY-FOUR

Paige

I'm in the bath, loving the soothing feeling of being enveloped by the warmth and the bubbles, putting my troubles aside and unwinding.

My temporary bliss is interrupted by a loud knock on the locked door. 'Are you in the bloody bath again?' Lucas's voice demands.

'Yes.'

'Seriously? How long are you going to be? I need a shower. Some of us have to get up for work tomorrow.'

'What? Are you kidding? It's not even ten o'clock. Since when do you go to bed this early?'

'Since now. Today was rubbish at work and tomorrow's going to be even worse. I need shut-eye. Who even has baths at this time of year, you big weirdo?'

'You're not going to charm your way in by talking to me like that,' I reply, wiping foam from my chin. 'And who says you can't have baths in summer? That's nonsense.'

'Whatever. How long are you going to be?'

I let out a sigh loud enough that I hope it might reach my annoying brother's ears. 'Fine, I'll hurry up. Give me half an hour.'

'What? That's way too long. I'm telling Mum.'

I giggle to myself. 'How old are you? Calm down. I'm kidding. I'll be out in twenty-five, okay?'

'Very funny. How about five? You've been in there for ages already.'

'Ten minutes, final answer. Now leave me alone, please.'

'Fine, but it better had only be that long.'

Once I'm out of the bath and back in my bedroom, I check my phone. I'm hoping for a message from Carmen, but no such luck. Instead, I find one from this creepy dude I met during my last few days in Sydney, asking if I'm still around and fancy 'hooking up'. In his dreams. How did he even get my contact details? Not from me. Thank goodness I'm on the other side of the world. He actually reminded me a bit of Zack next door. Aloof, like he was better than everyone else, and never very nice to me. Block and delete. Done.

I can't resist messaging Carmen.

Hi. Lovely to see you earlier. Any news re the laptop? X

She replies straight away.

You too. I'm on it now. No luck so far. Proving tricky but I'm not beaten yet. Keep the faith x

There's a knock on my bedroom door. I'm expecting Lucas, probably doing something gross to get me back for hogging the bathroom, but it turns out to be Dad, who I've barely seen today.

'Hey, how's my favourite daughter?'

'Not bad.'

'How was it seeing Carmen today? Is she well?'

'Yeah, she's good. It was really nice to catch up.'

'Seeing her didn't unearth any, er, bad memories, did it?'

'Um, maybe a bit.' I'm surprised and even touched by this perceptive question from Dad. It's more the kind of thing I'd expect Mum to ask, but she didn't when we spoke earlier. She seemed distracted. 'Don't worry,' I add. 'Nothing I couldn't handle.'

He nods, looking relieved. 'Good. I know the whole Jenna thing has stressed you out already, so...'

'Thanks for asking, Dad. I'm fine.'

He strokes his stubble, still leaning in the doorway. 'I, er, tried contacting Jenna myself today.'

'Really. Any luck?'

He shakes his head. 'I could do with her back at work... yesterday, preferably. Getting cover at the moment is a nightmare.'

I nod, wondering if this is another hint that he wants me to step up. If it is, I ignore it. 'Do you admit now that it's weird how she's disappeared, especially after that awful scream during the barbecue?'

He shuts the door and comes to sit next to me on the bed. 'We've been through this, love. My instinct says that she really needed to get away, maybe because of this break-up. Who knows? Perhaps she wanted to cut herself off from life back home for a while and deliberately chose somewhere isolated. Sometimes people need time alone. It *has* only been a few days, and she has at least replied to you. I see no reason to panic, particularly as she's done this before. And she was totally out of contact then.'

I wonder whether to tell him about the emails and what happened when I was in Jenna's house. But I can't bring myself to do it yet. I feel like I need to build a stronger case first, because of my doubts and the lack of hard evidence at this moment. Maybe if Carmen manages to get the laptop working again, or at least finds a way to access the emails. Perhaps if returning to the house, as I plan to do tomorrow, turns up something tangible. At least my lost cardigan ruse worked with Becky and I have the key again.

'I hope you're right, Dad. I just want my friend back and to know she's okay.'

He puts his arm around me. 'I do understand, darling. I worried about you all the time while you were travelling. But I knew you needed to go on that trip, and I had to give you the space to do it. It was hard, but it worked out for the best, right?'

Yeah, but that's not the same, I think.

'Anyway,' he goes on, 'now you're here, I need your help with something. It's about a trip away I'm planning as a surprise for your mum, to celebrate our wedding anniversary.'

'Oh?'

'Yeah, I think I've found what I want to book, but I'd like to run it by someone else first.' He pulls his phone out. 'Can I show you?'

'Sure.'

After Dad's left, I go to get a glass of water from the bathroom, only to find the door locked. I can hear the shower running, so Lucas must still be in there, which is ridiculous after he made me rush out of the bath. Brothers: who'd have them?

I take the opportunity to nip into his bedroom and return the cable I borrowed for Jenna's laptop, since I don't need it at the moment and would rather not have to explain why it's in my room if he comes looking for it.

I sit down on the swivel chair in front of his desk and open up the drawer where I found the cable. It was originally buried under various other rubbish, so I dig deep to return it to a similar position. As I do so, something golden glitters in the light, catching my eye.

What's that? Lucas isn't one for wearing jewellery. Could it be something he's bought for his girlfriend, Sylvia? Surely not. Why would he keep it loose in a drawer?

My fingers grab hold of a delicate gold chain. Baffled, I pull it carefully out from among the collection of junk.

I gasp when I spot the charm attached to it.

Oh my God. I recognise that straight away.

How could I not when it's Jenna's favourite necklace?

A slender gold chain with a gorgeous coffee bean charm, it was an eighteenth birthday present from her mum, inspired by her childhood pet name, Jenna Bean. She wears it more or less constantly. She had it on when I saw her on Saturday afternoon, I'm sure of it. Now the clasp is broken, so no wonder it's no longer around her neck.

The burning question is: why the hell does my brother, Jenna's ex-boyfriend, have it here in his bedroom desk drawer?

FORTY-FIVE

THEN

Paige

I was surprised when we got to Jeff's office to find someone already in there: a smartly dressed woman around his age with immaculate straight blonde hair in a long bob. She was standing at the far side of the room, watering one of several plants by the window.

'Oh,' I said. 'Do you already have another appointment? I'm sorry. I didn't realise. Would you like me to come back another time?'

'No, not at all,' he replied. 'It's fine, honestly. This is my wife, Gail. I'm taking her out to lunch later; she's earlier than I expected.'

He gestured for me to take a seat at the side of his desk, away from the door, which he pushed to, leaving it slightly ajar. Then he walked over to greet his wife with a kiss long and lingering enough for me to feel awkward and divert my eyes towards his bookshelf, as if I was genuinely interested in its contents.

Did this behaviour strike me as odd, considering my presence in the room? Yes, but I told myself they were obviously a very loving couple; that it was sweet they were still behaving that way at their age, especially if they'd been together a long time.

'Gail, this is Paige, one of my second-year students,' he said eventually. 'She grabbed me at the end of my lecture and wanted a word about an essay she wrote for me. You don't mind if I have a quick chat with her before we head out, do you?'

'No, that's fine,' she replied with a smile. 'Hello, Paige. Aren't you a pretty little thing?'

'Hello,' I said, feeling my cheeks turn pink. 'Um, nice to meet you.'

'The pleasure's all mine. Please, pretend I'm not here. As you can see, I'm watering Jeff's plants before they die an untimely death. He always forgets to do it.' She rolled her eyes. 'Too busy, apparently.'

I smiled politely as Jeff walked over to his desk, leaving Gail tending to the plants. I noticed her stroke one of the leaves in an almost sensual way before I turned my attention back to my lecturer.

'Can I get you a tea or coffee, Paige?' He nodded towards a kettle on the other side of his desk to where I was sitting.

'No thanks,' I said. 'I don't want to keep you long.'

'It's not a problem.'

'No, I'm fine, honestly.'

'Gail, darling? Would you like a drink?'

'No, I just had one, thanks, love.'

Jeff nodded, crossing his legs and then throwing an intense look in my direction. 'So, Paige. What would you like to discuss about your essay? Please, fire away.'

I took a deep breath, as discreetly as I could, feeling my heart start to race in my chest. 'Well... I'm a little disappointed with my mark.'

'I see,' he said, leaving a long pause after this, which I took as a request for me to elaborate.

I was about to do so when Gail suddenly exclaimed: 'Oh dear.'

Jeff and I both looked in her direction; she was giggling. 'Sorry, I didn't mean to interrupt. It's just this plant here is looking particularly sad.' She pressed one finger to her lips. 'I'll be quiet now. Please, pretend I'm not here.'

I continued. 'It's quite a bit lower than I usually score and, er, well... I wondered if you could possibly check it's correct. And if it is, fine, but could you then perhaps give me some further pointers as to why? That way, hopefully I'll be able to do better next time.'

'Right,' Jeff said, nodding slowly and scratching the tip of his nose as he squinted pensively in my direction. 'I suppose I'd better pull it up and remind myself what you wrote. Give me a few moments, please.'

'Of course. Thank you. I appreciate it.'

He slid his glasses out of his top pocket and then rooted around in one of his desk drawers for what felt like for ever. Eventually he pulled out a small green cleaning cloth and proceeded to use it to thoroughly wipe each lens. The silence in the room was oppressive by this point; my sense of awkwardness grew with every passing second.

I found myself looking down at my hands, which were gathered in my lap, and scratching at the fingertips of one with the nails of the other. I could sense Gail's presence behind me. I imagined her eyes burning holes in the back of my head. Hurry up, Jeff, for God's sake, I thought. This is excruciating.

But he didn't do anything at more than a snail's pace, so when he eventually reached the point of switching his computer on and waiting for it to boot up, I knew we were still far from getting to the job at hand.

Why was he putting me through this painstaking process,

particularly when his wife was here, waiting for him to take her out? It had to be a deliberate attempt to make me feel uncomfortable, presumably because he felt I was questioning his authority.

I was about to say something to emphasise that this wasn't the case when he beat me to it and broke the heavy silence. 'Remind me of your surname, please.'

I replied, holding out hope that we were now getting somewhere.

But it was another long wait that followed, interspersed by occasional mouse and keyboard clicks, plus the odd sigh and grunt, until Jeff finally spoke again. In the meantime, I didn't hear a peep from Gail, still behind me. I wondered what on earth she was doing. Was she standing there, hands on hips, scowling at me for interrupting their plans? That was certainly what I pictured as I continued to examine every detail of my hands, wishing I could magically blink myself away from this agonising situation.

'Right, I've had a quick look over your essay,' Jeff said, removing his glasses and looking in my direction for the first time in several minutes.

'Okay.'

'I'm afraid the mark is most definitely correct.'

'Right.'

'It just isn't particularly good, Paige. To be frank, it reads like something an average A-level student might write. It certainly isn't what I'd expect of someone in the second year of their degree. Not to worry. We all have off days. I must admit, though, it does concern me slightly that you feel it should have been scored higher. Do you genuinely believe it's a decent essay?'

I hadn't expected him to be this blunt. I was used to my uni lecturers being encouraging and open to debate; his harsh comments cut through my defences and left me vulnerable.

'Um, I don't know. I'm not sure. If you say it isn't good enough, I guess I'll have to accept that.'

'You guess... Hmm. I would never encourage a student to waste time on guesswork. Either have the courage of your convictions and properly argue your case, or don't. How about you tell me what you think is good about your essay?'

'I, er...' My mind went blank. Totally blank. Initially, I couldn't get any words out at all, and then when I did finally manage to speak, it was to say: 'Sorry. I shouldn't have bothered you. I, er... I should go.'

I was embarrassed and incredibly frustrated to feel tears pricking the corners of my eyes, doing little to dispel his opinion of me as an immature charlatan. And it felt even worse, somehow, knowing his wife was behind me, observing everything.

I was about to get up to leave when Gail spoke for the first time in ages, apparently coming to my rescue. 'Jeff, don't you think you're being a bit tough on poor Paige? It must have taken some courage for her to come to you and challenge your marking. Is there any need to be quite so dismissive?'

Suddenly, unexpectedly, I felt her hands on my shoulders, making me jump.

'Gosh, look how uneasy you've made her,' she said, removing her hands for a moment and then placing them back. She bent down and, with her mouth just a couple of centimetres away from my ear, so I could feel the heat and flow of her breath, whispered: 'Don't be intimidated by him, love. He pretends to be all authoritative, but what he really enjoys is to be dominated by a strong woman.'

She shifted position behind me, and next thing, her hands started moving, rubbing and kneading my shoulders and neck. 'Ooh, so tense. Someone needs to unwind.'

I froze, a deer caught in the headlights, as she let out a long, quiet moan, the sound of which made my insides squirm. I willed myself to shift forward in my seat as her fingers slid beneath my bra strap, but shock, fear and revulsion continued to paralyse me. I could barely breathe.

Time stopped.

This was really happening.

Too shocked to properly process the enormity of what was going on, I glanced towards the door, still ajar. I prayed for someone to walk past in the corridor outside in order to bring an end to this harrowing nightmare scenario. But no one did. It remained stubbornly empty.

Placing her mouth next to my ear again, Gail gave a little groan of pleasure. 'I'm sure there must be something a slutty little student could do to improve her mark, right, Jeff?'

I looked at him, sitting on the other side of his desk, eyes fixed on us. To my horror, I saw a smirk creep across his face. His hands slid snake-like off his keyboard and down into his lap.

FORTY-SIX

NOW

Kate

She slips her phone into her pocket as she hears Paige coming down the stairs just after ten o'clock.

'Morning, love.' She stands up from her seat at the kitchen table and walks over to the kettle. 'Sleep well? Body clock finally adjusting?'

'Hmm, not really. I woke from a bad dream in the middle of the night and couldn't get back to sleep for ages.'

'Oh dear. It's as well I didn't wake you this morning, then. You probably needed to catch up. What was the dream about?'

'I don't remember.'

Kate doesn't buy this for a second. There was a time when she would have pushed her daughter for an answer: a time when she was seriously worried about her mental well-being, in the aftermath of what that awful lecturer and his wife got away with putting her through. But it was amazing how quickly she picked herself up and moved on once she'd been removed from the situation.

When she initially mentioned travelling to Australia, even

when Jenna looked all set to go with her, Kate couldn't see how she'd be strong enough to do it. She'd been so broken when she'd first dropped out of uni. But planning the trip had given her something to focus on – a pathway to rebuild herself – and the recovery had been much faster than Kate had ever dared to hope. Her bounce-back was a masterclass in the resilience of youth, particularly when she decided to go ahead without Jenna, much to everyone's surprise, and went on to make a success of her solo trip.

Did Kate fret about her the whole time she was away? Of course, every day, especially at the start, although it got easier as time passed and Paige proved herself more than up to the task. Being able to stay in frequent contact with her while she was in Australia, thanks to the benefits of modern technology, was a big help. Before leaving, Paige had even set up her phone so that she and Danny could view her location at any time from their own mobiles.

'This way you'll be able to see where I am whenever you like,' she'd told them, demonstrating how it worked a few days ahead of flying out.

And although Kate's first thought had been that it wouldn't work if she lost her mobile or someone stole it, both she and Danny did end up using the function a lot. A frequent conversation starter became: 'Have you seen where Paige is today?'

Kate still worried about the unpredictable effect other people could have on her journey. Nasty people, like the pair who'd destroyed her university experience. But luckily, Paige avoided running into any more of those in Australia, hopefully restoring her faith in human nature, at least to some degree.

Despite all of this, Kate does still worry about her now. Her near-obsessive recent focus on Jenna's whereabouts is troubling. Jenna most likely needs a break from her day-to-day life, probably because of this bad break-up. People these days, particularly the younger generation, expect you to be available at all times, which can be exhausting. In the days before everyone had mobile phones, it would be quite normal to go several days without hearing a peep from even your closest friends.

Paige needs a new focus. A good place to start, as Kate's already intimated, would be to concentrate on herself and her next steps. Such as looking for a proper job that could lead to a career.

She almost brings this up again now, watching Paige make herself a bowl of cereal this Thursday morning. The words are on the tip of her tongue. But then she feels her mobile vibrate in her pocket and she's instantly distracted. She's almost certain who the message will be from, and she's dying to know what it says.

Or maybe it won't say anything. Maybe it will be another photo.

Her heart races at the thought of this.

She knows she's on a slippery slope.

She knows exactly where this is heading, and yet still she can't stop herself.

'Was that your phone?' Paige asks.

Kate tries not to look embarrassed or fazed. 'Um, yeah, I think so.'

'Aren't you going to see who it is?'

'When I'm ready. What's the rush? We don't have to live our lives on a schedule dictated by our phones, you know. I'll look at it when it suits me, thank you very much.'

'All right. Keep your hair on. Did you see Lucas before he went to work this morning?'

'No, he'd already left by the time I got up. Why?'

'Oh, I just wondered.'

'Right.'

'How come Sylvia wasn't at the barbecue on Saturday?' Paige asks.

'She's away for a few days. Some family thing down south.'

'Oh, okay. Lucas didn't mention that. I wonder if he's as keen on her as he used to be on Jenna.'

'That's an odd thing to say. You'd have to ask him, I suppose.'

'Do you think he's been a bit, um, weird the last couple of days?'

'How do you mean?'

Paige shrugs. 'Different to normal?'

'Not really. Why do you ask?'

'No reason. It's probably me.'

'Have the two of you been quarrelling?'

'No. It's fine, honestly. Forget I said anything.'

Kate drops it, but only because she's itching to get a moment alone to check her mobile.

FORTY-SEVEN

Paige

Mum is in a weird mood. She nearly bit my head off a few minutes ago when I was having breakfast, purely because I queried if she was going to check her phone when it vibrated.

I only asked because I wondered if it might be Dad contacting her to tell her about the romantic return to their honeymoon destination that he's booking for their anniversary. Lake Como looked gorgeous in the photos he showed me last night. It's so cute that he's planning it all by himself. She'll be over the moon, I reckon.

I've found them a bit prickly and cold with each other since I got back from Oz. Hopefully, this will inject a spark back into their relationship. Not that I want to think too hard about how they might achieve this on holiday. I'll leave that to them, behind closed doors. Good on Dad for making the effort.

As for my brother, I've still to challenge him about why he had Jenna's necklace, with its broken clasp, in his desk drawer. It's not there any more. I moved it to my own jewellery box for safe keeping while he was still in the bathroom last night. He can't have noticed yet. Initially, I was all for having it out with him on the spot. But when he was finally back in his room, he got on a video call with Sylvia. Then, before I knew it, Mum and Dad were upstairs, everyone was heading to bed and the moment was gone. Sleep on what to say to him, I told myself. I'll definitely be confronting him later today. One hundred per cent. He'd better have a damn good explanation.

It's ten past twelve by the time I'm ready to return to Jenna's house.

'I'm going out for a walk,' I say out of the open kitchen window to Mum, who's sitting in the garden enjoying the sun with a cuppa and a paperback. The book is currently closed, perched on the arm of her garden chair, as she types something into her mobile.

'Sorry?' she replies, looking startled.

'I said I'm going out for a walk.'

'Oh. Okay. Where? Are you going to be long?'

'Not sure. Why? Do you need me for something?'

'No. But I, er, might pop out to the shops in a bit, so take a key.'

'Will do.'

I head to Jenna's house, but not in a rush. I take the long route. I'm not looking forward to this.

I'm in her street, a few houses away, when I spot something – or rather someone – that makes me halt dead in my tracks and gasp. He walks out of Jenna's front door, clear as day. Eh?

What the hell has *he* been doing in there? How did he even get inside? And what business would he have doing so?

He can't have anything to do with this... can he?

That would change everything.

Instinctively, I duck down behind a nearby parked van so he doesn't spot me. I watch as he walks through Jenna's front garden and then – shit – turns onto the pavement and heads right towards me.

FORTY-EIGHT

Kate

She presses send and exhales.

Oh my God. Her heart is beating out of her chest and she's perspiring far more than she ought to be sitting in the garden in this temperature.

Her guilty conscience makes her look around to see if anyone might be watching, from a nearby bedroom window or something. But they're not. Not that she can see, anyway. And it's not like they'd have been able to catch sight of what she just sent on her phone. She's being paranoid.

The photo she fired off a moment ago – showing her doing something intimate in the bedroom earlier, after Danny had left for work – was carefully shot so as not to contain any details that might make her identifiable. But she still can't believe she's sent it... to *him*. She's never even sent a photo like that to Danny. And how many times has she warned Paige not to do the same, telling her it could easily end up on a porn website.

So what on earth is she thinking?

Is she having a midlife crisis?

She stares at the screen of her mobile, still on the messaging app, waiting for him to see the sexy snap. As soon as he has, she's planning to delete it for both of them. Partly to tease him and partly for her own peace of mind.

Frustratingly, he no longer appears to be online.

She almost deletes it anyway, but a part of her doesn't want to: would rather throw caution to the wind and wait until he *has* seen it. Because what was the point of taking the photo in the first place and building herself up to sending it otherwise?

She decides to put her phone to one side – face-down, out of reach – and try to read her book for a few minutes to distract herself. She'll chicken out if she doesn't, probably losing her mind in the process.

But almost as soon as she picks up the paperback, before she can even finish one page, her mobile starts vibrating. Not a message this time, but a call. Wow. This will be another first, to actually speak to him on the phone. He must have only just seen the picture, so she's guessing he likes it.

She gets up to retrieve the device from where she tossed it on the grass, and when she looks at the screen, she panics. Oh shit. It's not him at all. It's Danny.

Hang on. She didn't send the photo to *him* by accident, did she? No, she knows she didn't. She's always extra careful not to do anything like that. But still, the paranoid side of her wonders. It's not like her husband makes a habit of calling her when he's at work.

'Danny, hi.' She answers the call as casually as possible. 'Everything okay?'

'Fine. How are you? What are you up to?'

'Nothing much. Chilling in the garden.'

'With Paige?'

'No, she's gone out for a walk. How's work?'

'Fine, apart from Jenna still being AWOL, which remains a

headache, but I won't bore you with the details. I wasn't ringing about work. I have a surprise for you.'

'Oh?' Kate feels the phone vibrate against her ear, presumably indicating she's received a message, which she duly ignores.

'Yes. It's to do with our wedding anniversary.'

'Right.' Kate thanks God this isn't a video call, meaning Danny can't see the look of panic on her face as she realises she's totally forgotten about this – for the first time ever.

'I've arranged something to celebrate,' he says. 'I did wonder about keeping it totally secret, but I thought you'd appreciate a heads-up so you can look forward to it and properly prepare.'

'O-kay.' She has literally no idea where he's going with this.

'I was going to wait until I got home tonight, but what can I say? I'm too excited. I've been planning it for quite a while, and now everything is booked. I think it'll be great fun and also really good for us as a couple. When was the last time we had a night out, just the two of us?'

'A long time ago.'

'Exactly.'

Hang on. Surely he can't be making such a big deal about having booked a table at a nice restaurant. Can he? What else could it be: a show or concert of some kind?

'So? Are you going to tell me, or what?'

'Drum roll,' he says. 'Are you ready for it?'

'Yes, I think so. Hope so. Although, honestly, you *are* making me a little nervous.'

'Ah, nothing to stress about. Quite the opposite. Because... I've booked us a little break in... Can you guess?'

'Not really.'

'Blackpool!'

'Oh. Okay.'

'Yep. Right on the prom, a stone's throw from the Pleasure Beach. It'll be mint. What do you think?'

'I, er, I don't know what to say, Danny. Really?'

'No, of course not really. Are you kidding? Do you actually think I'd get this excited about telling you that? I know we've not been at our best recently. I know we need to work on a few things, but come on now. You know me better than that, surely.'

Kate rolls her eyes. 'I'm getting really confused now, Danny. Please could you just tell me what you do have planned?'

'Okay. I've booked us a five-night trip at the end of this month, including the date of our anniversary, to...' He makes the sound of a drum roll with his tongue this time, before finally coming out with it. 'Lake Como.'

Kate nearly falls off her chair. 'I'm sorry, what? Seriously? Where we went on our honeymoon?'

'Yep. Not the exact same hotel, I'm afraid. That was fully booked. But just down the road. A lovely romantic place with fantastic views of the lake. I think it'll be perfect.'

'Wow. I really am at a loss for words now. That sounds amazing. You're full of surprises. Where did this come from?'

'The bottom of my heart,' he replies. And although he says this in a cheesy voice that flags his tongue being firmly in his cheek, it still brings tears to Kate's eyes.

Her husband hasn't done anything this lovely and romantic in goodness knows how long, and she so appreciates it. It melts her heart to imagine him secretly planning it by himself, excited about surprising her.

Meanwhile, what's she been up to, other than forgetting their anniversary?

Sexting another man, that's what. A man who's probably messaged her while she's been on this phone call to comment on the spicy photo she just sent him.

A man she's led to believe that things are about to move to the next level and get physical in person.

A man who's well known to Danny and the rest of her family, so now has the potential to blow up her life.

Shit, shit, shit.

How the hell can she get herself out of it?

How can she fix this?

Once the call is over and she's thanked Danny, saying it's an amazing surprise and she can't wait to go back to their special place in Italy together, she gingerly opens up her messaging app.

As feared, Helen Work has replied to her photo.

Bloody hell, that's so hot! Are you trying to give me a coronary? When can I touch you there for real, you minx? Let's meet up today, somewhere we can be alone x

Kate groans, drops her phone onto the ground and holds her head in her hands.

FORTY-NINE

THEN

Paige

As soon as I got out of there, on the pavement in front of the history department building, I broke down in floods of tears.

People were staring at me; a couple of them even stopped to ask if I was all right.

I told them I was, because I wanted to be alone, but of course I wasn't. After moving to a nearby bench, so I wasn't such a spectacle, I was overcome by a wave of nausea and vomited on my trainers.

As if I didn't already feel dirty enough after what had happened in my lecturer's office.

To make matters worse, about ten minutes later, I saw Jeff and Gail exit the front of the building, holding hands.

I cowered into the bench, shaking, huddled up in the hope they wouldn't see me. Not like they appeared to be looking. They were chatting and smiling like everything was normal. Totally unfazed. Presumably heading out for their lunch date, as arranged. Because why would they alter their plans on account of me and what had just taken place?

Oh my God. How could it have been real, what I'd witnessed; what I'd been put through?

I pinched myself to check this wasn't a nightmare, because it all felt so weird. So creepy, so... off.

Uni was somewhere I was supposed to be safe. Especially in the presence of one of my department's most respected senior staff. And now I felt anything but safe. I wanted to run far away, puke-covered trainers or not, but I was petrified. What if I accidentally bumped into them?

I did the only thing I could think of: I pulled my mobile out of my pocket and called my best friend.

'Hi, Paige.' Jenna answered on the second ring. 'How's it going?'

'Um...' My voice broke and I started sobbing again. 'Not good.'

'Oh no, Paige. What's wrong? What happened?'

'Where are you?' I said after taking a deep breath and trying to pull myself together. 'Can you talk?'

'Yeah, yeah. Of course. It's fine. I'm at home. I'm not working this afternoon. What's going on?'

I was totally on edge, flinching at the slightest noise or person passing close by, wired like I'd taken something. 'I'm okay,' I said, even though I wasn't. Not even close. And then I started crying again. It felt like everyone in the vicinity was gawping at me: the weeping girl on the bench. But being on the phone seemed to stop anyone from trying to speak to me, at least.

'Oh, Paige.' Jenna said, her calm, soft voice a soothing snippet of home. 'What's going on? Please talk to me. I need to know that you're all right. Please tell me what's happened. I'm here for you.'

So I lowered my voice to a whisper to tell her. And, as shocked as she was, she stayed calm for me. She reassured me, as I'd known she would, and told me exactly what I had to do next, even though I didn't really want to hear it. That's Jenna for you: wise beyond her years. She's been dishing out advice to me for as long as I can remember.

'You need to report this straight away,' she said. 'To the university and to the police.'

'Really? Do you think so?'

'Absolutely. You have to. You can't let them get away with this, Paige. Especially your lecturer. He's in a position of responsibility. This was a total abuse of power. You say he's pretty senior?'

'Yes.'

'Have you heard any rumours about him?'

'No, nothing.'

'Hmm. He's probably been getting away with it for years, the bastard. He needs to be stopped.'

'What if I misunderstood what happened? What if I unconsciously gave off the wrong signals, Jenna? Like how I was dressed, or my make-up, or... I don't know. Something must have caused them to do this to me.'

'Paige. Stop that right now. You're in no way responsible for this. It's entirely on them. Feeling guilty is a normal human reaction, but you must try to ignore it and face up to the truth: you've been sexually assaulted.'

'Have I, though?' I asked. 'I managed to get myself out of there before things got out of hand.'

'She was touching you inappropriately and getting off on it. He was visibly hard and rubbing himself through his trousers. You just told me all that, and I'm sorry, but it's disgusting. It's absolutely sexual assault, Paige, without a shadow of a doubt. And it took place in the office and under the supervision of one of your senior lecturers, which is why you need to report it. Today preferably.'

'But who do I go to? What do I say? It's so embarrassing. I feel ashamed. How could I tell someone about it?'

'You told me.'

'That's different.'

'I know what you're saying, but you have to, Paige. Otherwise, it could happen again; if not to you, then to someone else, who might not escape before it gets even more serious. Listen, I'd come over and do this with you if I could. But you're not around the corner. I need to take Mum for a hospital appointment later today. Is there someone else who can help? What about that nice girl you live with, Carmen? Or maybe there's a special team at the student union that could advise you.'

'Yeah, I guess. What's up with your mum? Is she okay?'

'I'm not sure. She's been a bit off again lately, so they're sending her for some more tests. Fingers crossed it's not... bad news.'

'Oh God, I hope not,' I said, wincing at the unspoken fear of it being a cancer resurgence. 'Give her my love.'

'I will, but don't worry about that. Get yourself sorted, Paige. I'm here any time if you need to talk, and I'll call you later, whatever, to check how you're doing.'

'Thanks, Jenna. You're the best. I love you.'

'Love you too.'

Ten minutes after our chat, as I was waiting for a bus back to my student house, feeling miserable and unsure of what to do next, Carmen phoned me.

'Hey,' she said. 'I got a message from your friend Jenna saying to call you. She didn't say why. What's going on? Everything all right?'

Wow. I didn't even know they had each other's details. They must have exchanged them during one of Jenna's visits. Anyway, Jenna did good reaching out to Carmen. She was my rock from that moment forward.

If only reporting what Jeff and Gail had put me through had resulted in the outcome both friends predicted.

FIFTY

NOW

Paige

I step out from behind the van and onto the pavement before looking up and pretending to be surprised to see him.

'Paige,' he says, a look of shock and confusion flashing across his face. 'Um, hello. What—'

'Hi, Adrian,' I say slowly to my next-door neighbour and family doctor, no idea how to play this. He's dressed for work in smart navy trousers and a white open-necked shirt, carrying a leather satchel over one shoulder. So why isn't he at the surgery? Why's he here? 'How's it, er, going?'

'Yes. Good, thanks. You? Nice summer's day today, isn't it? Not the, er, kind of heat you got used to in Australia, though, I'm sure.'

I nod, knowing I have to ask him what he's doing here while I have the chance. Before he can talk his way out of it.

Heart thumping in my chest, I say: 'I just saw you coming out of Jenna's house. Is she home? I'm heading there myself to check something, but I was under the impression she was away. I've borrowed Becky's spare key.'

'Oh, um. Right. Yes. I see. No, er, she's not. I was hoping she would be, but, um... no. That makes sense, then. I hadn't realised she was away.'

'Do you also have a spare key? How come?'

Red-faced, he shuffles his feet and avoids my eye. 'Ah, yes. This must look a bit, er, odd. I do, as it happens. Back from when Jenna's mother was ill... in case of emergencies and so on.'

'So you let yourself in with it?'

'I did. Don't worry, it's nothing untoward. Jenna said to do so if she wasn't home. If she was at work or whatever. I was picking up some unused medication of her mum's, as we arranged. I said I'd take it to be disposed of for her. So now I've got it.' He pats his bag with one hand. 'At last. I've been meaning to call around for a while and, well, I was in the vicinity today visiting another patient. It seemed like a good opportunity.'

'Couldn't she have returned it to a pharmacy herself?' I ask.

Adrian smiles unconvincingly. 'Well, yes, of course. I was just trying to be helpful. She's been through so much, poor girl. And little things like these are harsh reminders of the reality of life without her mother. I was trying to lighten her load, that's all. To help her move on.'

'Right,' I say, nodding to disguise the fact I'm not convinced. What else can I do? Demand to see proof of these pills inside his satchel? Hardly. I might as well just come out and accuse him of being up to no good.

'Anyhow, nice to see you, Paige, but I must dash. Duty calls. I have a busy afternoon at the surgery ahead of me.'

He darts to his car, which is parked a couple of spaces away, and drives off.

Adrian seemed so uncomfortable, like I'd caught him red-handed. But doing what?

Could this mean that *he* is Jenna's mystery ex?

No way.

Surely not.

And yet the more I think about it, the more I realise that would actually make a certain weird kind of sense. For one, it would explain why she was so adamant that she couldn't attend our barbecue last Saturday, knowing he and his wife would be there. She claimed to have other plans, which I never believed, only to walk past not long before that awful cry.

If Jenna did have some kind of affair with Adrian, it would also make sense why she was so secretive about the relationship. He's married, for a start, and old enough to be her father. Plus, he's her GP. Boundaries would most certainly have been crossed.

Would Adrian really do that? I thought he and Sarah were happy. They've always come across that way. I know he was a huge support to both Jenna and her dying mum, arguably going above and beyond his duty of care as their family doctor. Even getting his own house key, apparently. So I suppose he and Jenna could have fallen for each other at some point around then. It's not inconceivable. He's good-looking for a man of his age, I guess, although I couldn't imagine falling for him myself.

That said, I'm struggling to imagine him writing that horrible, threatening email to my best friend.

Adrian has always seemed like such a nice, caring man. I've never forgotten the time he came to my rescue after I fell off my bike outside his house as a young child. He was mowing the front lawn when it happened. He was so kind, so good at calming me down, while I sobbed away, shocked and upset. He sat me down on a garden chair, gave me an ice lolly and made a point of checking me over, cleaning and putting a plaster on my grazed knee, before wheeling my bike home as he returned me to the safety of my parents.

That memory lingers in my mind as I let myself into Jenna's house. After locking the front door behind me, I take a seat on the bottom step of the staircase. Try to gather my thoughts.

Nope, I can't get my head around the idea of Jenna and Adrian being together. I can't picture it, no matter how hard I try. That's not to say it didn't happen, but... Oh, I'm so confused. He was definitely behaving strangely outside. Like a man with something to hide.

Running a hand through my hair, I get up to have another look around. That's why I came here after all. There is no favourite cardigan to locate.

So what *am* I looking for?

Good question. Signs that someone has been here between now and my last visit. Like Adrian, for instance...

I also might have missed something before, particularly after getting such a scare.

All the lights are still off, as I left them last time, so that's one thing to check off the list.

Next, I enter the small lounge. No change here either as far as I can see. The open cola can remains where I last saw it on the coffee table. And at least I'm ready this time for the movement caused by my reflection in the circular mirror, so no unnecessary jump scares.

The kitchen is as I left it too, nice and tidy; no obvious sign of anything being moved or tampered with, as far as I can tell.

I have a root around in the cupboards and drawers, in case something else significant, like the laptop I previously uncovered, might be stashed here. No luck.

I'm nervous about heading upstairs after last time, but I put my fears aside and force myself forward.

FIFTY-ONE

Paige

The landing and bathroom are all clear. Phew.

Next up is the spare bedroom. It's small, and other than the pile of sympathy cards I spotted on the bed last time, there's not much to search through, apart from a cupboard filled with towels and bedding, plus a bookshelf lined with a dozen well-thumbed paperbacks.

Jenna's bedroom is my next stop: the place I spent most of my time in this house over the years.

The first thing that strikes me is that the bed's made. This stops me in my tracks. I'm sure the duvet was balled up on my previous visit. Did I make it myself and, in the stress and confusion, forget I'd done it? I rack my brains, but try as I might, I can't recall ever doing that.

Could Adrian have done it? That would be very creepy.

Could it have also been him in the house with me last time, before he shut me in the bathroom, ran down the stairs and out of the front door? Surely not. And yet, now I know he has a key, I can't totally rule that out.

Sitting down on the bed, I look all around me, desperately searching for clues. But nothing jumps out.

Instead, I'm thrown back into the past, to the last time I was in here with Jenna, the day before I flew to Australia. I remember our conversation like it was yesterday.

We were lying next to each other on the bed, top and tail, as we so often did, totally comfortable in each other's company, gossiping away with zero reservations. Soulmates. We'd been finishing each other's sentences for as long as I could remember; me going to uni had done nothing to change that. If anything, our time apart and our respective traumas had only brought us closer. I frequently told Jenna things I wouldn't dream of telling anyone else. I spoke to her in the same breath I spoke to myself.

'I'm really going to miss you,' I told her.

'Me too.'

'You're going to miss yourself?'

'Shut it, pedant. You know what I mean. I wish I was coming, as we planned.'

'I still feel bad going without you; leaving you now, when you need me.'

'Don't. Just because I wish I was coming doesn't mean I don't want you to go. It's exactly what you need after everything that's happened to you. I'll be able to enjoy the journey through you, as long as you stay in contact like you say you will.'

'Of course. You'll get bored of hearing from me.'

'Never. I was thinking earlier...'

'Oh? Thinking what?'

'You'll probably never see my mum again after today.'

'God, don't say that. You don't know for sure. Some people live for ages, despite what the doctors say. She's a fighter.'

'I hope so. I'm not ready to lose her, Paige. You and Mum, you're my whole world.'

'You've got Becky and your nieces too. And your dad, kind of.'

'He's a waste of space. He only cares about his new family. I adore Jess and Amber, of course, but Becky... Well, Becky's Becky. You're far more of a sister to me than she ever will be.'

Tears pricked the corners of my eyes. 'I feel the same. Me being away for a year, it won't change anything between us, will it?'

'Never. We're BFFs, remember? Clue's in the final F. Not that you'll be thinking about me while you're down under, surrounded by hot, horny boys.'

I laughed at the breathy voice she used to say those last three words, even as the tears ran down my cheeks. 'We'll see about that. What about you? Got your eye on anyone to keep you busy while I'm out of town?'

Jenna shuffled onto her side, looking away from me and out of the window. 'Um. No, I don't think so. I need to focus my attention on Mum. Make the most of our remaining time together.' She giggled. 'Remember that time *we* kissed?'

'Oh my God, yeah.' I covered my mouth, also laughing. 'How weird was that?'

She was referring to a brief moment a couple of years earlier, in the summer holidays, before I went to uni. I'd bought a load of white wine one night when Jenna's mum was away visiting a relative. We'd got smashed, and, in a moment of madness, I'd put it on her. We'd had a brief drunken snog before both bursting into laughter, realising that wasn't for us. Afterwards, we swore to keep it our secret.

'You should try everything once, right?' I continued. 'I'll say one thing: you did have very soft lips compared to some of the lads I've kissed. And it was nice not to have stubble chafing my skin. Did you ever tell anyone else about that?'

Jenna shook her head. 'You?'

'Nope. Why did you bring it up?' I winked. 'Are you getting the hots for me now?'

'Yeah, right. In your dreams. No, I don't know. It just came back to me, for some reason.'

She went on to open up about how hard she was finding it being strong for her mum.

'No one expects you to carry the weight alone,' I said, turning around to sit next to her and holding her tight as her whole body shook while she wept. 'You've got Becky to help too, and the various medical professionals. There's Adrian, for a start. You said earlier that he'd been really supportive.'

'He has. He's actually been amazing. It's not even his responsibility any more, since she's under the care of various specialists, but he's always popping around and keeping in touch. He's even given me his personal mobile number in case I have any concerns or questions. I doubt many GPs would be so attentive. How did Adrian and Sarah end up with such a creepy oddball as a son, by the way? They're both so lovely and he's... Well, we've both noticed the way he stares. I saw him looking at me out of the window, this intense expression on his face, when I was visiting your house the other day. I wouldn't be surprised if he was playing with himself.'

'Eww, don't,' I said. 'That's disgusting.'

'*He's* disgusting.'

'Yeah, I can't deny that. He's always been odd, as long as I can remember.'

'Maybe he's adopted. He could be the Devil's child, like in that horror movie we saw, *The Omen.*'

It was strange how quickly Jenna could move from being heartbroken to making jokes. I'd noticed this a lot lately. It seemed to be her way of dealing with everything she was going through, so I did my best to roll with it.

'Oh my God, yeah,' I said. 'Zack the Antichrist. That's a scary thought, considering he lives next door to me. It makes me glad I'm leaving tomorrow.'

Back in the present, as the memory fades, I feel a horrible

sense of Jenna's absence here where she belongs. One particular thing stays with me: Adrian having given her his mobile number. Suddenly this, together with his spare key, feels like a big deal. Did she start calling him a lot? Did she grow even closer to him when she was alone, after her mum's death, leading to something more between them?

I want to say no. I really do.

I want to dismiss this idea out of hand – especially considering his lovely wife, Sarah but my friend was grieving, without me there to support her. And before that, she was struggling to cope with the enormity of her precious mother fading away before her eyes. Plus, she had been more or less abandoned by her dad, so wanting a father figure in her life wouldn't be that strange.

He should have known better and never allowed it to happen. But he's a man, and in my experience, even the nicest men in the strongest-seeming relationships can become weak and vulnerable to cheating, given the right circumstances. Not least when someone as young and attractive as Jenna is involved.

I've been right through her bedroom cupboard and drawers in my hunt for information, but I've drawn a total blank.

What was I hoping to find: a diary, love letters? Yeah, right. Only in some corny old movie. Photos of her and her mystery man? They'd be on her phone, if anywhere. Unless she got herself one of those instant cameras, but I've seen no evidence of that.

Hmm. I move on to her mum's room.

In here, everything looks much as I recall: floral duvet; unfinished romance novel on the bedside table; personal belongings – reading glasses, hairbrush, dressing gown, and so on – still in place, like she could return at any moment.

I feel even sadder seeing it now than I did before. As painful as it will be, Jenna needs to sort through this stuff so that she can start to move on. She either needs to begin the process of making this house her own or selling it for a fresh start.

I've not had a good look through the cupboard and chest of drawers here yet, so respectfully I do so. It brings tears to my eyes as I recognise clothes and jewellery she used to wear. I find one drawer full of paperwork – mainly bills and so forth – that I avoid looking at in detail for fear of snooping. The same goes for her underwear drawer.

What am I doing? This feels so intrusive. But I push on, focusing on my drive to help Jenna, or at least get some clue as to where she's gone.

It's as well I do, because what I discover in the next drawer I open blows my mind.

FIFTY-TWO

I let myself into the ramshackle cottage again, having taken the usual precautions so as not to be spotted on the way here. The problem with living in a small village is that everyone knows you and your business, so even outside the area, here in the nearby countryside, it would be far too easy to be recognised. The popularity of hoodies is a godsend, because even if you wear the hood up when the weather is fine, like today, no one thinks too much of it. It's such a common sight. I did also consider a hi-vis jacket, because nobody ever gets questioned while wearing one of those. But fearing it could make me stand out and thus more memorable, I decided to skip that.

It's quiet when I step through the back door, but as I climb the stairs, a loud thumping sound starts up. I hear her cry: 'Hello? Is someone there? Help me! Please help me!'

The drugs must have worn off already. Maybe she's developing a tolerance, and I need to up the dose. Anyhow, nice of her to flag this fact to me. At least I'm prepared. I put my hand in the left pocket of my hoodie and pull out the Swiss Army knife I brought with me. It should suffice to keep her under control.

And I will hurt her if it's required.

She must know that by now.

What we had together is over. That person she said she was in love with is gone.

Was I ever in love with her?

I thought I might be for a while. But the main reason I said those words was because I knew she wanted to hear them.

I was definitely infatuated with her at one point. I was hooked; couldn't get enough. Until fate or chance or whatever decides life's challenges stepped in and changed everything in the blink of an eye.

Now? I mainly hate her for turning me into this person I can barely look at in the mirror. Her captor. Someone actually considering how hard and messy it would be to slit her throat with this knife.

Could I go through with that and live with the consequences, the guilt?

In some ways, assuming I could get rid of her body without getting caught, it would make life so much simpler than it is now. This drawn-out mess is awful. It can't carry on for much longer.

I still hope that I won't have to kill her.

That I will, eventually, come up with a better solution.

But time's ticking, and the longer this carries on, the more likely it is that I'll get found out. Especially if she's shouting and screaming like she is now, pushing me ever closer to the darkest part of myself. All it would take would be for some off-piste walker to pass a little too close by and hear her, then...

'Shut up!' I bellow as I thump on the locked bedroom door with my fist. 'No one will ever hear you, and you're giving me a headache. If you're still making that racket when I come in, I'll shut you up once and for all. Do you hear me? No one else is here. No one is coming to save you. Nobody cares where you've gone or what's happened to you. There's only me. And you're pissing me off, which is not a good idea. I'll gag you when I leave *this time, if I have to. Is that really what you want? There will be no eating or drinking then.'*

The noise stops, replaced by a pathetic whimpering.

That's a point. It would be a really easy way to kill her, if I had to. No one can live long without water. And I wouldn't have to get my hands dirty then, would I? I'd simply have to wait.

I'd still be a killer, though. And a cruel one at that.

I couldn't reasonably write off her death as an accident like the last one.

I unlock the padlock on the door, and before turning the handle, I tighten my grip on the knife.

The first few times I came here after capturing her, I had to steel myself for the sight before walking into the bedroom. It upset me to see her tied up and helpless, but I didn't want her to know this, for fear of looking vulnerable. I'm used to it now, though. I've adapted.

'Right,' I say. 'I'm coming in. And just to warn you, in case you're planning any funny business, I have a knife. Don't think I won't use it.'

FIFTY-THREE

Paige

I can't believe what I'm looking at: a drawer literally stuffed full of boxes of prescription pills in Jenna's mum's name.

If that's what Adrian was supposedly picking up from the house – the whole reason for him dropping by, so he said – why are they all still here? He'd need a large bin bag to fit this lot in. They'd never squash into his satchel. But why would he take some and not the rest?

Oh God, my head hurts.

The thought of him and Jenna together makes me feel queasy. He's older than Dad, for God's sake. Gross.

I must say, though, I've never once caught Adrian looking at *me* that way. And it's not like I haven't seen others do it. Ahem, Scott from next door. At least *he's* only in his thirties, rather than his fifties, but still... He's also married with two young daughters.

Scott hasn't been handsy with me so far, thankfully. But I've definitely seen him behaving inappropriately with other women after a few drinks. Like the way he said goodbye to Mum and

Sarah at the end of last Saturday's barbecue. His hugs lingered too long; his hands reached too far, while just about staying decent. I disappeared to the bathroom before it was my turn, taking no chances.

I wonder if Becky notices. You'd think so. She's an intelligent woman. And yet she often seems detached, like her mind's elsewhere. She's rarely quick to notice what's going on with her sister. So it could be the same with her husband. Who knows? Maybe she's oblivious, or perhaps she just doesn't care because she accepts that's how he is: a touchy-feely kind of guy.

As I'm thinking this, my phone starts to vibrate. I pull it out of my pocket and see that it's Carmen calling.

'Hi,' I answer. 'How's it going?'

'Good. You?'

'Yeah, not too bad.'

'I'm calling about the laptop,' she says.

'Right. Any luck?'

'There's good news and bad news.'

'Okay.'

'So the operating system is screwed. It needs reinstalling from scratch.'

'Shit. That sucks. What does that mean for the emails? Are they lost?'

'So far, but I've not given up yet. Now, like I said, there is also good news... if you can call it that.'

'Spill.'

'I've been trying to recover what I can from the hard drive, and I came across a few video files. I was hesitant to open them, in case they were, like, sex tapes.'

'Oh my God. They weren't, were they?'

'No, don't worry, it's not that. It's, er, more like a video diary, confessional type thing – Jenna talking to the camera. All the entries seem to have been recorded recently. Like in the last few weeks.'

'Seriously? That sounds a bit weird. Why would she do that? I never came across them.'

'Yeah, they were stored in an odd place,' Carmen says. 'I think she must have recorded them on her phone, then copied the files across to the laptop and deliberately hidden them in a random folder.'

'So have you watched any?'

She clears her throat. 'I've, er, had a quick scan through. Enough to tell that it's pretty personal what she's saying. I think that's more something for you to do, Paige. I'll send them to your phone, yeah?'

FIFTY-FOUR

Kate

She feels like she's losing her mind. Ever since she received that last message in response to her sexy photo, she's been tearing her hair out.

After going back inside the house, she deleted the image – for both of them – keeping her fingers crossed that he hadn't already made a copy. Then she cleared the conversation. That was a start, but now she needs to find a way to pour cold water on the whole thing. Draw a line under this embarrassing episode and hope it never comes back to haunt her.

Why the hell did she let it go so far?

Why did she lead him on?

Because she never really planned to actually do anything in person... right?

Whatever. The past is the past, full stop. Danny arranging this amazing anniversary surprise, like a bolt from the blue, has shaken her and brought her to her senses. It's reminded her of everything she's lucky enough to have, which her ridiculous behaviour was putting seriously at risk.

Oh Lord, what a mess.

But how to bring it to a close, once and for all, without causing offence and resentment, thus running the risk of some kind of stupid retaliation?

Should she ghost him and simply stop sending messages?

Probably not. That could well lead to a confrontation.

So what, then? Send one final message; see him in person to explain?

She lies down on the sofa in the lounge, picks up a cushion, places it on her face and, groaning, thumps it several times in frustration.

'I'm such an idiot,' she says to the empty room.

Then her phone vibrates with a new message.

She takes a deep breath before opening it, and when she sees it's from him, her heart sinks.

You deleted it! Gutted. A glimpse of heaven. Wow. Just as well I have a good memory. I can't stop thinking about you, sexy. I'm dying to rip your clothes off.

Bloody hell. She's got him even hornier than he was before. And now she's not feeling it – guilt and loyalty to her husband having taken back control – she sees his words very differently. It's like she's finally sobered up after a crazy, boozy night. What she previously found edgy and dangerously hot now seems sad and pathetic.

She feels sad and pathetic: the bored middle-aged housewife throwing caution to the wind, seeking reckless thrills to make her feel alive again. Such a tired cliché.

So what's she going to do about it? How's she going to end it?

As she continues to ponder this, Kate hears the front door. 'Is that you, Paige?' she calls, switching off her screen and tucking the phone out of sight.

'Yeah. Where are you?'

'In the lounge. How was the walk?'

Her daughter sticks her head through the door. 'Good. Too hot for you in the garden?'

'Yeah. I thought I'd come inside for a bit. Guess what: your dad and I are going away at the end of the month. He's booked us a surprise trip to Lake Como, where we spent our honeymoon. So you and your brother are going to have to fend for yourselves for a few days.'

Paige smiles. 'Ah, he's told you, then.'

'You knew?'

'Maybe.'

'Sneaky. Does your brother know too?'

'I'm not sure. Dad mentioned it to me last night, all cloak and dagger. He was really excited about surprising you.'

'Bless him.' Kate feels the knot in her stomach tighten.

'Don't worry, by the way. I won't let Lucas turn the house into party central.'

'That's my girl. Come here and give your old mum a hug.'

Paige sits down next to her on the sofa, and Kate pulls her into a tight, reassuring squeeze. 'It's so lovely having you home again,' she says with an unexpected catch in her throat.

'It's good to be back.'

Once she trusts her voice again, she asks: 'How's everything with you?'

'Fine. I do have some things I need to do, though, so I'm going to head up to my room.'

'Okay.' She plants a kiss on Paige's forehead. 'What are you up to? Anything exciting.'

'I'm helping Carmen plan her travels. She's interested in going to Australia, among other places, so I'm sorting her out with some tips.'

'What a shame you weren't able to go at the same time.'

'Yeah, well, it is what it is.'

'It's lovely that you've connected with her again, despite...
you know. It's not, um, brought back any bad memories, has it?'

'No, no. That's all water under the bridge. Are you up to
much today?'

'Not really. Same old, same old.'

'Still planning to go shopping?'

'Oh, um, yeah, probably.'

'Please could you get me some more of that cereal I like?
We're nearly out.'

'Sure.'

Before Paige leaves the lounge, Kate adds: 'Sorry for biting
your head off this morning. You know, when you were having
breakfast. About checking my phone. I didn't sleep too well last
night, so I was a bit narky. I'm feeling better now.'

Once she's alone again, Paige in her bedroom with the door
shut, Kate reminds herself how lucky she is to have a thought-
ful, caring husband and two happy, healthy children still living
under her roof. Sometimes she grumbles about this fact, especially in the case of Lucas, who does have a tendency to treat
the place like a hotel. But in truth she'd be bereft without at
least one of them around. Her family is everything, despite
what her recent actions might suggest. Apparently, she needed
a shock to the system to remind her of this fact.

Seeing Paige so independent and self-confident, back to her
old self – how she was before the awful injustice of what
happened to her at university – is incredibly rewarding. Fortu-
nately, her unhealthy fixation on Jenna's supposed disappearance, aka holiday, seems to have waned. That was Kate's one big
concern about her since she returned home.

She's come such a long way from the broken shell of a girl
that she and Danny had the heartbreaking job of bringing home
after the roof caved in on her time as a student.

FIFTY-FIVE

THEN

Kate

It felt like they were on an emergency rescue mission. She and Danny were both wired and incredibly anxious as the car raced along the motorway to get their girl home. To pull her out of her misery, following a teary, desperate phone conversation a couple of hours earlier.

'Mum, I need you to come and get me. I'm dropping out.'

'What?' Kate had answered. 'Why, love? Not because of what happened with that horrible man? We've been through this. He'll be gone in no time. They'll turf him out on his ear, and he'll probably face criminal charges too. You've done all the hard stuff. You've told us. You've reported it to all the right people. Now you just have to be patient and wait for justice to be served.'

'No, Mum,' Paige had sobbed. 'There is no justice. The police and the university don't believe me. They all think I made it up.'

'Of course they don't. Why would anyone say that? It makes no sense.'

'Well, that's what they believe. They think I was trying it on because I got a bad mark and was afraid of failing. There was only one of me and two of them, and they've taken their side. There's no evidence it happened. Apparently, I'm some kind of fantasist. The policeman who told me said I was lucky not to be charged with wasting their time.'

'That's outrageous. When did this happen?'

'The other day. I wanted to tell you, but I was too upset. I've hardly left my bed since. I'm a total mess.'

'Darling. You should have come to us straight away. That's what we're here for. We're your family. We'll find a way to fight this. We'll get a lawyer. Whatever it takes. We'll make this vile man and his disgusting wife pay for what they've done.'

'No. I've thought long and hard about it, Mum. I'm done. They've beaten me. They've won. I want to come home and never return here.'

'But what about your future? It's not fair on you. You have to fight this.'

'I've no fight left in me. Please. Come and get me. I can't stay here one more night. Please, please, please. I need you and Dad.'

As her firstborn had said this, in a shaky, weepy voice that blew her heart to pieces, Kate had never felt more devastated, frustrated and angry.

'Okay, love,' she'd said. 'I'll contact your father right away.'

'So you're coming? Today?'

'Yes, of course. We're always here for you when you need us. I'll let you know when we're leaving.'

'Thank you,' Paige had whispered. The relief in her voice was palpable.

Now they were almost halfway there.

Danny, who was driving despite the fact they were in Kate's car, asked: 'She'll be all right until we get there, won't she? How bad did she sound? She's not going to do anything stupid, right?'

'Calm down, love,' Kate said, despite feeling a million miles from calm herself. 'You've asked me that already. Concentrate on driving. She knows we're on our way. She'll be fine.'

'Maybe you should give her another call to update her.' Danny looked so pale and fraught. He'd been beside himself ever since she'd explained the situation earlier. He'd dropped everything at work and come home immediately.

Kate reached across and squeezed his hand where it was resting on the gearstick. 'I'll message her, okay? Try not to worry.'

'I want to lay into that prick,' he said. 'Make him and his wife pay for what they've done to my little girl.'

'Trust me, I know exactly what you mean. But how would that help?'

'It would make me feel better. Like there had been some sort of justice.'

'And then you'd be the one to end up in a cell. Brilliant.'

Danny let out a long sigh. 'I know. You're right. Don't worry, I'm not an idiot. I'm not actually going to do anything like that. But I can't help thinking about it. I'm Paige's father. I should be able to protect my daughter. I feel helpless.'

Kate looked across at him and squeezed his hand again. 'I know. I feel exactly the same. But right now, I think the best and only thing we can do is to be there for her. Support her. Focus on what she needs, which is for us to take her home. Then we'll help her to recover and find a new way forward.'

They didn't say much to each other for the rest of the journey, both lost in their own thoughts. But when they pulled up outside Paige's student house, Kate said: 'Let's both stay strong and positive. We won't hound her with questions yet. We'll gather her stuff, load up the car and make her feel loved, yeah?'

'Agreed.'

It broke Kate's heart when her daughter answered the door, deathly pale and so gaunt, like she hadn't eaten for days. She looked shattered, devoid of her usual energy and warmth. Kate immediately pulled her into a cuddle and felt her bony, fragile form shake in her arms as she started to sob. 'I'm so glad to see you both,' she said once she'd composed herself a little. 'I can't wait to get out of here and back home.'

Only one of her housemates was present. Carmen. While Danny and Paige were outside, organising space in the car, Kate asked her: 'How's she been? She looks awful.'

'Not good,' Carmen replied. 'She's barely left her bed for the last few days. I was getting worried. As much as I don't want her to leave, I think she needs this. I think she needs her mum and dad. I know I would. It's so awful what she's been through. I can't get my head around how it's all panned out. I don't understand why the police and the university aren't taking her side. I wanted to get people together to organise a protest or something – to bring the truth to light – but she wouldn't let me. I feel like I've let her down.'

Kate shook her head vigorously. 'No, love. Please don't feel that way. Not for a second. From what Paige has told me, you've been an amazing friend. You've been the one here, on hand, supporting her throughout all of this. The system is what's let her down, not you. I can't thank you enough for what you've done for her.'

Kate spent the whole of the journey home trying to be upbeat, talking about anything that came to mind other than the devastating reason for the trip. But it was tough. Danny stayed focused on the driving, and Paige was almost monosyllabic.

She'd not been this worried about either of her children for a long, long time. She prayed that eventually, with the right support, Paige would be able to lick her wounds, dust herself off and find a new sense of purpose. But she feared it would be tough. She'd never seen her daughter this broken before.

Thankfully, the first glimmer of hope came when they arrived home to find Jenna waiting with Lucas. There were tears, naturally, but there was also a smile or two at being reunited with her best friend. If anyone, other than her family, could help Paige get over this, it was optimistic, wise-beyond-her-years Jenna.

'Everything's going to be all right,' she told Paige, embracing her and stroking her hair. 'I've got you now. We'll work this out.'

Later, as they were all sitting around the kitchen table over a takeaway pizza, Jenna asked: 'Any idea yet what's next for you, Paige?'

Danny threw Kate a concerned glance; a subtle headshake was enough to stop him intervening.

Paige cleared her throat. 'I, er, need some time to get my head together first. It's been a tornado, everything that's happened. I need to heal for a bit before I start looking ahead. But don't worry about me. I'll get there. I'll get past this.'

Jenna put her arm around her. 'I know you will. You're amazing, Paige. Don't ever forget that. You got shafted, thrown under the bus. None of this is down to you. It's great to have you home, anyway. I wish it was under happier circumstances, obviously, but their loss is our gain.'

'Yeah, screw university,' Lucas chipped in, mouth full of pizza, drawing frowns from both parents. 'Who needs it?'

'I actually have something exciting I want to talk to you about,' Jenna told Paige. 'It'll cheer you right up, I reckon. But not today. Soon. When you're feeling better. And you will, trust me.'

I hope so, Kate thought. I really hope so.

And yet when Jenna revealed this exciting idea of hers a few days later – for the two of them to take a trip to the other side of the world – Kate was far from convinced. She thought it sounded like a terrible idea.

FIFTY-SIX

NOW

Zack

He's not expecting anyone to be home when he gets back mid-afternoon on Thursday. He rang ahead for that very reason, having stayed at Erin's last night, and he was glad when no one answered. He took that to mean both his parents were out.

So he's annoyed to see a car in the drive: his dad's, unusually. Bollocks. Now he'll have to explain why he's not in work, having taken a second sick day with his supposed chronic diarrhoea and vomiting.

'I'm a bit better,' he whispered into the phone to his boss this morning. 'I didn't have a great night, but I think I'm on the mend, thank God. My arse is red raw, though. I've barely been able to keep any food down, but somehow it keeps on coming.'

He pledged, in a suitably pathetic voice, to do his utmost to get back tomorrow. And he will, as planned, making himself look nice and dedicated in the process. Hopefully all his colleagues – not wanting to catch his lurgy before the weekend – will leave him in peace as a bonus.

Perfect.

Unlike his dad being home.

'Hello?' he says, walking through the front door into the hallway. 'Dad?'

A muffled reply from somewhere upstairs: 'Zack?'

'Yes.' Stupid bloody question.

'You're back early,' Adrian says, appearing at the top of the stairs a minute later, scratching his head and generally looking flustered.

'You too,' Zack replies.

'I'm returning to the surgery in a minute. I, er, popped back to sort a couple of things out. What about you? Didn't you already have a day off yesterday?'

'Yeah. They owed me some time in lieu, so I got to knock off early today too.'

'Right. Wouldn't it have made more sense to do that tomorrow, ahead of the weekend?'

Zack rolls his eyes. 'My thoughts exactly, but it wasn't convenient, apparently. Too much on tomorrow. The joys of being a trainee.'

'Right. Do you know where your mum is?'

He shrugs. 'No idea. I haven't spoken to her. I tried ringing the house phone before, to see if she wanted me to pick anything up for tea tonight. But she didn't answer, and then I got distracted, so I never got round to trying her mobile. She probably wouldn't have answered, anyway. You know what she's like. It's always on silent.'

Once his dad has left, Zack makes himself a cup of tea and, after nipping into the garden for a quick vape, heads up to his bedroom to watch some porn. Might as well make the most of being the only one home while it lasts. Hang on, he thinks. That couldn't be what his dad was doing upstairs when he got back, could it? Gross. Surely not. No, he must be too old for that kind of thing.

Pushing all thoughts of his father out of his mind, he makes himself comfy on the bed and opens up a couple of his go-to websites on his phone.

He's getting into it when he hears someone at the front door. Shit. He's tempted to ignore them, but fearing it might be one of his parents – not using their key for whatever annoying reason – he makes himself decent and heads downstairs.

When he swings open the front door, it's Paige he sees looking back at him, which sets his pulse racing. God, what does she want? What has Lucas said to her?

'Oh. Zack. Hi.' She frowns. 'I, er... Did I see your dad around earlier?'

Zack rubs his chin, relieved to be off the hook. 'Yeah, he was home, but he's back at work now. That's why his car's not on the drive. Mum's not home either.'

'Right.'

There's a long, uncomfortable silence before he adds: 'Was there something you wanted to speak to Dad about? Because if it's a medical thing, you'd be best going through the proper channels.'

'Yes... No. Um... Don't worry. I'll catch up with him later.'

She's wearing a sexy, tight top, and he can't stop staring at her. 'Okay. Fine.'

He imagines himself inviting her in and leading her up to his bedroom for a live re-enactment of the sleazy scenes he was watching moments ago. But instead, he stares at her and nods, no more words leaving his mouth. Once she's gone, following a typically awkward goodbye, he takes that thought back upstairs with him.

FIFTY-SEVEN

Paige

That was fun, as always. God, Zack's weird. So creepy. I could feel his eyes crawling all over me when I was at the door, not being invited in. Yuck. I wouldn't have said yes even if he had. I wouldn't want to be alone with him.

Maybe his dad is secretly the same but hides it better. Dammit, I was desperate to challenge Adrian again about why he was really in Jenna's house, considering all those meds were still there.

Anyway, I've got those videos through from Carmen, and it's time to start watching.

It's nearly five full days now since the barbecue, and apart from that one message she sent me – if it really was her – I've heard nothing.

My gut feeling that something isn't right gets stronger every day.

I desperately need answers. And one of those has to come from my own brother, about Jenna's necklace, the moment he gets home from work.

For now, I shut myself in my room. With a deep breath and a racing heart, I pull out my phone, pop on my headphones and click on the first of the eight video files.

Jenna's face fills the screen, and I instantly spot that she's wearing the same gold necklace with the coffee bean that's now burning a hole in my jewellery box. She's at home, wearing a summery T-shirt, propped up with a pillow against the headboard of her bed, much like me now.

Hi. It's me, Jenna. How's it going, future me, or whoever you are? I hope you're watching this for a good reason rather than a bad one. I have so much I want to say.

I'd usually confide in my best friend, Paige, but she's not here. She's travelling around Australia, lucky thing. We're in frequent contact, via messages and video calls, but I'm afraid to say anything about this over the Internet. It's too sensitive. I can't risk it getting out.

Paranoid much? Tell me about it. That's what happens when you fall in love with someone you shouldn't. When you get involved in a secret relationship that lots of people – even Paige – might struggle to understand. And when you know that the relationship would almost certainly be over if the truth ever got out.

What about Becky, my sister? Couldn't I tell her? No way. Not this. She'd never understand in a million years, even if she wasn't a workaholic and could spare me the time to listen. No, we've never really had a confiding-type relationship. Not even since Mum died.

The thing is, it's killing me not being able to chat about this with someone. So here I am, talking to my phone, with no intention of sharing the recording. Does that make sense? It's kind of a diary, I suppose. The lazy kind where you can chat to the camera rather than having to write or type anything. Like a vlog, only not posted online.

So yeah. I've met someone.

Actually, you can't meet someone you already know, can you?

I'm seeing someone. That's better. And I'm head over heels. But it's really complicated and risky, which is why I'm so paranoid.

Hang on. I've had a thought. I'm going to stop this for a minute. Back soon.

FIFTY-EIGHT

Jenna

Hi. I decided to do this another way. Same place, same day, same me. Different audience. Or imagined audience, at least. So no more chatting to future me. From now on, I'll be addressing this kind-of-vlog to... drumroll ... YOU.

Yeah, you – the 'risky' person I'm seeing. The one I'm mad about. You know who you are, but no one else does, and we need to keep it that way.

I had a brainwave about this while recording the previous video. So I stopped and took a beat to think it over. See? I do listen to your advice. Just like I've also cut back on my social media posts and stopped sharing my location with friends on Snapchat. Privacy first. That's important when you're in a situation like ours. I totally get that now, which is why I won't be sharing these recordings with anyone, including you. I won't even be keeping them here on my phone. I'll store the files somewhere else for safe keeping. They're meant purely as a kind of video diary. A way for me to safely chat about us and our secret relationship; to offload all the emotions I'm feeling, positive and negative.

Let's start by saying that I'm really happy.

But I feel bad about that because I'm supposed to be grieving for my mum. It's still not long since she died, and when that happened, I felt so bereft, I couldn't imagine ever being happy again.

And yet here I am, thanks to you.

Of course I am still grieving. I miss Mum almost every moment of every day. I often dream about her like she's still alive. Then I wake up and remember she's not. That's the worst. Mornings are tough, because I'm always alone. But you help with that, calling or messaging to say hi. You did it even before we became a thing. You knew what I was going through, and you were there for me, more than anyone else, even my own family. That meant so much.

I already had a crush on you then, but I never dreamed you felt the same. I thought you were just being kind; that you felt sorry for me. Even when you started coming round to the house and helping me look to the future.

Then we kissed, and you backed off for a bit, because you felt guilty, which I understood. I agreed it was a mistake. Not that I could stop thinking about you.

So when you returned, saying you couldn't bear to stay away, things progressed really fast. And wow, it's mind-blowing. Like nothing I've ever experienced before.

We have to be so careful that no one finds out about us, though. You're already in a relationship, for starters.

The two of us hooking up wasn't planned. We felt a connection – a magnetic attraction, too strong to ignore or resist.

We fell hard for each other. Nothing else mattered.

Neither of us has dropped the L-bomb yet, but surely it's only a matter of time.

I want to shout about us from the rooftops. But I know I can't, at least for now. There's too much to lose.

You say your official relationship has run its course and it's only a matter of time. Yeah, that's what cheaters always say. But still, when you look me in the eyes and tell me so, I know you mean it.

You're the reason I get up in the morning. You believe in me. You encourage me to plan ahead: make a life for myself beyond living here in this village, working as a cleaner to make ends meet, missing Mum all the time.

'But I messed up my A-levels,' I tell you.

'So what?' you reply. 'You were going through so much. You've got a brilliant brain. You could do anything you want. Take them again, or do something else. Whatever you want. Sky's the limit.'

And so I dream of a future far away from here. A future for the two of us, where we can be together in public with no judgement, no restrictions. Free to be ourselves.

Is that naïve of me?

Perhaps it's all part of my grief process, becoming so attached to someone like you. But honestly, whatever it is, I don't care.

You make me happy. You fill me with hope.

Plenty of people would say what we're doing is wrong, but it doesn't feel that way. It feels so right.

I'm counting down the seconds until we're together again. Until I can hold you, kiss you... and the rest.

You. Are. Amazing.

And on that note, I'm signing off. Bye for now.

FIFTY-NINE

Paige

Wow. That was something. How on earth did Jenna keep all of this from me when she was so consumed by it? She didn't give anything away at all when we were messaging and video calling. I bet it would have been different in person. If I'd been here.

I watch the next two videos straight after this, and although it's interesting to hear about the relationship developing, I'm frustrated not to get any closer to discovering Mr888's identity.

My ears prick up when she talks about them planning a weekend away. She says: 'I can't wait to spend three days, two nights, just the two of us. No prying eyes. Out in public with none of the usual secrecy.'

In the fifth video, recorded the night before this trip away, Jenna is bouncing around in front of the camera, smiling ear to ear. 'I'm dying to be able to hold your hand and kiss you in full view of other people,' she says. 'Spending the whole night with you, waking up next to you; having breakfast together. I'm going to cherish every moment. I also plan to tell you that I love you for the very first time. I wonder how you'll react. Will you say it back? Oh, I can't wait. I have butterflies.'

When I finish watching this instalment, I have a bad feeling about what's coming next. There are only three more videos left, and I know from what Jenna told me before the barbecue that the relationship is about to hit the rocks on the back of something 'really bad'. I suspect this took place while they were away.

Oh, Jenna, what happened? What did he say or do to you?

I need to watch the sixth video right now. I'm about to press play when Lucas, who I didn't even hear come home, barges into my bedroom.

'Jeez.' I remove my headphones and put my mobile aside. 'You scared the crap out of me.'

My brother laughs.

'That's not funny.'

'It totally is.'

'You're home early. When did you get back from work?'

'Just now. Have you heard? Mum and Dad are going away at the end of the month. Party time!'

I sigh.

'Oh, come on, sis. Don't be boring. Where's Mum gone, by the way?'

'Food shopping.'

'More veggie meals. Yum.'

'Whatever. I need to talk to you about something important.'

He rolls his eyes. 'Can it wait? I'm knackered. Some of us have been out working.'

'No, it can't. I found Jenna's necklace in your bedroom yesterday. Why do you—'

'What? Why were you snooping around in my room?' His face turns red and he gets fidgety, a furtive look in his eyes. 'Shit, Paige, that's bang out of order.'

'It wasn't like that. I was, um, returning a pen I'd borrowed. The necklace was just there. It caught my eye and I recognised it straight away. It's her favourite, Lucas. She was wearing it the last time I saw her, before the barbecue. So how did it end up in your bedroom, and how come the clasp is broken? What's going on? Do you know where she is? Do you have something to do with all of this?'

Lucas scowls at me. 'No, I do not. I knew you'd think that. That's why I didn't mention it to you. Anyway, I've only had it since yesterday. I got it from someone else. Okay?'

'Who? And why didn't you tell me about it? You know how worried I am about her.'

'I'm telling you now, aren't I?'

'Only because I found the damn necklace. Don't you lie to me, Lucas.'

'I'm not, swear to God.'

'So who did you get it from and why did they have it?'

'If I tell you, you have to promise not to overreact. To hear me out.'

'I'll do my best.'

'Right.' He pauses before adding: 'It was Zack next door.'

SIXTY

Becky

'Mummy?'

Becky shuts her eyes and runs a finger down her nose, determined to stay calm despite yet another interruption. 'What is it, Amber?'

'When will Daddy be back?'

'We've been through this. He's having a day to himself. I'm not sure when he'll be back. Mummy's home but she's also working. Like Daddy does when he's writing in his study. So unless it's important—'

'But you're not in the study. You're in the kitchen.'

'I know. But for today, let's consider this my study, okay?'

'Okay. What's for tea?'

'I'm not sure.'

'Are you making it, or is Daddy?'

'If you're good and let me get on with my work, maybe I'll take you and Jess to the drive-thru for tea. Does that sound fun?'

Amber pulls a sad face.

'What? I thought you loved burgers.'

'I used to, but I prefer pizza now.'

'Fine, we can order a takeaway pizza. If you leave Mummy to do her work.'

Amber pouts. 'Daddy's home-made pizzas are the best.'

'Well, I'm sorry, love. They're not on the menu tonight. But trust me, I know an amazing pizza place you've never eaten from before. The best you'll ever taste. Normally they're so good only adults are allowed them, but just this once, I'll make an exception.'

'Really?'

'Absolutely.'

'Okay. I'll go and tell Jess. Thanks, Mummy.'

No Parent of the Year prizes for me any time soon, Becky thinks.

Wife of the Year, on the other hand... she could still be in contention for that.

Working from home isn't something she does often, but today she's juggled things around to make it happen, purely to give Scott a day to himself out of the house.

Yes, he technically had one yesterday too, when his parents took the girls to the zoo. But apparently he spent most of that time cleaning the house and doing food shopping. And last night – out of sight of the girls, thank goodness – he had a meltdown.

The tears came out in full flow. The multiple writing rejections had got to him far more than he'd previously let on. He confessed he was really struggling to settle on the next idea, which he considered his last chance to snag a publishing deal.

'I feel like such a loser sometimes,' he said. 'A fraud. It eats away at me that all the stuff I write is so crap no one wants it. I love being at home with the girls, but I need more. I need my own purpose beyond looking after them. My writing really helps, but only when I believe in myself – when I feel like I'm heading somewhere positive. And at the moment I feel lost. My doubts are like wounds, sapping my creativity. I'm lucky to have the chance to even try to succeed. I know that more than anyone, love, and I appreciate you so much for giving me the space to do so. But equally, that adds to the pressure I feel, because I'm terrified of letting you down after you've shown so much belief in me.'

'How can I help you?' she asked. 'What about a day off tomorrow? A chance for you to get out of the house alone and do something different; to clear your mind and refocus?'

'That sounds like bliss. But my opportunity to do that was today, and I wasted it, like an idiot. It felt like there was so much to do around the house. I couldn't see the wood for the trees.'

Hence her offer to work from home. She insisted. Because the last thing she wants is to see Scott's mental health deteriorate like it did when he was stressed in his old job. She knows the warning signs. And while she might not totally understand how he's got himself into this state by doing the very thing he's always wanted to do – writing – she's not an overthinker like he is. That character trait is, ironically, one of the things that makes his writing, which she genuinely loves, so perceptive, honest, emotional and funny. Like she's told him on numerous occasions, his work just needs to land on the right desk at the right time. She's convinced of that, even if he isn't.

It's been as challenging today as she expected, trying to get anything done with frequent interruptions from the girls, asking her to adjudicate on quarrels and so forth. She might have been better setting up in the study rather than a family room like the kitchen, but Scott's stuff is all over the place in there. It's basically a man cave. And at least in here she has everything handy for the frequent cups of tea and coffee she needs to stay sane.

Also, part of her enjoys the interruptions, because it's only one day, and she doesn't get to do this often. Could she handle it on a regular basis? No way. She doesn't know how Scott manages to get anything done during school holidays. It's a constant juggling act.

Anyway, hopefully he's enjoying himself today. She's no idea where he's gone. Somewhere in the car – that's as much as she knows. As long as he's finding a healthy way to unwind. That's the important thing.

Last time stress got the better of him, it drove him to the bottle.

He says that's not the case now, but when she thinks back to the way he necked that wine last night...

She nips through to his study to have a quick nose around, and sure enough, she finds a half-empty bottle of whisky and a used glass hidden in the back of one of his cupboards.

A sliver of unease slides down her spine. Oh God. Nightmare. Alcohol drives Scott to do stupid things, and she realises that he *has* been secretive recently. Shit. Not this again, please. How has she not noticed? The two of them need to have a serious discussion once the girls are in bed tonight.

In the meantime, she forces herself to shelve those concerns and focus on work. She turns her mind back to the mountain of unanswered emails in her inbox. Five minutes later, Jess is at the kitchen door.

'Mummy?'

Becky flashes her elder daughter a pursed smile. 'Yes, love?'

'When are we next seeing Aunt Jenna?'

'She's still away. We'll arrange something when she gets back.'

'When's that?'

'I'm not sure.'

'Where's she gone again?'

'I don't know.'

'How come?'

'That's just how it is, love.'

Lowering her voice, Jess asks: 'Do you think it's anything to do with that fight she had with her, um, boyfriend?'

'I honestly don't know, but I'm sure she'll be back soon. Listen, I'm really busy with work stuff. Please could we do this later?'

Jess leaves the room with a sullen look on her face.

It sparks Becky to message Jenna.

You good, sis? When are you coming home? Your nieces miss their fav aunt!

SIXTY-ONE

I'm checking her phone in the car, a safe distance away from the cottage, when a message arrives from Becky.

Good timing.

She wants to know when her little sister is coming home, although she asks the question in the context of her nieces missing her. Does that mean she doesn't? Hmm. Sounds about right. The two of them aren't exactly close. Becky did next to nothing for their mum when she was dying, leaving all the heavy lifting to Jenna.

Usually, you'd expect blood relatives to be the ones most concerned about a young adult's sudden disappearance. But I knew that wouldn't be so in Jenna's case.

I didn't think anyone would make much of a fuss. If she hadn't been so alone since her mum's death, she and I would never have got close like we did. She wouldn't have needed someone like me watching out for her in the first place.

For the record, my intentions were good. I felt sorry for her after everything she'd been through. I wanted to help her to cope, to manage alone, and to make the best of her life rather than throwing away her potential on a dead-end cleaning job. I certainly had no designs on starting a relationship with her. That just happened. I think it surprised both of us. A magnetic attraction that was impossible to resist.

I knew it could never go anywhere long-term, but I gave into it regardless and enjoyed it. Right up to the moment when it all went wrong. The accident. Then I found myself in survival mode, doing things I'd never thought I was capable of. I wasn't prepared to lose everything I'd built over the years on the back of one misjudged affair and a cruel twist of fate that put us in the wrong place at the wrong time.

My actions might not have been the right thing to do morally, but pragmatically they were, without doubt.

Jenna didn't see things the same way, and that led to the unfortunate situation in which we now find ourselves.

At least dealing with Becky's message is easy enough.

I type my reply into Jenna's phone.

Ah, bless. Tell my fav nieces I miss them too and I'll be back soon. All good here x

Job done. Knowing Becky, that'll easily satisfy any minor concerns she might have about where Jenna's gone or what she's doing.

If only it was that simple to throw Paige off the scent.

SIXTY-TWO

Scott

Becky's been good enough to give him a day to himself after he lost the plot last night, the weight of everything on his mind temporarily getting too much to carry. And what's he doing with this much-needed downtime? Propping up the bar in a country pub, chatting up the curvaceous twenty-something bartender, Josie, and trying not to drink too much that he can't get back behind the wheel of his car in a bit.

He did have a walk prior to this, which helped clear his head a little, but that only lasted for about an hour.

'Day off today?' Josie asks him

'Yes,' he replies, readying himself for the inevitable next question.

'What is it you do?' she asks on cue.

'Whatever I like,' he says with a cheeky smile.

He's had that one up his sleeve for ages but not had the right opportunity to use it before.

'That sounds nice,' she replies. 'So you're a man of means?'

'I wouldn't go that far.'

'Come on, then,' she says, leaning towards him across the bar, eyebrows raised. 'I'm intrigued. What do you actually do?'

'I work in IT,' he says, as he has so many times before, to nosy barbers and the like. It's a fairly reliable way of getting them to lose interest and stop asking questions. Whereas if you tell people you're writing a book... well, everyone has an opinion about that.

'So you turn things off and on again for a living?' Josie asks with a playful wink.

'Something like that,' he replies, looking down at his pint rather than making the obvious flirtatious reference to turning her on.

He's lost the energy to keep this pretence going. He has enough on his plate already. So he's actually glad when an elderly couple come in to order food and drinks, commandeering Josie's attention and giving him the opportunity to move to a quiet table in a corner.

From there, he ruminates on the catastrophe that is his life today. Wallows in self-pity and regret about how he's boxed himself into a corner as a burnt-out, talentless has-been. And how, on top of the failed literary career, he's got himself into such a bloody mess in so many other ways.

If Becky knew the truth, she wouldn't be giving him a day to himself, she'd be kicking him out of the house and dumping his sorry ass for good. That or worse.

He doesn't deserve her or the girls.

All three of them are far too good for a loser like him: a waste-of-space fantasist with so little self-worth that he needs other women to fall for him just to validate his own existence.

They'd be better off without him, he thinks.

Then he gets a message on his phone that makes things even more complicated. Sends his brain into a spin.

'Another drink?' Josie asks, appearing at the side of his table. 'You look like you need it.'

'Yes, please. Same again.'

SIXTY-THREE

Jenna

God, where do I start? I'm in two minds whether I should be videoing this at all, considering what happened on our trip away. The worst thing ever. I still can't get my head around it. It was... There are no words.

I have to do this, though. I must. There's so much on my mind and still no one I dare speak to about it. Worse than before, actually, because now I'm afraid of incriminating us.

You'd lose it if you knew I was recording this. You've been clear that I mustn't say a word to another soul. Scarily so. And truth be told, that actually makes me want to continue with this vlog even more. Because what happened has changed everything, including you, and I'm not sure I trust you any more.

I can't believe I'm saying this, but maybe I even need these videos now as a way to protect myself. Against you. A security blanket in case you turn on me.

You were determined from the start that we couldn't, under any circumstances, report what had happened. Even though it was a terrible accident. 'We're not supposed to be here,' you said, 'Especially not together. No one can find out. We need to get out of here now. Get as far away as possible and pray no one's seen us. Otherwise, we're screwed. Do you understand? We're not supposed to be here.'

I saw a wild-eyed, ruthless side of you then that I'd never seen before, and it scared the crap out of me.

Hours earlier, I'd told you I loved you.

I just don't think I can live with what we've done. It's eating away at me. I want to confess. Do the right thing. But you're having none of it. How can you be so cold and calculated?

I get there's a lot at stake – way more for you than for me – but the fact remains, WE KILLED SOMEONE.

Bloody hell. I can't believe I said that out loud. Recorded it on my phone.

But that's the truth. It's what happened.

We didn't do it on purpose. We both know that.

And yet we still did it. Then ran off like criminals.

I'm getting ahead of myself...

Jumping back to the beginning, the weekend got off to a great start. You picked me up on the edge of the village early on Friday, supposedly visiting an old school friend. We enjoyed the drive up to the remote cottage I'd booked, tucked away in the Cumbrian hills. We didn't do much that first night other than walk to the local pub, where we enjoyed good food and wine, like two people in a regular relationship. Kissing and cuddling you at the table felt fantastic. Sure, we drew a few funny looks – not surprising considering the quiet rural location – but we didn't care.

Back at the cute ivy-covered cottage – all stone floors, low ceiling beams and quirky, cosy furniture – we soaked together in the gorgeous roll-top bath before enjoying the most amazing, passionate, unrushed night. I was so happy. I almost dropped the L-bomb there and then. But instead, I waited for the next night, when we had a nine-course tasting menu at a romantic Michelin-star restaurant a short taxi drive away.

It was gorgeous. I've never experienced anything like it before. So inventive and luxurious; super bougie. I felt like a celebrity, the way the staff attended to our every need, even brushing away our table crumbs with a miniature silver dustpan and brush. There was a different wine paired with each course. It was simply WOW.

Afterwards, I felt light-headed and giddy as the cab sped along the country lanes back to our little cottage. And the minute we were alone again, before we'd even stepped through the front door, I spilled my heart to you, breathless with excitement.

'Wait, I need to tell you something,' I said, taking your hand in mine before you had a chance to reach for the lock.

'Oh?' You flashed me a big smile.

'I love you. I've been holding it in for the right moment. You're amazing. You make me so happy. I love you, I love you, I love you. Oh, it's so nice to finally get that off my chest. I—'

Before I could finish, you pulled me into an embrace and gave me the most passionate kiss. And then you made my night complete by telling me you loved me too.

I was bursting with joy. I don't think I stopped smiling for the rest of the night, even when I dropped off to sleep, naked, wrapped in your arms, dreaming of our future together.

If someone had told me how drastically my mood would change by the following morning – how darkness would descend on us from nowhere, like a thick storm cloud – I'd never have believed them.

But change it did, from delight to horror, in the blink of an eye.

And so did you, from the person I felt closest to and most comfortable with in the world to someone I didn't recognise. Someone terrifying.

It was so awful. I've only seen one dead body before this: Mum's, just after she passed away. That was dreadful too, but in a different way. It didn't feel like a body, if that makes sense. It still felt like Mum.

But the body we saw after the accident. That was twisted and battered and bloody.

I'm riddled with guilt. That poor man must have a family, and they must be beside themselves. Desperate to know what happened. Whether he suffered. And to see the perpetrators – us – brought to justice.

At least I got to prepare for Mum's death. I can only imagine the excruciating pain and misery of losing a loved one out of nowhere, in such dire circumstances.

No wonder living with the guilt of our actions hanging over me, which I'm only doing at your insistence, because I love you, is proving so difficult to bear.

The violent way you shouted at me when I got upset and suggested we turn ourselves in. It's like a knife to my heart whenever I think back to it. 'Stupid little girl,' you spat. 'Are you really so naïve that you think everything will end up fine and dandy just because you've done the right thing? Bloody hell! This is the real world, Jenna. Not some bullshit fairy tale. We'd be fucked.'

Yes, you calmed down eventually. You apologised for being so 'intense' in the heat of the moment and tried to reason with me. But the genie was out of the bottle. I could not unsee what I'd witnessed. And even more chilling than your rage was the fact you seemed so unmoved by the man's death. Saving yourself was your only concern.

'Don't you feel bad?' I asked you later.

'Of course,' you replied. 'But he's dead. Whatever I feel,

*say or do, it won't bring him back. His life is over. Ruining our
own lives to ease our consciences won't change that.'*

'But we killed him.'

*'Don't you say that ever again,' you hissed. 'He should
have been more careful what he was doing up there. Made
himself more visible, at least. It was like he had a death wish.'*

I was too horrified to reply.

SIXTY-FOUR

Paige

Holy shit. Jenna and her lover killed someone.

It's one bombshell after another.

What the absolute fuck?

I can barely even get that idea to sink into my mind.

How can it be so?

And yet I know it is, because I could tell that Jenna was absolutely telling the truth in that video; I could see how utterly destroyed she was by it.

My brother assured me earlier that Zack definitely isn't Jenna's ex. But if Lucas is to be believed, that means Zack somehow got his dirty hands on her favourite necklace right around the time she went missing.

'Why would *he* have it?' I asked him. 'What's that weirdo been up to?'

'Ah, Zack's not that bad when you get to know him. We actually, um, hang out sometimes.'

'I'm sorry, what? Since when?'

'I got to know him a bit when you were away. We're hardly

best mates or anything, but – you know – he's all right. I was round there yesterday and... Listen, you really need to hear this from him.'

'You need to tell me right now why he had her necklace,' I said. 'And how come you ended up with it. This all smells like bullshit, Lucas.'

'It's not, trust me. I'll get him to come round and explain, like he did to me. I'll message him now.'

'My trust is running out,' I said. 'It has to be today, and it has to be very soon, or I'm going to his mum.' Sarah was the only realistic option, considering my suspicions about Adrian, which were already spinning off towards a freak-show father-and-son conspiracy theory.

'There's no need for that. I'll sort it. I promise.'

'I still don't see why the hell you can't just tell me.'

'Because I wasn't there, and he was. Honest, sis, I wasn't buying it to start with either, but you'll see.'

SIXTY-FIVE

Jenna

Where was I? I had to stop videoing to catch my breath. I panic when I think too much about what happened. What we did. So I broke off and went for a walk. My head's clearer now. As much as it can be in the circumstances.

So back to our weekend away. On Sunday we woke up together again after another passionate night. We squeezed in one more lovemaking session before you surprised me with a gorgeous champagne breakfast. Then we checked out. The plan was to have a long walk in the nearby hills, followed by a late pub lunch on the way home. The weather had other ideas. It was so wet and windy, you suggested a drive through the hills instead.

'Are you okay to drive now?' I asked, bearing in mind all the alcohol we'd consumed the night before, followed by that morning's champagne.

'Yeah, I'll be fine. I didn't have a lot, and I doubt there will be much traffic on such a miserable day.'

You were right about the traffic, but with hindsight, you

shouldn't have been driving. We've not talked about this. I daren't bring it up. But I suspect that's a key reason you wouldn't report what happened to the police. Because if they breathalysed you, you'd have been in even more trouble. If only I'd been more insistent that you shouldn't drive yet, this awful mess would never have happened. But the truth is, we've never had that kind of relationship, have we? You've always been the decision-maker.

So yeah, we drove into the hills in bad weather. It wasn't the best idea, we soon realised, because visibility was poor, meaning we were hardly taking in the sights. All the same, we pushed on, and I got a bit frisky. Nothing much at the start: just stuff like tickling your thighs and leaning over to kiss you here and there. But things soon stepped up a gear, probably because of the breakfast champagne, and I was really getting into it. Distracting you from driving, which I've been beating myself up about ever since.

Because, as I was doing this and you were driving around a tight bend, high up in an isolated spot, we heard a loud thump, and the car kind of lifted up for a moment.

'What the hell was that?' I asked.

'No idea,' you said, pulling into the side of the road. 'I think we hit something. Maybe ran over a rock or... I don't know. We'd best get out and have a look.'

And that's how we came to find his body, slumped partway down the steep incline on the left-hand side of the road, about one hundred metres back.

We didn't spot him immediately. The dark green cagoule and waterproof trousers acted like camouflage against the grass. It was his shock of white hair that first stood out.

'Oh my God,' I said with a horrified gasp. 'Look, over there. It's a person. We hit someone.'

'No, that's not possible,' you replied. 'I'd have seen them if they were walking. And I didn't spot anyone.'

Maybe he was sitting down or kneeling or something, I thought afterwards, desperately trying to make sense of what had happened. Could he have been doing up a bootlace? A stupid thing to do at the side of a road. More likely he actually was walking there, and you didn't see him, like I didn't, because I was busy distracting you. Plus, you weren't sober.

But this all came later. In the moment, my only concern was if he was all right.

I rushed over and you followed, after stopping for a brief moment to check the car. We both wobbled down the sharp incline to where the elderly man was lying in a twisted heap: a gory, mangled mess. I couldn't stomach looking more than once.

I got to him first, but he was unresponsive.

I expected you to take charge – to know what to do – and you did, but not how I imagined.

You pushed past my petrified form and knelt at his side, checking to see if he was breathing or had a pulse. Then you shook your head. I thought you'd start CPR, but instead, you stood back up, declaring: 'He's gone.'

'What? No way. That's not possible. There must be something you can do.'

'Like what? Look at the state of him. It's too late.' You glanced back at the parked car. 'We need to get out of here. No one's driven past so far. Best keep it that way.'

I was stunned. 'What are you talking about? We need to call an ambulance, the police. We can't just go and leave him here.'

'We can, and we are.' Your eyes narrowed, face hardened. The look you gave me at that moment is ingrained in my mind. Then you launched into that spiel I've already mentioned, about how we weren't supposed to be here, and no one could find out.

You grabbed my arm and pulled me back to the car.

I wish I could say I fought you. But you were so determined, so insistent. And I was so shocked. I didn't even get my phone out until we were driving away.

'I could ring the emergency services anonymously,' I said. 'Block my number. We have to do that at least, right?'

But you were having none of it. And we were in such an isolated spot, I didn't have a signal.

As you drove, I started to cry. Stony-faced, you gave me the silent treatment for the next hour or so. It was all I could do to get you to stop several miles down the road, where I got out of the car and puked into a bush.

'Where's my phone?' It was no longer where I'd left it, between the two front seats.

'I have it,' you said. 'I'll give it you back in a bit, when you're less... het up.'

'What? Bullshit. Give it back now.'

'No.'

Your tone was so menacing, I didn't dare to stand up to you.

You didn't ask if I was all right until much later, when we stopped for petrol at a motorway service station.

'We did the only thing we could realistically do in a difficult situation,' you told me after getting back into the car and handing me a bottle of water.

'But we did a terrible thing,' I whispered. 'They'll catch us.'

'No they won't. There's next to no visible damage to the car, and no one else was around at the time to see us. No one knew we were there. Now we're miles away.'

'But a man is dead because of us. How can we live with that?'

'We'll have to find a way. If I give your phone back, can I trust you won't do anything you'll regret?'

I nodded, and you reached into your pocket before handing it to me.

I was furious at you for that: treating me like a naughty child who couldn't be trusted. Normally I'd have given you a piece of my mind. I'd have started our first-ever proper row.

But these weren't normal circumstances.

I was still too busy reeling from the fact we'd killed a man.

I was devastated, terrified, confused. I felt more guilty than ever before in my life. Had no clue what to do next.

You're the one I've been turning to for advice since Mum's death, but you have more blood on your hands than I do.

And I'm scared stiff of saying a word to another soul.

I'm terrified of what you might do if you found out.

SIXTY-SIX

Paige

Watching that – Jenna's penultimate video – was gut-wrenching. My heart goes out to her. I can't believe the trauma she's been through. It's staggering what happened. And the fact she ended the recording, still wearing her favourite necklace, so afraid... I'm devastated.

Why didn't she say something when we met up before the barbecue on Saturday? The shit must have hit the fan. I could see she was unhappy and distressed. I should have pushed harder to get her to open up. Who knew that would be my only chance?

If it was Adrian who went away with Jenna that weekend – and that's still a big *if* – he'd have had a heck of a lot to lose. Killing someone while drink-driving on a secret trip with a young patient. That's major. He'd end up in jail, surely. He'd stand to lose his job, marriage, reputation, the lot.

Mind you, so would anyone.

Whoever Mr888 is, he's clearly desperate. That was

obvious from the disturbed, menacing tone of that last email he sent Jenna.

If she threatened to come clean to the police, that could have sent him over the edge.

He'd already killed once by that point.

What if he was ready to kill again?

As I'm thinking this, sitting up on my bed, I hear the door-bell sound.

Moments later, there's a knock on my door. 'Paige?' Lucas says from the other side. 'I've got Zack here. Can we come in?'

What? Zack in my bedroom. No thanks.

'Hang on,' I say. 'I'm in the middle of something. Can we do this in your room, Lucas? I'll be there in a minute.'

'Sure.'

When I get there, Lucas is sitting on his bed, and Zack's on the desk chair. 'Hi,' I say, going to sit down next to my brother.

'Hi,' Zack replies with a blank expression.

'So what's going on?' I ask, skipping the small talk. 'Lucas says he got Jenna's necklace from you. What were you doing with it in the first place? If you know anything about where she is, what's happened to her, you need to tell me right now.'

Zack glances at my brother and then back at me, making eye contact for a brief moment before looking down at his own bare feet as he shuffles them around in his sliders.

'I, er, don't have a clue where Jenna is right now, honestly. The last time I saw her was, um, on Saturday evening. When the rest of you were at the barbecue.'

'What?' I ask. 'How come? I thought you were out with your fiancée.'

That word sounds ridiculous to me as it leaves my mouth. Who on earth would ever want to marry a weirdo like Zack?

'I was, but not until later on.'

'Did you speak to Jenna that evening?'

'Yes.'

'And you never thought to mention this before? You know damn well I've been trying to find out what happened to her, Zack.'

He shrugs.

'Do you know anything about that awful cry we all heard; that haunting scream?'

He looks at Lucas again, who gestures for him to continue. Zack gives a sheepish nod.

'What? Seriously?' I throw daggers at the pair of them. 'And you knew about this too, Lucas?'

'Only since yesterday.'

I can't believe what I'm hearing.

'So?' I say to Zack. 'Are you going to tell me what happened? You have some serious explaining to do, because let me tell you, this all sounds dodgy as hell.'

'Tell her, mate,' Lucas says.

Frowning, like it pains him to do so, Zack starts talking.

SIXTY-SEVEN

LAST SATURDAY: THE EVENING OF THE BARBECUE

Zack

He'd been due at Erin's flat forty-five minutes ago. They were going to a party together at the house of one of her friends, and he was dragging his heels because he knew it would be a complete yawnfest, having been to a do there before. The host and her boyfriend were more into tea and elderflower than beer and wine, for a start. Zack knew from bitter experience that he had little in common with either of them or their other friends. Their last party had involved bloody board games. Enough said.

He'd already messaged Erin with a fake excuse.

Dad's roped me in to help him with something. Gonna be a bit late. Sorry! Love you x

She hadn't been happy, replying straight away:

What? You're joking. How late?

Not too long, hopefully. Can meet you at the party if you prefer x

No. I'll wait. Hurry up!

No kisses on her messages. Not a good sign. Never mind. He'd smooth things out later.

Having had a couple of beers in front of the telly, enjoying an empty house for once, with his parents at the barbecue next door, he was thinking about getting an Uber when, to his shock, a face appeared at the front window, peering in.

It was that hottie Jenna, Paige from next door's best mate and Becky's sister. What was she doing? What did she want?

'The barbecue's next door,' he said in a loud voice, waving her away.

She looked as surprised to see him as he was her. She said something in reply that he couldn't make out. Then she walked away, or so he thought, only for her to ring the doorbell. Goddammit.

With a heavy sigh, he got up off the sofa and stomped towards the front door.

'Yes?' he said.

'Oh, hi, Zack,' Jenna replied with a tired half-smile. 'Sorry for peering in at you.'

'It's fine.'

'Did you say something to me through the window? I couldn't make it out.'

'Just that everyone's at the barbecue next door.'

'Are your parents both there?'

'Yeah.'

'Are you going too?'

'No. I'm heading out in a minute.'

Jenna's face fell, like she was about to cry. She appeared to lose her balance and steadied herself on the door frame.

'Are you all right?' Zack asked.

He expected her to say yes and leave. But instead, she replied: 'No. I'm not sure I am. Do you think I could come inside for a moment and have a glass of water? I feel really dehydrated.'

'Um...' He wanted to say no, but at the same time, Jenna *was* looking sexy. She was wearing a skimpy floral summer dress that looked like it could blow off in a strong gust of wind. Plenty of leg and cleavage on show. If he let her in, perhaps she'd collapse in his arms, and one thing would lead to another. 'Okay, sure,' he said. 'Come in.'

He led her through to the lounge and offered her a seat. 'So you want a glass of water?'

'Yes please. If it's not too much trouble. I think I'll be all right in a minute. It's... I'm not sure what's going on.'

'From the tap okay?'

'Sure.'

As he brought her the water, he noticed her dress had risen high up her thighs, which he couldn't help glancing at, his imagination running wild.

He realised she'd asked him something, which he'd totally missed. 'Sorry, what was that?'

'Did you say you were going out?' Jenna said. 'I'm not delaying you, am I?'

'I am, but it's fine.' As long as you get down on your knees and make it up to me, he thought from behind an innocuous smile. 'Are you feeling any better?'

'A bit.'

'My dad's only over the fence if you need someone to check you over.'

'No, no,' she said, looking somewhat alarmed at this suggestion and taking a big swig of her water. 'I'm sure I'll be fine. I could do with using the bathroom, though, if that's all right.'

'Oh, um, okay. It's next to the front door.'

'Thanks.'

She got up, looking a little unsteady on her feet, and disappeared into the hall. He thought about following her, but that felt too weird, so he stayed where he was and waited.

Ten minutes passed and she still wasn't back.

What the hell?

He crept into the hallway and peered at the toilet door, which was shut.

He almost said something but couldn't bring himself to do so yet. Too awkward. So he slipped back to the lounge to wait a bit longer.

After another five minutes had passed, though, he was getting really antsy. What if she'd collapsed in there or something?

He picked up his phone and walked back to the hall, calling out: 'Everything all right?'

There was a long pause before a reply finally came. And when it did, it wasn't from the downstairs loo. It was from upstairs. What? Why had she taken herself up there? He'd told her exactly where to go.

As he stormed to the bottom of the stairs, he saw her dart shamefaced out of his parents' bedroom.

'What the fuck do you think you're doing?'

'Sorry. I, er... thought it was the bathroom.'

'What? Are you joking? For the last fifteen minutes? I'm not an idiot, you know. I'll ask you again: what were you doing up there? Are you trying to steal something?'

'No, of course not. I... Can I just leave now, please? I want to go home.'

'Yeah, right. Not until I've checked your pockets, you're not.'

'I haven't got any pockets.' She walked cautiously down the staircase towards him.

'You have a handbag,' Zack said, spotting it hanging from one shoulder.

She clamped her hand over it. 'There's nothing to see, I swear.'

'You won't mind me looking then, will you?' He moved backwards so he was standing in the way of the front door, blocking Jenna's exit.

'Let me go,' she said, facing off against him, hands squeezed into fists and a defiant look on her face.

'What happened to you not feeling well? You look fine to me now. Was that just an excuse to get inside and snoop around? What are you up to, you sneaky bitch? You're going nowhere.'

'Is that right?' Without warning, she lurched forward and kneed him hard in the balls, shoving him to one side as he doubled up and yelped in pain. She pushed past him and swung open the door, but despite Zack's agony, he managed to grab her upper arm and hold on tight.

'Let go of me right now,' she said, standing there in the open doorway for anyone walking past to see. 'Or I'll scream.'

'No,' he groaned.

And then she let rip with a deafening, eye-watering cry that the whole neighbourhood must have been able to hear. Anyone would think he was trying to rape her or something. It shocked him into losing his grip for a moment. He clawed out again a second later, but only managed to grab her necklace, which snapped off in his hand as she jerked free and raced into the distance without so much as a backward glance.

SIXTY-EIGHT

NOW

Paige

I stare in silence at Zack after he finishes speaking, weighing up what he's just told me. If I'd heard these same words leave his mouth yesterday, I wouldn't have believed them for a second. But that was before I saw his father leave Jenna's house earlier today.

The possibility of Adrian being Jenna's ex could explain – especially in light of his threats and refusal to speak to Jenna any more – why she might have cause to sneak around in his bedroom.

'Well,' Lucas says eventually. 'What do you make of that? Weird, eh? Doesn't really sound like Jenna, does it? But why would Zack make up such a story? What do you reckon she was up to?'

'I'm not sure,' I lie. 'What do you think, Zack?'

He shrugs. 'Beats me.'

'Who've you told about this, other than me and Lucas?'

'No one.'

'Not even your parents?'

He shakes his head. 'What would I have said? Especially after Jenna screaming, which made me look bad. I couldn't see anything obvious missing from their bedroom. The whole thing was just weird. And I was worried what Erin would think if she found out. She gets jealous easily. I figured keeping quiet was the best move all round.'

'How come you told Lucas, then?'

My brother replies. 'I was at his house yesterday, dropping off a couple of vapes I owed him. The necklace fell out of his pocket when we were in his bedroom. I recognised it as Jenna's and asked him what he was doing with it. He eventually came clean and told me what he's told you.'

'So you took it home and hid it in your desk drawer. Brilliant. Why didn't you tell me about it straight away?'

Lucas sighs. 'I wanted to, but... I dunno. It wouldn't have helped you track down Jenna, would it? We've no idea what she did next. And I didn't want you going after Zack, all guns blazing. Besides, you found it about five minutes after I stashed it there.'

'No thanks to you,' I tell him. 'Hang on, though. You went round the front after we all heard the scream on Saturday. How come you didn't see Jenna or Zack?'

'I wasn't quick enough, I guess. She must have already run off by then, and he'd closed the front door. Right, Zack?'

'Yeah.'

'What did you do for the rest of the night?' I asked Zack.

'I went to Erin's eventually,' he said. 'Once I could stand up straight again. Then we went to that party as planned.'

'And you haven't seen Jenna since?'

He shook his head. 'Where's, um, the necklace now?'

'I have it. And I'll be keeping hold of it until I can give it back to her in person.'

I picture him walking around with it in his pocket beforehand like a trophy, touching it with his disgusting hands; getting off on having it. The image sends shivers down my spine.

He might not have done anything bad to my friend on this occasion, but I still wouldn't trust that creep as far as I could throw him.

SIXTY-NINE

Kate

She's taken the bull by the horns, so to speak, and arranged to meet him. She really hopes he's not expecting it to lead anywhere – like a sordid fumble in a car park. But after the photo she sent him earlier, that's probably exactly what he's hoping for. Hence she's suggested somewhere public but not too close to the village: a farm café she and Danny have been to previously, a fifteen-minute drive away. She'll have to pick up some food shopping on the way home so that what she told Paige stands up.

She's hoping this won't take too long. The plan is to knock things on the head while avoiding a nasty fallout.

How on earth did she get herself into this mess?

She spots his car parked outside when she pulls up. It sets her heart racing with nerves, but she pushes on regardless. She has to. As she walks into the café, she sees him straight away, sitting alone in a booth, perusing the menu.

It's busy. She scans the other tables, looking for familiar faces; thankfully, apart from him, there aren't any.

He doesn't notice her approaching, or maybe he pretends not to, so she just slides onto the seat opposite. 'Hi.'

'Ah, there you are.' He glances up with a warm smile. 'You look nice.'

'Thanks.' She doesn't return the compliment, even though he looks handsome, as usual. Not at his best, though. A bit frazzled?

'Alone at last,' he says, shifting around in his seat, eyes briefly on her and then wandering into the distance.

'Have you ordered anything yet?' Kate asks, picking up the menu from where he's left it open on the table.

'No. I haven't been here long. I thought I'd wait for you. I'm going to have a coffee: a cappuccino or whatever. You?'

'Um, just a cup of tea, I think. Is it table service or do we need to order at the counter?'

'There's a girl coming around taking orders. There she is.' He reaches a hand into the air to signal her; when she walks over, he places their order.

'So this is weird,' he says. 'Next-door neighbours driving here to meet up in secret. Anyone would think we were up to no good.'

Kate clears her throat. 'Yeah, about that, Scott. I need to be clear why I'm here, before this gets awkward. I'm really sorry, but it's not what you think. I... I know I sent you that picture this morning, and everything I said before that, but I can't do it. I'm really sorry if I led you on. I didn't mean to. It just happened. I enjoyed our, um, interactions. I guess I got off on the thrill of what we were doing, but I don't want to take things any further. I don't want to actually cheat on Danny. Well, not any more than I have already. I—'

'It's okay. Don't sweat it, honestly.' To Kate's surprise, Scott laughs.

'You're okay with that?' she asks. 'I thought you'd be mad. That you'd accuse me of being a prick tease, that kind of thing.'

'Honestly,' he says, 'I'm relieved. It didn't feel real when we were messaging. More like a fantasy. Even when we were exchanging, er, photos. I know I banged on a lot about meeting up and doing it for real, but I never thought you'd agree to that. So when you did, I was like... well, I can't back down now, can I? Then you sat down opposite me here, in real life, and it felt immediately different. I mean, we've always flirted, haven't we?'

Kate nods.

'And we clearly find each other attractive, right?'

She nods again, feeling her cheeks redden. 'Although I'm probably a bit old for you, realistically. You're not even close to forty yet. Or was that all part of the allure: the older woman thing?'

'You say cougar, I say toy boy.' Scott throws her a playful wink. 'I think we were both a bit bored, lost maybe, and we let the flirting get out of hand. Is that fair?'

'Yes, I totally agree.'

The server arrives with their drinks. Once she's gone, Kate continues: 'So where do we go from here? We've both seen more of each other, physically and mentally, than we should have. I'm guessing neither of us wants to fess up to our other halves. I know I don't.'

'No, definitely not. Becky would lose it.'

'Danny would probably storm round and try to knock your block off.'

'Bloody hell.' Scott pulls a face like he's terrified, and they both start chuckling.

'Oh my God, we really shouldn't laugh. How do we draw a line under this?'

'How about we both delete whatever's left from our chat and remove each other's contact details from our phones? That would be a good start, right?'

'Okay. Let's do it.' She pauses. 'What am I saved as in your contacts? You're Helen Work in mine.'

'Mick Joiner,' he says, pulling a puckered-up face that makes them both giggle again.

Kate takes a sip of her drink. 'Anyway, moving on. How are you, Scott? Don't take this the wrong way, but you look tired. Everything all right?'

He says he's fine; that he didn't get much sleep last night. She has the feeling he's not telling her the whole truth. She could swear there's alcohol on his breath, but she doesn't mention this. It's none of her business.

'How's Paige?' he asks. 'Did she find her cardigan?'

'Sorry, what cardigan?'

He explains about her taking Jenna's key again to retrieve the lost piece of clothing.

'Right. Yes, of course,' Kate says, feigning knowledge of this. It's immediately clear to her what's actually going on: that her daughter is still secretly obsessed with her best friend's whereabouts. Oh God. What's Paige doing to herself? This doesn't bode well at all. She needs to speak to her. 'Has Becky heard anything from Jenna about when she'll be home?'

'Not that I'm aware of, although she'll be back soon, no doubt.' He winks before adding: 'When you're as old as we are, twenty seems young, but she's a fully grown adult. She's very independent.'

'Yeah, Paige too, especially since her travels. I wish I could say the same for Lucas, but I fear he'd live on takeaways and microwave meals if he wasn't still under our roof. I'm not sure he even knows where the washing machine is, never mind how to use it.'

Later, saying goodbye outside the café, the pair exchange a jokey handshake and pledge never again to mention this awkward period of shared secrecy.

'Are you heading straight home?' Scott asks.

'No, I need to nip to the supermarket on the way.'

'Good. Best we don't arrive back in convoy. Anyway, goodbye, neighbour. I'll see you around.'

'See you later, neighbour.'

Kate watches him drive off and waits a minute before leaving. Looking at her reflection in the side window as she sits
behind the wheel, she breathes a long sigh of relief. 'You had a
lucky escape there, missy,' she says under her breath. 'No more
nonsense now. Act your age. Embrace what you have.'

As she's walking from her car to the entrance of the
supermarket, Kate spots another of her neighbours sitting in the
driving seat of his own car, busy typing something into his
mobile. As childish as it is, she can't resist the urge to bang on
his window and give him a shock.

It has the desired effect – and more. He nearly jumps out of
his skin, dropping his phone into the footwell. When he looks
up, it's with an irritated frown on his forehead, which makes
Kate feel bad. She waves and mouths 'sorry' before he winds
down the window.

'I didn't mean to scare you,' she fibs. 'I was walking past and
saw you sitting there, so I thought I'd say hello.'

'Hi, Kate,' Adrian replies, his expression calming. 'Wow,
that didn't half give me a fright. I was miles away.'

'I noticed. Sorry again. Is your phone all right?'

His eyes flick down to his feet, but he doesn't retrieve the
device. 'Oh, it'll be fine, I'm sure. It's survived much worse than
that. How's it going?'

'Good. You?'

'Ah, you know. Can't complain.'

They make small talk for a minute or two before Kate asks:
'Are you heading inside?'

'Me? No, no. I've already got what I need. I just got sucked
in by my phone before starting the car. You know how it is.'

'Right. Well, I'll let you go, then. If I don't get a shift on, everyone will be moaning that their tea's late. How's Sarah, by the way? I haven't seen her since the weekend.'

He nods. 'Fine. She's out and about a lot, enjoying the summer weather. I'll say you were asking after her. And thanks again for the barbecue last Saturday. We both really enjoyed it.'

As Kate heads into the store, she finds herself wondering what Adrian was up to on his mobile to be so jumpy and apparently not want to pick it up in front of her. Then she berates herself for being nosy and judgemental. Get a life, she thinks, and mind your own business. Not everyone's busy misbehaving, sending raunchy pictures to their neighbours. He was probably dealing with some work stuff.

SEVENTY

Paige

I press play on Jenna's eighth and final video.

Her face appears on my phone screen. This time she's sitting in the lounge at her house.

The accident has changed everything. It's like you suddenly went cold on me because I felt terrible about what we did. Because I dared to question you. And apparently because you see me as a liability who might get you sent to jail.

How many times have you warned me not to go to the police or else? How often have you threatened that if you go down, I'll go down too?

'What's so hard?' I can hear you asking me with that cold look that rarely leaves your eyes these days. 'All you have to do is stay quiet. No one has a clue we were there.'

I'll tell you what's so hard: I have a conscience.

I've searched the local news to find out who the man was and what happened after we left. Not that I've dared to tell you this. You'd say I was running the risk of identifying myself.

But I'm not as stupid as you seem to think. I covered my tracks online with a VPN. Do you even know what that is?

I bet you've looked too, even though you've told me it's better – easier – if we don't know anything more than what we saw on that awful day.

Now I know his name, Arthur Smith, and the fact that he was a much-loved seventy-two-year-old retired head teacher, who enjoyed walking in the hills of his native Cumbria. And yes, this makes it even harder to live with what we did. He leaves a widow, three children, six grandkids and countless other family and friends. They're all beside themselves, natu-rally, and appeals have been made for anyone who might have seen what happened to come forward. Police suspect a hit-and-run, and the whole community is in shock. At least it wasn't too long until he was found. A couple of hours after we sped off into the distance, by my calculations. No thanks to us.

We killed that poor, poor man. It's because of our actions that his grieving family has been left in the dark about what happened, adding to the weight of their sorrows.

And you're okay with that, apparently.

You sent me such a nasty email in response to the various ones I've sent, because that's the only way I have left to communicate with you. You don't visit any more. You've blocked me on your phone. If I was spiteful, I'd call round at your house and have it out with you in front of your unsus-pecting family. But that's not me. I still care about you, for some reason I barely understand.

But I am really struggling with my guilt over what happened. I can't rule out the possibility of turning myself in. Perhaps there's a way I can ease my conscience without impli-cating you, even though you don't deserve it.

That's what I really need to discuss with you. But all you did was send me that horrible email, telling me it was your final reply, our relationship was over, and if I tried to approach or contact you again, I'd regret it.

I'm losing my mind. I'm a mess.

How could you, of all people, abandon me right when I need you most?

What have I ever done to you other than love you; protect your secrets?

Was our relationship one big game to you? Was I a bit of fun that you ditched when things got tough?

It seems that way.

So why am I still protecting you, even here?

I should say your name out loud, and then if you do kill me, someone might find this and track you down.

I want to, you know, but I can't. Because I'm a good person, unlike you, and I try to do the right thing by everyone.

That's why I can't live with Arthur Smith's death on my conscience. What must his family be going through?

I'm so miserable. I wish Mum was here to advise me. She'd know the right thing to do.

At least Paige will be home very soon, although, honestly, I think it might be too late to go to her with this. Where would I even begin? What would she think of me? And would it be fair to burden her, freshly back from the trip of a lifetime?

Oh, I need to stop this now. I want to curl up in a ball and cry myself to sleep.

I'm done.

I put the phone down and hold my head in my hands. Is that why she didn't talk to me when she called round last Saturday: because she didn't want to burden me?

What happened to her after she did whatever she did in Adrian's bedroom on Saturday evening and kicked Zack in the balls before running off? Adrian was right there with us for the rest of the night. Well, up until late, anyway. When did he and

Sarah leave? Eleven, twelve, something like that. Everyone left around the same time. Could he have done something to her afterwards; even early the next morning?

I need hard answers. And as insightful as these videos of Jenna's have been, they've not named Mr888 as I'd hoped they would.

I mean, it has to be Adrian, right? All clues are pointing towards him, especially in light of Zack's account of his run-in with Jenna on Saturday evening. Why else would she be rooting around in his dad's bedroom? There's also the small fact that I caught Adrian red-handed leaving *her* house earlier.

And yet still, for whatever reason, I have my doubts.

I need to speak to him again, somewhere private but safe, so I can be totally candid. I think I've come up with the perfect way to do that... although it is extreme.

I must talk it through with someone first. Jenna herself would be my first choice, especially after seeing so much of her in her videos. But at least I'm lucky enough to have a great alternative.

I give Carmen a call.

SEVENTY-ONE

Adrian

He peeks at his phone in between Friday-morning appointments. Stares at the blank dark screen for a moment before waking it up and, with a heavy sigh, going to one of the usual apps: the ones he keeps well away from the home screen. Is luck going to be on his side today?

He's about to place a quick bet on the gee-gees, hoping to end a recent streak of bad luck, when an overwhelming sense of self-revulsion takes hold, not for the first time.

'What the hell am I doing?' he asks himself under his breath. It's 10.26 a.m., and he's supposed to be working. This gambling thing is getting out of control. Stuff that: it's already well out of control. He needs to take a break, or better still, delete all the life-sucking apps once and for all and permanently stop.

If only it was that easy.

When he's winning, he feels like he's untouchable and needs to keep going to maximise the streak. When he's losing, like now, a change in fortune always seems imminent, waiting around every corner. And when he's doing okay – somewhere down the middle, breaking even – it's all too easy to tell himself that everything is fine; that he likes a bet, but it's a hobby rather than an addiction.

Yeah, right.

He's amazed Sarah hasn't got wind of it. He tries to steer clear of using their joint account to fund his gambling, but he's backed himself into a bit of a corner this month. Mind you, she's been pretty distant with him lately, particularly since the glitch that means he can't take time off for them to enjoy a summer holiday together. She's been drinking more than normal, which he hopes isn't a way of drowning her sorrows about their life together. About him. He's been too busy concealing his own vices to say anything, but it does seem to run contrary to her usual yoga-inspired restraint and healthy lifestyle. At least she's always active, out and about, running her classes, meeting up with friends, going for walks.

He decides not to place that bet on the horses, for now at least, despite having had a good tip. He pockets his phone before wiggling the mouse on his desktop computer, bringing the screen to life. Who's next? Oh God. It's Paige from next door. That's a surprise, and incredibly awkward in light of their last conversation, when she caught him leaving Jenna's house. He had to think on his feet to explain why he'd been in there; luckily, she seemed to buy his bullshit explanation about old medication.

The real reason he was there was money, to help him get past this current bastard losing streak. He'd heard Jenna was away and he'd remembered a pot in the kitchen that her late mum, who was pretty old-school, used to keep full of banknotes. It was a long shot that it was still there, but in a moment of madness, he'd convinced himself that if it was, he could borrow enough to get himself back winning again, or at least to see him through until payday. Then he'd return it, with interest.

God, what has he become, trying to steal from a grieving twenty-year-old?

Anyway, he'd found the pot empty – probably no longer in use as a cash float – so he'd left without any money. And then, to his horror, immediately bumped into his young, busybody neighbour.

Now here she is again.

Paige must have rung up first thing this morning and snagged one of the urgent same-day appointments. Stay professional, he tells himself. Focus on the job.

He buzzes her through and awaits the imminent rap on his door.

'Come in,' he says on cue, flashing her a smile full of bravado as she enters. 'Ah, Paige. Hello there. Nice to see you again. Please have a seat.'

'Thanks.' She sits down at the side of his desk, a nervous energy about her.

'So how can I help you today?' he asks, leaning forward with his hands clasped together.

'I'll get straight to the point,' she says, eyeballing him in a way that feels weirdly uncomfortable. 'The symptoms I mentioned to whoever I spoke to on the phone were made up. There's nothing wrong with me, but I do need to speak to you urgently.'

Adrian gulps. 'I'm sorry, that's totally unacceptable. I'm afraid I'm going to have to ask you to—'

'I'm not going anywhere until you hear me out. If you don't, I'll scream and create a right fuss. Trust me, you don't want that to happen.'

'Paige, I'm not sure what's going on here, but it sounds like you're upset about something.' Head reeling, he reaches towards his desk phone. 'Why don't I call one of your parents and—'

'Don't you dare,' she snaps. 'I know what you've been up to.

I know your big secret, and if you don't sit back and listen to what I have to say – answer my questions – I'm going to tell all to Sarah, Zack and whoever else will listen.'

This most definitely gets his attention. Shit. He sits back in his seat.

How the hell does she know?

How *much* does she know?

SEVENTY-TWO

Paige

'Let's talk about Jenna, shall we?' I say.

'Jenna?' Adrian replies. 'What about her?'

'How about we start with where she is?'

'I'm sorry? Am I supposed to know that?'

'Don't play dumb.'

'I'm n-not,' he stutters, apparently on the back foot, although it could be an act. 'I don't know where Jenna is, honestly. Why do you think I do? Because you saw me coming out of her house? I already explained why I was there.'

'Hmm. So why is there still a drawerful of prescription pills in her mum's room? How do you explain that? And what about the previous time I was at her house, on Monday evening? You were there too, weren't you? You're the one who shut me in the bathroom. Where is she? What the hell have you done to her?'

He stares at me, a bewildered look on his face, mouth open, eyes skittish. 'Um. I, er... I'm afraid you've lost me. The pills I took were from, er, a cupboard in the kitchen. If there are others upstairs, I wasn't aware of them. As for Monday, I'm not sure what you're talking about. I wasn't there then. I've only visited once recently. And I certainly haven't done anything to Jenna. Look, is everything all right? You seem very worked up.'

I ignore this question and try a different tack. 'Okay, you said you called there because you were in the neighbourhood. How come?'

Adrian frowns. 'I made a house call to one of her neighbours.'

'How convenient. Who were you visiting?'

'That's none of your business, Paige. I can't tell you that.'

Is he being truthful, or is he trying to manipulate me? I want to believe him, but he looked genuinely scared when I told him I knew his big secret. So maybe I should blurt it out, then try to gauge his reaction.

I'm afraid of what he might do to me, though, if this is the same person who killed that elderly rambler and then threatened Jenna. That's the beauty of confronting him here. I might be alone with him in this room, but there are plenty of people, staff and patients, on the other side of the door, plus a record of my appointment. I'm also recording this conversation on my phone, at Carmen's suggestion. And I have a small kitchen knife hidden in my handbag, in case things get really messy.

'Look, why would you think I'd do something to Jenna?' Adrian asks. 'I'm very fond of her. I saw a lot of her when her mother was sick. She's a lovely girl. After the funeral, I suggested she should try Sarah's yoga classes as a way to relax and help process her grief; she found them very helpful. Sarah took her under her wing and the two of them were close for a while. She wanted to help Jenna achieve her true potential. To find a rewarding career and so on. It was all going well, and then, I don't know... Jenna lost interest. She quit yoga and stopped returning Sarah's calls. Such a shame.'

He's staring at me now, lips pursed, like he's expecting a response. But I don't know what I'm supposed to make of this stuff about his wife helping Jenna. If true, it's the first I've heard of it. Jenna never mentioned a thing to me about taking up yoga or getting close to Sarah.

'I don't understand what's going on,' Adrian adds. 'I thought you said Jenna was away somewhere when we last spoke. Is everything all right?'

'Far from it. As you know.'

'N-no. That's not true.'

'Let's cut the bullshit,' I say. 'I know exactly what was going on between you and Jenna. I know the two of you were having an affair. That you went away for a secret weekend in Cumbria together. And that you were involved in a hit-and-run, killing an elderly man. And now I think you—'

'Hang on, what the hell are you talking about? This is nonsense. These very serious allegations are utterly baseless. I'm so taken aback, I hardly know how to respond. Honestly, this whole thing is making me very concerned about you, Paige. About your mental health. Especially in light of your, um, past issues. I think I need to get one of my colleagues in here to assist.'

He reaches towards his desk phone, and I panic. 'No,' I say. 'Don't you dare do that. Don't you try to turn this back on me, making out I'm unhinged.' I reach into my handbag and touch the cool steel of the knife blade.

SEVENTY-THREE

Paige

'Stop,' I say, squeezing my fist around the handle of the knife. 'Don't you touch that phone. This is between me and you. I don't want anyone else in here.'

Adrian's eyes stretch wide open. The colour drains from his face and his hands start to shake as he holds them up in a surrender gesture. 'Whoa. Let's calm this right down, Paige. This is me you're talking to – your neighbour, your doctor. There's no need for that.'

I back up in my seat and tell him to do the same, fearing he might try to grab the weapon from me. My grip is so tight as I keep it pointed at him, I can feel my pulse throbbing against it. 'Speak.'

'What do you want me to say? I don't understand why you think Jenna and I have had an affair. She's what: twenty? I'm old enough to be her father. And as for this business about a hit-and-run, I don't know where that's come from. It's not true. I do my best to save lives, not take them away. Look, should we get Jenna on the phone? Would that help to clear things up?'

'If only we could. She's been missing since the weekend.'

'Missing?'

'Well, officially she's gone away, but she's barely contactable. Nothing at all by video or voice. Just the occasional message. And who can say if that's really her? It could be you, for all I know. Have you done something to her? Tell the truth, or I swear I'll—'

'Please. Calm down, Paige.' Adrian looks convincingly flummoxed by everything I've told him. 'If I promise not to call anyone else in, do you think you could maybe put the knife down?'

I shake my head. 'No, not yet. But if you talk to me and tell me the truth, you won't have anything to worry about.'

He nods gingerly. 'I *am* telling you the truth. You have the wrong man. If Jenna has been having an affair with someone, honestly, it's not me. Did she tell you it was?'

'Not specifically,' I whisper. It dawns on me how deranged I might sound to Adrian if he does happen to be telling the truth and really had nothing to do with any of this. 'She's been protecting the identity of the person she's been seeing. But from what she's said, you fit the bill better than anyone else.'

'Maybe there's some way I can prove to you it wasn't me. This hit-and-run you mentioned – this secret weekend away – when was it? *Where* was it? Because I haven't been away anywhere in ages.'

I know the exact date, having looked up the details of Arthur Smith's death online, so I tell him.

'Right. Well, how about we look in my diary? I have it here on my desk. Do you mind if I open it?'

'Go ahead. But I'm watching you. No funny business.'

'Of course. Stay calm, please. We'll get to the bottom of this, Paige, I promise.' His anxious eyes linger on the knife in my hand before looking down at the diary. His hands are shaking as he turns the pages. 'Right, let's see what I was doing then... Oh yes. That was the weekend Sarah was away for a couple of nights in Stratford-upon-Avon.'

He holds up the black A5 diary to show me the entry, written in blue biro: *Sarah Stratford, Fri–Sun.*

'She was away all that weekend, and I was home. I remember that Zack and I had a couple of boys' nights, watching sport and films. In fact, your dad joined us for a few hours on the Saturday night, when the cricket was on. You can check with him.'

He points out another entry, for the Sunday: *Optician, 11.15.*

'I went for an eye test on the day you say this hit-and-run happened. I still have a printout of the results at home, which I'd be happy to show you if it helps. So if Jenna was away in Cumbria that weekend, it wasn't with me. It does all sound very troubling, though. Do the police know? Could this be something to do with her disappearance?'

Oh crap. He could have covered his tracks here, but is that likely? Have I got the wrong man? Have I pulled a knife on Adrian for nothing?

My heart sinks. I feel light-headed, like I'm about to faint. 'I, er...'

'Paige,' he says. 'Are you all right? Please, talk to me.'

'Shit.'

'Paige,' he repeats. 'What's going through your mind? Please don't panic or do anything rash. We can sort this out.'

Yeah, right. How? He'll have to call the police on me for this. Then I'll be utterly screwed, especially after what they accused me of doing at uni. They'll think I've lost the plot. They'll probably have me sectioned. And then who will find my best friend?

'Jenna's in trouble,' I say. 'Big trouble. If it's not you behind it, then it's someone else – and I need to work out who. I have to get back out there and find my friend.'

'No, wait, please.'

I jump to my feet, keeping the knife firmly pointed at Adrian and gradually backing away towards the door. 'I'm sorry, I really thought it was you. Jenna *did* have an affair with someone, and it ended badly. There *was* a hit-and-run. I have hard proof. I'll work out the rest somehow. I have to.'

'What are you doing?' Adrian asks as I reach my spare hand behind me and feel for the door handle to let myself out. 'We need to talk about this. I can help you.'

'If you really want to do that,' I say, 'don't grass me up. Don't come after me. I needed your attention, that was all. You know I'd never have used this.' I toss the knife into the waste-paper bin next to me as I swing open the door.

Then I make a run for it.

SEVENTY-FOUR

Paige

The speed at which I race down the corridor, back into the waiting room and then out of the front doors of the GP surgery must attract attention. But I don't have time to notice. The only thing on my mind is getting out of there. As I exit the main glass doors, having had to halt for a precious couple of seconds for them to slide open, the warm sun and a gentle breeze kiss my skin. It feels like freedom. I expect someone to shout something after me as I dart across the tarmac to Mum's car. My hands are shaking when I pull out the keys, unlock the doors and then jump in and start the engine.

I reverse out of the space, and that's when I see Adrian and another male staff member. They're standing in the main entrance, looking for me, but apparently they haven't spotted me yet. Luckily, the car park has two exits, so I head for the one in the opposite direction, driving normally so as not to draw attention to myself.

My heart's pounding so hard I can hear it in my ears.

By the time they do see me, I'm nearly out of there, only for traffic to back up on the road I want to join.

'No!' I shout, banging my hand on the steering wheel. 'Come on. Move, for God's sake.'

I'm watching them get closer and closer in the rear-view mirror. I've locked the doors, but I can hear Adrian calling my name, telling me to stop and talk to them.

His hand reaches for the back windscreen.

And then, in the nick of time, the traffic shifts and I pull out and away, speeding into the distance.

What now?

Adrian's probably on the phone to Mum or Dad already. If not the police.

Shit.

I reach for my mobile and switch it off. I don't want anyone to be able to contact or locate me.

I need time alone to think.

At least I'm in the car rather than on foot.

Although if Adrian does get the police involved, that won't be much help. They'll be looking out for this number plate before long.

I drive round and round, circling the same streets, heading nowhere. My mind is a jumbled mess. I don't trust myself to travel far in this state. The last thing I need is to stumble my way into a car accident. I daren't go home either, but not knowing what else to do – where else to go – I pull into a quiet spot just around the corner from our street.

What now? I need time to think. To work out what happens next.

I'm mulling this over, while fighting not to slip into a major panic attack, when I notice a familiar car coming towards me: Sarah's.

My heart skips a beat. I duck down in my seat so she doesn't see me as she drives past. She couldn't be out looking for me, could she, after what just happened at the surgery? Surely not this soon. And if so, how come she drove past Mum's car without a second glance?

No, it must be a coincidence.

But there are no coincidences, an intuitive voice in my head tells me. Maybe it's a sign. And Adrian *did* say that stuff about Sarah getting close to Jenna while teaching her yoga.

Next thing, without totally understanding why, I'm following her, keeping a couple of other cars in between so it's hopefully not too obvious. What have I got to lose? I'm already in the shit up to my neck. I might as well keep going.

After several minutes of driving, we're out of the village and in the countryside on a twisty lane. But then Sarah unexpectedly pulls her car to the side of the road, and I have no option but to drive on by.

Brilliant. That went well.

Just around the next bend, however, I get lucky, spotting a dirt track off to the left, probably leading to a farmer's field. I make a snap decision to turn onto it, following it as it curves off to one side behind a high bush. I stop the car out of sight of the main road and jump out. Not an ideal parking spot if a tractor comes along wanting to get past, but I'll take my chances.

I return to the road on foot, having fished Mum's green raincoat out of the boot as a makeshift disguise. Hood up, despite the warm weather, I dart back to the bend in the road to see if Sarah's car is still parked up.

It is. And Sarah herself is kneeling in front of it, doing the strangest thing.

SEVENTY-FIVE

Paige

I drop to the ground and scuttle into the undergrowth at the side of the road, baffled as I watch Sarah, now wearing a dark hoodie and sunglasses, stick an alternate number plate on top of her real one. I memorise the new number. Then she walks to the back of the car, where, as far as I can tell from my limited viewpoint, she does the same again.

What *is* she up to?

I expect her to get back behind the wheel next and drive off to do something dodgy. But instead, she removes a small rucksack from the boot, straps it over her shoulders, shuts and locks the vehicle, then strides purposefully in my direction.

Staying as low to the ground as possible, I turn around and crawl through the undergrowth until I'm well around the bend. Then I get up and run back to the safety of the bush where I've hidden the car.

What have I just witnessed?

It's nothing to do with her looking for me, that's for sure.

Cogs start to whir and turn in my head.

Adrian's earlier words at the surgery, which barely registered at the time because of the sheer stress of the situation, shift into position and take on new meaning.

Sarah took her under her wing, his voice echoes in my memory, *and the two of them were close for a while.*

It couldn't be.

Could it?

That was the weekend Sarah was away for a couple of nights, I recall him telling me, like he's whispering it into my ear right now.

My thoughts are racing.

When I saw Jenna on Saturday, before the barbecue, and she was talking about her bad break-up, did she ever specifically refer to her ex as a man? Or was that my own interpretation?

I can't remember – not for sure – but the more I think about it, the more I'm convinced she didn't specify. The same with the videos, which are fresher in my mind.

What about the emails? I may only have managed to actually read one, but they were all sent to and from this male-sounding Mr888. Perhaps that was the idea. A convenient cover to help hide the truth, which the pair of them were so desperate to conceal at every turn.

So Jenna was having a secret relationship with Sarah, my neighbour and, apparently, her yoga instructor?

I guess it's as believable as her being with Adrian, her GP. And it would certainly explain why the pair of them were so secretive about the whole thing.

I need to follow Sarah, that's for sure. That way lies the truth about what's happened to my friend, I'm sure of it. But if Sarah is the person I now suspect her to be – as ludicrous as that still sounds to me – I need to be incredibly careful. I mustn't underestimate my seemingly relaxed, friendly neighbour or what she's capable of.

If Sarah killed an elderly walker and showed no remorse; threatened Jenna not to speak out... what has she done now?

What have you got yourself into, Jenna?

I pray I'm not too late to help you.

SEVENTY-SIX

Sarah

Here I am again, on my way to the abandoned cottage I've visited daily since it became the hiding place for my dirty little secret. My ill-advised affair with Jenna has spiralled into chaos, thanks to the death of that bastard bloody rambler.

The old git should have been more careful about where he was walking. Although the truth of the matter, which I haven't told Jenna, is that I did actually see him when I was driving. She was too busy getting frisky to be looking up ahead. I saw him striding along the road like he owned it. I thought it would be funny to give the idiot a scare. Teach him to use the footpath like he should have been doing. So I drove really close to him... and, well, the rest is history.

Did a part of me want to kill him?

I didn't think so at the time, but with hindsight, maybe a little bit.

When I realised he was dead, I certainly didn't feel remorse. My main concern was not getting caught. And that turned out to be surprisingly easy, particularly as my car somehow suffered barely a scratch and no one else passed by, like fortune was shining on me, protecting me. Like I deserved to get away with it. The only potential weak spot was Jenna.

Despite the respectable face I present to the world on a daily basis, there's always been a darkness within me.

I kept it buried for a very long time. Tried to pretend it wasn't there. But you can't repress your true nature for ever. It never gives up trying to find ways to break free. And once you open that door, even a crack, there's no going back.

It started with me doing risky things because I got off on the thrill. They made me feel alive after long years of restraint and boredom.

Like deliberately going for a drive after a few drinks and getting away with it.

Or secretly using dating apps to have casual sex with strangers, male and female. I've always liked both.

Or taking advantage of a vulnerable, attractive twenty-year-old and having an affair with her.

Or, most recently, finding my way onto the dark web and using it to order fake car number plates, the right drugs and the kind of items you need to restrain a person for an extended period of time. All delivered to my front door, discreetly packaged, by a reputable courier service while Adrian and Zack were out at work.

Anyway, I've been keeping Jenna in this ramshackle old property for nearly a week now – and it has to end. I'm heading there with fresh purpose this time.

When I spoke to her yesterday, she said all the right things.

'Please let me go,' she pleaded. 'If you do, I swear I won't tell anyone about any of this. I'll keep quiet about our relationship and the hit-and-run too. For good. I promise. I won't say a word ever. Please, I'm begging you. You don't need to do this.'

But I didn't believe her. She would say that, wouldn't she? Anything to get free.

'What about your guilt?' I asked her. 'I thought you couldn't live with it.'

'I was wrong,' she said. 'I can. I will. If you just let me go, I'll forget it all. I'll leave you alone. I'll even move away, out of the area, if that's what it takes, so you never have to see me again.'

She was simply telling me what I wanted to hear. If I was to set her free, she'd run straight to the police and tell them everything, the lot, no question about it.

I don't doubt she was really in love with me when we were together, particularly towards the end, before it all went wrong. But still. How could she see past everything I've put her through since? How could anyone in their right mind ever let that go?

I was fond of her once, I really was, before she started to annoy me with her whining emails and constant self-reproach. Sure, a lot of the initial enjoyment came from the illicit nature of our affair. But for a while I felt happy and fulfilled. I bathed in her warmth and kindness. I hoped her virtue and love might be enough to save me from the dark, destructive desires that still simmered deep within me.

She wasn't enough, though. I doubt anyone ever could be. Adrian came damn close. That's why I married him, had his son and played at being the good wife and mother for so many years, in the hope it would eventually become true. Look how that turned out. If the good doctor couldn't save me from myself, then how could a grieving, messed-up twenty-year-old?

I realised that up in Cumbria, as I swerved the car and felt it make contact with human flesh and bone. And in that fateful moment, I sent the pair of us hurtling towards this pitch-black present where we now find ourselves.

The one in which I intend to kill Jenna today.

SEVENTY-SEVEN

Paige

I've been tailing Sarah on foot for a while now. I'm hanging back as far as possible without losing sight of her, staying close to the hedgerow at my side. Luckily, she's barely looked behind her; she doesn't seem to have spotted me.

She's moving at quite a pace along the country road and shows no sign of slowing down, changing course or approaching a destination.

It's the corners, when the road ahead twists out of sight, that bother me. Every time she disappears around one, I worry she'll have vanished when I get there. Or, worse, she'll be waiting for me.

I regret leaving the knife behind in Adrian's consulting room now. I was trying to demonstrate to him that I wasn't a threat. That he didn't need to call the police on me. Little did I know then that I'd soon be tailing someone genuinely dangerous – his wife, of all people.

Adrian doesn't know about Sarah, does he? He can't, or he'd never have fed me the information that finally led me to put the pieces together, to see the villain hiding in plain sight. I suspect no one knows other than Jenna. I also suspect that's why she's gone missing.

Sarah disappears around yet another bend in the road, and I wince, sucking air in through my teeth. There's a temptation to speed up my pace, but I know I shouldn't, or I'll potentially get too close. So I try to stay consistent and pray she'll still be in sight, the usual distance ahead of me, when I round the bend.

It'll be fine. It'll be fine.

Like the previous times.

But thinking this doesn't reduce the speed of my pounding heart as I approach.

And then... Shit!

She actually has disappeared this time. The road immediately ahead is straight as a ruler, and there's no sign of her at all.

Where has she gone?

I jog forward, my panic at having lost her overtaking my fear of getting too close, eyes scouring either side of the road, desperate for clues.

A rusty metal gate on my right is the first possibility. But a quick scan of the large, empty field beyond suggests it's unlikely.

If she's spotted me, she could be hiding somewhere in there, I guess, but I don't think so.

I continue forward. To my huge relief, hidden behind a large tree on the left is a muddy old track, leading off to goodness knows where. Only the first few yards are visible before it takes a sharp turn to the right and down an incline. That has to be it, right? That has to be where Sarah has gone.

I'm no tracker, but I turn my eyes down to the mud, which is mainly dry with the odd damp section, and look for footprints. There definitely are a few, although whether they're recent and belong to Sarah is another matter.

I hesitate for a minute or two, looking all around again to

ensure there are no better options. But I can't see any. Not without continuing further along the road. And I'm really afraid of losing her. I need to make a decision, so I take the turn and follow the mud track, hoping beyond hope that I'm right.

'I'm coming for you, Jenna,' I whisper under my breath, longing for this to be true.

SEVENTY-EIGHT

Sarah

I'm getting close to the old cottage now, at last. I parked even further away than usual this time, so it's been a fair old walk, but I'm off-road now and a decent way down the track.

I barely looked around me as I marched along the main road, keeping my eyes firmly on the ground ahead. I wanted to look as inconspicuous as possible to people in the few vehicles that zoomed by in both directions. I didn't encounter any cyclists or other walkers today, thankfully. They've always worried me most, because the slower speed of travel means they're more likely to spot something they might remember.

In an ideal world, I'd have done this further away from home. But I knew I'd need to visit frequently, and it's not like I have a portfolio of abandoned, isolated buildings at my disposal.

I started formulating my contingency plan as I drove Jenna home from the scene of the accident in Cumbria. I feared she was going to be a liability when I had to confiscate her phone to stop her from calling the emergency services.

Obviously, I hoped it wouldn't come down to kidnapping

and locking her up here in the middle of nowhere. But as time passed and she grew increasingly distraught and hysterical – refusing to leave me alone even after I'd taken the risky step of ending our relationship – I was glad I'd prepared for this eventuality.

I sent her my final warning via email, using the accounts we'd set up specifically to keep in touch while we were still seeing each other. I kept my fingers crossed that it would finally do the trick, but it didn't. She couldn't let go.

The very next day she called me from her mum's old phone, knowing I'd blocked her own number. She left a voicemail saying that I'd left her with no choice but to go to the police and tell them everything.

I couldn't have that, so I got back in touch and begged her not to do anything rash. If she'd ever truly loved me, I said, could she at least allow me a few more days to think the situation through?

'I'm racked with guilt too,' I lied, unashamedly manipulating her. 'Just because I don't show it like you do doesn't mean I don't feel it. Honestly, I haven't had a proper night's sleep since what happened. I've burst into tears I can't tell you how many times, and I'm constantly questioning everything that runs through my mind. Do you think I don't miss you just because I said we should end things? My emotions are all over the place. Maybe going to the police *is* the right thing to do, like you say. But I'm really scared. Please don't force me into this. I need a chance to breathe, Jenna. I'm suffocating. I'm begging you to do this one thing for me and hold off for a few days.'

And she did, because she's too nice for her own good. Certainly too nice for me.

Which gave me enough time to dot the i's and cross the t's on my contingency plan.

Before leaving Kate and Danny's barbecue on Saturday, I messaged Jenna from the bathroom:

I need to see you tonight. I think I've made a huge mistake. I miss you so much. I'll come round to yours as soon as I can, although it could be late. Please let me in and hear me out. I need to explain x

I waited until an hour or so after we'd got home, once Adrian was snoring in bed, before I covered myself up and sneaked round there on foot.

Jenna was raging initially. 'You've treated me like shit,' she spat. 'I thought you loved me, but the moment things got difficult, you turned on me. You were like a totally different person. Someone I barely recognised. That poor old man lost his life because of us. His family must be devastated. But for you it's only ever been about saving your own skin. You ditched me and left me all alone when I needed you most. You threatened me. And now you say you've made a mistake; you miss me. What am I supposed to do with that, Sarah: just forget all the crap you've put me through?'

'I know,' I said. 'I feel awful. I'm so, so sorry for how I've treated you, Jenna. I panicked. Lost my head. It was all too much, like my life was spinning out of control. I made some terrible decisions. Did some unforgivable things. But I know that now, and I want to make up for it. Do the right thing. Whatever it takes.'

'What does that mean? Why are you even here?'

I reached for her hand. She pulled it away at first, but then she let me take it. 'Because I miss you, Jenna. I love you, more than anything. More than anyone else. And I can't go on without you. I mean it. I need to be with you... all the time.'

Tears rolling down her cheeks, she whispered: 'You don't know how much I've wanted to hear you say that. I've felt so alone, so broken without you. You've really hurt me.'

'I know. I'm so sorry. Please give me another chance. Let me try to make it up to you.'

It took a while, but I talked her round. She was still in love with me, and I tapped into that, knowing I offered her the prospect of a lover and replacement mother figure all rolled into one, even if she didn't consciously realise that.

'Please can we make another go of it?' I begged her.

'But how? What about the accident? What will we do about that?'

'This is why I had to see you tonight. Hear me out. I have an idea. How about you come away with me for a few days so we can put our heads together and work it out?'

'Away where?'

'Leave that to me.'

'Work what out exactly?'

'Everything. Our response to the accident and a way to be together properly in the future, out of the shadows. That's all I've ever really wanted, though I lacked the courage to make it happen until now. Once I realised I couldn't stand to lose you.'

'But we killed someone. How could it ever be that easy?'

'We'll work it out. We'll find a way, trust me. We can do anything as long as we're together. I believe in us. Don't you?'

Basically, I offered Jenna everything she wanted on a plate, knowing she wouldn't be able to resist. She skipped right past the many flaws in my plan, as I hoped she would. She bought it.

'I'll pick you up first thing in the morning, same place as last time,' I said before leaving.

'You still haven't told me where we're going.'

'It's a surprise, but I know you'll love it. I took the liberty of booking it as a last-minute deal earlier today, praying you'd agree.'

'What about Adrian and Zack? What have you told them?'

'That's all sorted. Not your problem. Don't concern yourself about them.'

'Okay,' she replied, promising to message Danny and Becky to explain her absence.

'Perfect.' I kissed her goodbye like I used to.

'You're not... This isn't all just because I said I was going to the police, is it? You do really—'

'I love you. You must know that.'

'I used to think so. But it's not felt like that ever since... you know what. We still have to do something about that. We *are* going to, right?'

'Of course. We'll work it out together. We're a team.'

'Promise?'

'Promise.'

The lies were slipping out of my mouth one after another by that point.

I sneaked back home and into bed, where Adrian remained zonked out, exactly as I'd left him. And a few hours later, at 7.30 a.m., I left him again, dropping a note on the kitchen table saying that I'd gone for an early walk before a yoga class.

SEVENTY-NINE

Sarah

I collected Jenna as arranged on Sunday morning. I told her that before we left the area, I had to pick up some things I'd stashed nearby. Then I drove her to this hidden place I'd found and been secretly preparing for her. It was the one time I took the risky step of taking my car all the way down the mud track to the cottage entrance. It seemed like the only sensible option, and at least the track was dry, so there was less chance of long-lasting tyre tracks.

'Where *are* we?' she asked as we drew up outside.

'An abandoned cottage. Don't worry, it's not where we're staying, although honestly, after I came across it, I did wonder if it's somewhere we might be able to make a cute little den for ourselves to avoid prying eyes.'

'We already have *my* house,' she said. 'That's private enough, isn't it? Besides, I thought you were ready to discuss ways of being together properly in public. Like leaving Adrian.'

'Absolutely.' I threw her my best meaningful look. 'But it is a delicate situation, especially with me being married and significantly older than you, and both of us living in a small village packed with nosy gossips. We'll need to plan things carefully, and that might take a little bit of time. But it will all be worth it in the end, won't it?'

I stroked her cheek, and we kissed for what I sensed would be the last time.

'How come you're not wearing your coffee bean today?' I asked her afterwards, referring to her favourite gold necklace.

'Oh yeah,' she said, reaching up to her bare neck with one hand, frowning. 'I lost it recently. I'm, er, not sure where. It must have fallen off. Mum gave me that. I'm gutted.'

I changed the subject. 'Do you know what? I think this place, dilapidated as it is, has a certain romantic charm. And we have some lovely memories from the last time we were in a cottage together, right? Despite what happened afterwards. Anyway, I need to pop in and get this stuff. Are you going to give me a hand? It'll be quicker that way.'

'What on earth have you stashed here? This is a little odd, you know.'

I laughed. 'Oh, you'll see. Just a few treats for us to enjoy while we're away. Things I didn't want to risk being found at home. Trust me.'

And she did, more fool her, especially after the past few weeks. Love really is blind.

'What *is* this place?' she exclaimed while being unwittingly led to her prison. 'Oh my God. It's like nature has started to reclaim it. All that moss and ivy everywhere. And that battered old car. Wow. That's not driven anywhere for a very long time. Who owns this place? Someone must.'

I shrugged. 'No idea. I came across it by chance while I was out here one day looking for some solitude off the beaten track.'

'Well, you certainly found that.'

Less than an hour later, I left the premises alone, returned home, and, with the help of several drinks, did my best to behave like it was a regular Sunday.

I won't pretend I wasn't thrown by Paige's unannounced appearance that afternoon. She was asking about our doorbell camera in relation to the piercing scream everyone had heard at the barbecue the night before. Her turning up like that so soon after I'd abducted her friend was really troubling. I feared she was on to me already: that Jenna might have confided in her about our affair and maybe even the car accident. But Paige gave no indication whatsoever that she suspected me of anything. So despite my racing heartbeat, I think I managed to retain the illusion that I was calm and unfazed by her questions. I prayed she was scrabbling around in the dark and I was off the hook.

When she and Zack had a tetchy run-in outside our house on Wednesday, I seized the opportunity to be the peacemaker. It was quite the relief to look in Paige's eyes again and see that she still didn't suspect me, despite the near disaster that had unfolded two days prior.

Would-be Nancy Drew had turned up at Jenna's house on Monday evening, letting herself in while I was upstairs. Still in possession of a spare key, from when we were sneaking around during our affair, I'd been looking for Jenna's laptop. She'd used it to email me, so I wanted to destroy it to get rid of any evidence it might contain of our relationship. Anyway, it was touch and go for a spell at the house, but I seized an opportunity to make a run for it and, thankfully, escaped unseen, without having to hurt Paige.

I never found that damn laptop, even though I did sneak back for another look. By that point, I'd scared Jenna into telling me it was in a kitchen drawer, but either she was lying or someone else had found it first. The most likely scenario seems to be that Paige came across it and took it home. Thank God my email account was created with fake details. But is there really nothing at Jenna's end to identify me?

Unless Paige has been scuppered by the password. I know it, but does she? Do best friends share that kind of information with each other? Let's hope not.

And what about Monday? I shut her in the bathroom before running down the stairs and out of the front door. And yet I've heard nothing about her encountering an intruder. Wouldn't she have gone to the police, her parents or Becky and Scott for help? If so, surely news of this would have reached me by now. Weird.

Right, I've reached the cottage at last, and I'm a bundle of nerves. I need to concentrate. Keep my mind in the moment – on the task at hand – rather than in the past. Otherwise, I'll end up making a mistake. And that cannot happen.

Do I really have the strength to go ahead with this: to end Jenna's life?

I have to. If I don't, I'll lose everything.

I can't see any other way out of this mess. Not now. Not after all the things I've done.

As I follow the overgrown path past the now familiar sight of the long-abandoned Citroën, a crunching sound from somewhere behind me grabs my attention.

What was that? I lower myself into a crouch, hands balled into tight fists, and slowly, silently scan every detail of my overgrown surroundings, hunting for any sign of someone else nearby. I curse myself for not checking around me more frequently as I made my way here from the road.

After a few long minutes of waiting and watching, on full alert, I calm down. Tell myself it will have been a wild animal.

I continue towards the back door, spinning around a couple more times en route. But once I get there, I'm fairly satisfied that I'm just freaking out because of the daunting task ahead of me.

EIGHTY

Paige

Is Jenna here, inside this wreck of a place?

I turn my mobile back on, ultra-careful to ensure that it's muted first, with all notifications turned off. There's a weak signal, thank goodness. Only one bar, but hopefully that will be enough. I type a message to Mum and Dad, saying where I am; that I'm scared, in big trouble and need their help. But when I come to send it, the signal has dropped out. I can't get the stupid thing to reconnect, although I leave it trying.

Dammit.

Looks like I've no choice but to go it alone.

Moments later, I let myself in through the back door of the cottage, which is closed but not locked. There are fresh heavy-duty fixings on the outside so it can be secured with a padlock. Sarah must have removed this to enter.

The old wooden door feels solid despite the peeling black paint. I wince as it screeches open and shut, praying that wherever Sarah is inside, she can't hear it.

There's no sign of her or anyone else in the cold, bare

kitchen. I creep on tiptoe across the hard stone floor, terrified of coming face to face with her at any moment: round any corner, behind any doorway.

I've armed myself with a chunky stick I found outside. I hold it tight in my right hand, and yet I feel far from strong or brave.

Fake it till you make it, I imagine Jenna telling me.

I'm starting to wonder whether anyone else is actually in this grimy, dingy shadow of a house when I reach the bottom of the staircase and hear a voice. Or maybe two voices. Both female, I think. The sound is too muffled to make out what they're saying, but it's definitely coming from upstairs.

There's a grotty red carpet on the stairs, which I hope will mute my footsteps. And yet there are still too many creaks as I go up. I'm convinced Sarah must have heard me, although no one appears when I reach the top, brandishing my stick. The voices continue. Is that Sarah and Jenna? I tip my head to try to hear better, but I still can't make them out clearly. The sound seems to be coming from the other side of a door at the end of the landing. I inch my way towards it, passing by another closed door with padlock fixings similar to those I saw downstairs. I'm tempted to peek in there first, but that's not where the voices are coming from, so I push on, my heart in my mouth.

Leaning forward to listen, I can finally hear what's being said. And to my surprise, it's neither Sarah nor Jenna. It's... What? No, that can't be right.

As I reach forward to open the door, there's a sudden noise and movement behind me.

Fuck.

Before I can react, something heavy smashes into the back of my head, and...

Nothing.

EIGHTY-ONE

Paige

I come to with a thumping head, blurred vision and vertigo. I'm sitting on a hard wooden chair, hands tied behind my back. I shake them and they won't budge. My legs are restrained too.

'Paige?' A slurred voice speaks to my left before breaking into a coughing fit.

I look over and, at long last, see the face of my best friend. But this is no cause for celebration. She looks horrendous. Like a junkie. Lying in squalor on a mattress on filthy floorboards. Ashen-faced, hollow-cheeked, eyes glazed over. Defeated.

'Jenna,' I groan.

'Is it really you?'

'Yes.'

'You came for me. You found me.' The tiniest hint of a smile crosses her dry, cracked lips. 'I screwed up.'

With a leaden heart, I look around the dingy room, taking in the chains that have been holding Jenna here and the two grimy, smelly buckets that apparently serve as her toilets.

I turn my head as far as I can in either direction. The door must be directly behind me, out of my view. 'Where is she? Where's Sarah? Has she locked us in here? How long was I out?'

Speaking slowly and barely moving, like she's heavily doped up, Jenna slurs: 'Not sure. Sorry. It's hard to stay awake. Doing my best.'

'Has she given you something? Drugs?'

She replies with a slow nod.

'Have you been here the whole time, since you disappeared?'

Another nod.

Realising that the chains attached to her ankles must allow Jenna some movement to use the buckets, I wonder if she might be able to reach me and help me get loose. Mind you, Sarah's used thick cable ties to restrain me and she's fixed them tight. We'd need something sharp to cut through them. And if Jenna had such a tool handy, she'd surely have used it by now to remove her own ankle ties.

I say her name, but she doesn't answer. Her eyes are shut.

'Jenna,' I repeat, louder this time, but still she doesn't stir. Whatever drugs Sarah has given her must have finally knocked her out.

Panic sets in, and I start screaming for help.

Unfortunately, the only help that comes is Sarah, a few minutes later, by which time my throat is already on fire.

'You're wasting your time shouting. I'm the only person who can hear you. There's no one else.' She sneers at me, then looks over at my friend's inert form. 'Not even Jenna.'

'Go screw yourself. How could you do this to her? She loved you, for whatever reason. What have you drugged her with?'

'I'll tell you if you tell me how you worked out it was me. It was her laptop, right? Who else knows?'

'Just let us both go, Sarah. The game's up. You're finished. You're going to jail for a very long time.'

'Confident words for someone tied to a chair. I can't believe how easy it was to trick you, sending you to the wrong bedroom. Mobiles come in handy for all sorts these days, don't they?' She waves my phone in front of me. 'Thanks for unlocking this one for me while you were out of it. Good old biometrics. I saw the message you tried to send Mummy and Daddy. What a shame about the signal round here. So poor.'

'Why are you doing this, Sarah?' I plead, changing tack. 'Jenna and I both have our whole lives ahead of us. Please don't take that away. It's not too late to do the right thing.'

'Save it,' she snaps. 'Don't waste your breath. You got yourself into this, Paige. I left you alone even though I knew you were sniffing around. I could easily have hurt or kidnapped you when you interrupted me at Jenna's house, but I chose not to. I shut you in the bathroom and ran off instead. You wouldn't let it lie, though. You kept on beavering away until you followed me here and, well, forced me into this.'

'What? I didn't force you to do anything. You manipulated Jenna, seducing her when she was lonely and vulnerable, desperately missing her mum.'

'Shut up. It wasn't like that. We genuinely cared for each other.'

I nod my head at Jenna's unconscious form. 'Yeah, looks like it. Is that why you took her drink-driving in the hills? You didn't care much about the poor old man you killed, did you? And this was her punishment for wanting to do the right thing? Wow, no wonder Zack turned out such a charmer.'

'Leave my son out of it. He has nothing to do with this.'

'What about Adrian, then? Does he know you're into young girls? I'm guessing not. But he will do soon, especially after our chat in his surgery earlier. I thought he was the one having an affair with Jenna, so I confronted him. It didn't take me long to figure out the truth once he revealed you were away on the weekend of the hit-and-run. I'm sure he'll work it out too. So where's all this going, Sarah? What exactly are you planning to do with me and Jenna? You're going to get found out. You might as well give yourself up and let us go.'

She stares at me, a deranged glint in her eyes. 'No. Look around. I'm the one in control, not you. I'm not getting caught. I'm not going to prison. I'll run if I have to, but you're not going anywhere. Neither of you is leaving this place alive.'

She charges out of the room, returning a few seconds later with... Oh fuck.

A jerrycan.

'Please, no!' I cry. 'You can't do this. Seriously, I'm begging you. I'll do anything. I'll help you escape. I won't say a word. Whatever you want. Please.'

The smell of petrol greets my nostrils even before she starts pouring.

EIGHTY-TWO

Kate

'Keep going,' she tells Danny. 'It says she's down here.'

'Does it, though?' he replies. 'I thought her phone was offline. There's nothing to see this way, love. It's just a track to a farmer's field or something. I'll end up getting the car stuck if I'm not careful.'

'I don't care. Wherever it leads, keep bloody following it. This is the last location we have for her, and she was here not long ago. It's all we've got to go on. We need to find her urgently. She pulled a knife on Adrian, for God's sake. If it was anyone else, he'd have called the police. The only reason he hasn't is because I begged him not to, promising we'd find her and get to the bottom of this. Thank goodness she still has her mobile set up to send us her location.'

'I know we need to find her, love. That's why I dropped everything at work to be here with you, looking for her. But getting the car stuck isn't going to help anyone.'

'It won't get stuck. Carry on. I have a really bad feeling. We need to find her now. We'll be there in a minute.'

'Fine. Remind me what Carmen said when you phoned her before?'

Kate lets out a frustrated sigh. 'That Paige had strong evidence of Adrian being behind Jenna's disappearance.'

'What kind of evidence?'

'I don't know. I stopped listening. It's clearly nonsense, isn't it? Paige has lost the plot, and she's somehow persuaded Carmen to believe her.'

Danny frowns. 'There must be something in it, love. She's never done anything remotely like this before, even after what happened to her at uni. She's always been so sensible. If Carmen believed her, perhaps we should too. We should at least hear her out when we find her.'

'So you think it's true about Adrian? Oh, come on. I think it's more likely that she has delayed PTSD because of what happened at uni. Maybe it's been triggered by coming back from Australia. I told you before that I was worried she was getting obsessed about Jenna's supposed disappearance. I wanted to speak to her yesterday, but I didn't get a chance. I was going to say something tonight. Clearly I left it too late.'

'There's a building up ahead,' Danny says. 'An old farmhouse or something. Does that look about the right distance away on your phone?'

'Yes. It has to be there. See, I told you. Oh, I really hope she's all right.'

EIGHTY-THREE

Sarah

I wasn't intending to burn the house down like this. Before Paige showed up, my plan was to give Jenna a fatal overdose. Let her slip quietly away. Then leave her body here for a bit while I came up with a devious plan to get rid of it and escape scot-free. That said, I brought the petrol here a couple of days ago as a contingency measure in case things went to shit, as they clearly have.

Committing arson will draw attention to this place. It'll bring the emergency services here far sooner than they ever would otherwise, but it will also burn away lots of evidence. Plus, as long as I get to my car quickly enough, before the cottage really goes up and the smoke becomes noticeable, it will act as a nice distraction while I flee. That's why I did all the petrol dousing upstairs, so I can start the fire down here and hopefully it won't spread too fast initially. Then once it hits the first floor: *whoosh*.

Perhaps I could go home and pretend like nothing's happened for a bit. That would be bold, wouldn't it? But I fear what might come out after Paige's visit to Adrian earlier. Plus, there's that bloody laptop in play, wherever she left it. And I have no idea what she might have told her family and friends.

It was at least a stroke of luck that Paige's message to Kate and Danny didn't send.

So why haven't I started the fire already?

I'm at the back door, a windproof lighter in my hand, already burning, ready to drop onto the trail of old sheets and curtains I've laid out along the floor to the stairs.

But I can't let go of it.

I'm actually hesitating.

Have I reached my limit?

Sudden unexpected sounds from outside startle me. Make me jump. And in that moment, the decision is taken out of my hands. The lighter tumbles from my grip, and I flee in the opposite direction from the voices I heard. A man and a woman, I think.

EIGHTY-FOUR

Danny

'Over here,' he calls to his wife. 'There's a back door open. Something's burning inside.'

'Bloody hell,' Kate exclaims, raising a hand to her mouth as she catches up with him and peers through the back door. 'What's happening? What do we do? She's inside somewhere, Danny, I know she is. I can't tell you how, but I'm sure of it. We need to get her out.'

'We should call the fire service.'

'There's no time for that. The whole place will be ablaze before they can get here. We have to do something now. Paige is in trouble. She needs us. It looks like just a sheet or something that's burning at the moment. It can't have long started. See if you can put it out.'

'Okay. I...' Frantically, he looks all around, searching for something to try to dampen the flames. Before he can stop her, Kate pulls her T-shirt up over her mouth and nose, darts through the door, skirting the burning sheet, and disappears into the body of the house.

'Kate, no!' he calls, but it's too late. She's gone.

He's tempted to chase after her but decides he'd better concentrate on extinguishing the fire to ensure she can get safely back out.

Looking inside, it does just seem to be one burning sheet so far, assuming – hoping – there are no other seats of fire in the derelict cottage. But there is a pile of stuff in a row alongside the sheet, like someone put it there as part of a deliberate attempt to torch the place, which is very worrying.

He snaps a small branch from a nearby tree and, following Kate's example, covers his mouth and nose with his shirt. Then he darts inside and attempts to use the stick to drag the flaming sheet along the stone floor and out of the building.

To his horror, as he's concentrating on doing this without burning himself or inhaling smoke, the outside door slams shut with a bang, followed by a clicking sound like it's being locked from the other side.

'Hey, what the hell?' he shouts. 'There are people in here. You're going to kill us all.'

No reply.

Having confirmed the door is definitely locked, he slides the still flaming sheet into an empty corner. Should he use some of the other fabric stuff on the floor to try to smother the flames, like a fire blanket, or will that just spread it quicker? Crap. He's not sure. He should know this, but he's panicking. Can't think straight. Can't breathe properly. He runs in the direction Kate disappeared and shuts the inside door behind him, hopefully containing the blaze until they can find another way out.

He takes a big gulp of air. Oh my God, it reeks of petrol.

'Kate!' he calls. 'Where are you? We need to get out of here right now. Someone just shut us inside. We're going to have to smash our way out.'

'Up here. It's Paige. She's trapped.'

Thump.

Thump.
Thump.
Crash.
What now?

He tears up the staircase, where the smell of petrol is so strong it burns his throat. Kate has just shoulder-barged her way through a locked bedroom door. Inside, it's a scene straight out of his worst nightmare. Paige, wide-eyed and frantic, tied to a chair and gagged. And – no, it can't be – a deathly white Jenna sprawled unconscious on a mattress on the floor, also restrained.

'Danny!' Kate screams, snapping him out of his staggered stupor. 'We have to get them free. Do you have something sharp?'

'Um, I don't think... Hang on. Yes, I do.' As luck would have it, when Kate had called him out of work earlier, he'd been doing odd jobs about the business centre. Annoying little things the lazy-arse caretaker had skipped. He'd been using his multi-tool for this, which he'd stuck in his trouser pocket on the way out and forgotten about. Until now.

You beauty! It's perfect for cutting the girls free of their bindings, despite his shaking, sweat-coated hands. Moments later, he's carrying Jenna down the stairs in a fireman's lift while Kate follows, helping Paige.

There's no time for words. Explanations. Smoke is spreading, flames at its heels, and they have to get out.

Immediately. Any way possible.

It's all a blur.

He's on autopilot, barely conscious of what he's doing, as he gently places down Jenna's lifeless form and picks up a chunky old coffee table. Roaring a guttural war cry, he somehow finds the strength to hurl it through a half-rotten window, smashing it to pieces.

Then he's making sure everyone else is out before following them, coughing and gasping for air. Leading them all a safe distance away from the ramshackle horror house he never wants to see again.

Kate's calling someone. 'All of them,' she yells into her phone. 'Everyone.'

Paige is sobbing. Crouched at Jenna's side, desperately trying to wake her. Saying words that make no sense.

Danny can't speak.

Can hardly move.

What happened?

Little over an hour ago, he was fixing things at work. A dull, ordinary day.

Then his life imploded, like he'd crossed into a warped alternate reality where everything was messed up beyond belief.

Is he still there now, or back where he belongs, where things make some kind of sense?

He looks up to the incongruously calm summer sky and breathes. Just breathes. Says a silent prayer to the God he hasn't spoken to for so long.

And breathes.

EIGHTY-FIVE

Sarah

I was in a toilet cubicle in a service station on the M1, near Leicester, when they came for me.

I knew something was going on when I heard lots of whispering and shuffling about on the other side of the door. I prayed it was nothing to do with me, even though I knew in my heart it had to be. Next thing, cameras appeared above and below, and I was instructed in a no-nonsense police voice to come out, moving slowly and keeping my hands visible.

I think I was resigned to my fate by then. Possibly even before that. Having spent the previous night sleeping in my car in a grotty lay-by, I had started to realise that life on the run wasn't something I could realistically manage for long.

'No sudden movements,' I was instructed by the female officer whose head had appeared over the top of the cubicle.

Minutes later, I was arrested and put in cuffs.

I still don't know how they caught me. There I was, thinking I was doing all the right things to evade capture: those fake number plates on my car; not using my phone or bank cards;

heading somewhere random where I had no obvious links; not trying to leave the country. But they tracked me down in no time.

Should I have ditched my phone rather than just switching it off?

Who knows? Too late now.

So here I am in the back of a police van, travelling somewhere to be processed before the inevitable interviews begin.

Fuck.

It's mid-morning on Saturday. Not even a full day since I fled, having shut Kate and Danny in that dilapidated burning cottage together with Paige and Jenna. In for a penny, in for a pound, I thought, irritated by their sudden appearance, attempting to foil my plans. And yet it did surprise me how easily I threw them – my long-time neighbours, supposed friends – to the wolves. How I felt no hesitation, no remorse, no second thoughts whatsoever in doing so.

I'm not a very nice person, am I?

Anyhow, I heard on the news earlier that, against the odds, they'd all made it out okay.

I can't believe that whiny bitch Paige got the better of me. Although she did have help from her parents. If they hadn't shown up when they did, however they managed to track her down, she'd never have saved Jenna by herself. I'm sure of that.

With hindsight, it's probably just as well that they did find her. Better for me, now I've been caught, in terms of what I'll be charged with; what kind of prison time I might face. Not that I intend giving up without a fight. I'll be trying every last trick in the book to wriggle my way out of this.

I'm just getting started.

EIGHTY-SIX

TWO MONTHS LATER

Adrian

'Okay, that's the last of it,' he says to Zack, who's standing on the drive next to the car. 'The movers will meet us at the new place. Ready?'

'No.'

'Look, son, I know you don't want to leave, but it's for the best. We need a fresh start. Somewhere everyone isn't going to judge us all the time.'

'And somewhere you can afford without a doctor's salary.'

Yeah, that too, Adrian thinks, not rising to the bait. Not suggesting that, at the age of twenty-three, Zack could always get a place of his own instead. He might have moved in with Erin, his former fiancée, if she hadn't dumped him as soon as the news got out about Sarah.

Erin was one of many people who'd cut off all ties with him and his son because of what Sarah did. They were guilty by association in most people's eyes.

How could they not have known what she was truly like;

what she was up to? That seems to be the general consensus among former friends, neighbours, colleagues, the lot.

Neither of them had the foggiest. That's the truth. He and Zack are in total agreement about that. She hid that side of herself from them entirely, however implausible that might sound. Mind you, they probably weren't looking. Zack's still a young man, too wrapped up in himself to waste time thinking about his parents. And Adrian's been preoccupied with his own shit: work stress and his gambling habit, which he hasn't yet managed to knock on the head.

At least the work stress is gone for now. He's taken a sabbatical, on firm advice from above. But it's basically an easy way to leave his old surgery on the quiet. He'll look for another post elsewhere eventually, once money gets really tight. But the priority for now is getting himself and Zack settled in a place they can be invisible to ride out the inevitable storm of Sarah's trial, whenever that happens.

Apart from at early court appearances, neither of them has seen her since she was arrested. She's refused all visitors while on remand. And to be honest, Adrian's glad about that. It's probably easier this way. He has a million questions, like whether any of what she did was down to him, for a start. But he's not sure he's ready for the answers.

As for Zack, he wouldn't want to see her anyway. He's not once joined Adrian at court and barely speaks of his mother at all, other than to say how she's ruined his life.

Climbing into the driving seat of his car, Adrian spots a small shard of eggshell stuck to the outside of the windscreen. An unwelcome reminder of finding it covered in broken eggs after he parked it outside the supermarket the other day.

'For fuck's sake!' he cried out in exasperation at the time, drawing countless stares. 'It wasn't me. I didn't do anything. Why won't you all just leave me the hell alone?'

Back in the present, he addresses his son in a far quieter, more composed tone. 'Come on. Time to go.'

Zack gets into the passenger seat. 'No one, not one of our neighbours has come out to say goodbye. We're total outcasts. Thanks a bunch, Mum, you utter psycho.'

The irony of this bothering someone who barely made an effort with any of the neighbours isn't lost on Adrian. 'Don't talk about her like that,' he says, because he feels like he must. 'No matter what she's done, she's still your mother. She loves you like she always has.'

'Yeah, whatever.' Zack puts on his seat belt. 'Let's get out of this shithole and head to the next one.'

Adrian takes a deep breath. He can't muster the energy to reply. The lad's angry – and he has a right to be.

As he reverses the car off the drive for the final time, ready to leave this village he's given so much of his life to, Adrian scans the houses of his neighbours, thinking back to the barbecue at Danny and Kate's, which feels like a lifetime ago. They were his friends. He thought they had many years of summer barbecues ahead of them. And now they can barely meet his eye, never mind speak to him.

As for Jenna and Paige – the ones who suffered the most at Sarah's hands, along with the old man she killed – he has at least had the chance to apologise to them both in person. They were together at the time, at Jenna's house. They invited him inside, to the front room, which he hadn't expected. It was extremely awkward, but at least neither of them shouted and screamed at him or anything like that. In fact, Paige said sorry for pulling a knife on him and blaming him for Sarah's actions. Incredibly, Jenna also apologised for having an affair with his wife.

'It was nothing personal,' she told him. 'I just... fell head over heels for her. I guess I got what was coming to me.'

'Please, no. Neither of you have anything to apologise for.

I'm the one who's sorry. I should have seen what was going on right under my nose. I should have stopped her. Protected you both from her. Honestly, I had no idea what she was capable of.'

'Tell me about it,' Jenna replied.

Fragments of those words – that conversation – echo through Adrian's mind as he puts his foot on the accelerator and leaves their home behind.

The next time he'll see Jenna and Paige will almost certainly be at Sarah's trial.

EIGHTY-SEVEN

Paige

At least they caught Sarah. Her attempt to flee, thankfully, was no more successful than her attempt to kill Jenna, myself and both of my parents.

It's lucky I noted and reported that fake number plate she was using, because it was picked up on cameras at a motorway service station the morning after our rescue. The police pounced – doing their jobs very well this time; helping restore my faith in them a bit after what they put me through at uni.

As for what Sarah put us through, Jenna in particular... It would be easy to get consumed by that. To let the terrible memories eat us up and haunt us. Affect us for the rest of our lives. But we're trying not to let that happen, as best as anyone can. We're attempting to stay upbeat and to focus on the facts: she failed; she's now behind bars awaiting trial; she will, hopefully, remain in prison, where she belongs, for a very long time.

To try to take the edge off, we call her things like 'the psycho bitch' and laugh about her getting arrested while on the toilet.

You have to laugh. Otherwise, you'll cry. Something we've all done more than enough of since that awful day.

'I loved her,' Jenna told me, tears flowing during one such emotional moment. 'Like *really* loved her. I'd never felt like that about anyone before. It was my first time with a woman, and it felt so right, like everything suddenly made sense. And then it all turned to shit. Even after she treated me like crap, I let her back in, giving her the chance to abduct me. I mean, how could I love someone like that? I was so under her spell that on the night of the barbecue, when I knew she was out, I tricked my way past Zack into her bedroom so I could feel close to her again. To touch some of her things. To smell her perfume on her bedsheets. I even slipped one of her vest tops into my handbag, like a stalker. How weird and creepy is that? What does it say about me?'

'Nothing,' I told her. 'Her evil doesn't reflect on you at all. She fooled *everyone*. Not only you. You were human. You got to know her at an incredibly vulnerable time in your life, let her in and fell for her. You challenged her after the hit-and-run, told her it wasn't right, and she turned on you. You're her victim, Jenna. Her crimes say nothing about you. Nothing whatsoever.'

I can't tell you how many awful nightmares I've had since – and I know it's the same for poor Jenna. The slightest whiff of petrol is enough to make the hairs stand up on the back of my neck.

We're housemates now, by the way, Jenna and I. I've moved into her place rather than staying at home for ever, Lucas-style, like an eternal child. I'm in the spare room for now, although we've agreed I'll eventually have her mum's old room, once we find the right time to go through all her stuff together.

I'll also be urging her to go on dates with other girls, preferably not married and more age-appropriate, as soon as I think she's ready. She can't let what happened with Sarah stand in the way of her own happiness.

Right now, I don't think either of us has a clue about what we want to do with our adult lives, long-term. But we're still young, so time is on our side. Maybe more education is the answer. Maybe not. There could be further travelling at some point, although not for the time being. It would feel too much like running away, and neither of us wants to do that. Plus, there's the small matter of Sarah's trial to consider, in which we'll be the main witnesses. We intend to be as cooperative as possible with the prosecution to ensure she goes down and stays down.

We've been talking lately about the possibility of starting a small business together. Maybe opening a market stall or a little shop nearby. Nothing fancy. Just a way to get us out there, together, making a little cash and keeping us occupied. Baby steps. We haven't even decided what to sell yet. Try telling that to Jenna's excitable nieces, though. Jess and Amber have already allocated themselves Saturday jobs working for us; they won't even entertain the notion that they're still too young to be employed. They really do adore their Aunt Jenna, bless them.

As for Adrian and Zack, they moved out of the village the other day. I doubt they'll ever return. Who would want to?

Mum and Dad – my heroes for finding us and saving our lives – are doing okay, considering. They decided to delay the wedding anniversary trip to Lake Como, which was a shame, but they're still hoping to go in the near future. Thank God they came for us; that I'd given them the means to track me; that my location got shared despite the poor signal, like a guardian angel was watching over us. Otherwise, I don't see how Jenna and I would still be alive.

I could say 'I told you so' to everyone who dismissed my concerns about Jenna as fantasy, but what would that achieve?

They've all apologised to me so many times since, and so profusely – Becky and Scott in particular – I'm super over it. Becky's also been making more of an effort to be a big sister to

Jenna since all of this happened: checking in with her daily, popping around more often and inviting her over for meals and stuff. About time. I hope it continues.

She'll never have the same bond I do with Jenna, though, which is stronger today than ever. Becky might be her sister in blood, on paper, but I'm her chosen sister, and she's mine.

When Jenna disappeared, I *knew* in my heart, my gut, whatever you want to call it, that she wasn't all right.

I can't explain how. I knew, that's all.

Mum said much the same about me being trapped in that creepy old cottage, which was why she raced in there despite the flames. She *felt* I was inside. She was certain.

Some things can't be explained.

Others can, like Scott's eye for the ladies and lingering hugs, which I now think may have been caused, or at least worsened, by a drinking problem. He's suddenly, unexpectedly gone teetotal. According to Jenna, he attends AA meetings several times a week. And he's definitely more reserved than before. I've no idea how much he was drinking or how often. It's not something I ever picked up on. But good for him and his family that he's taken himself in hand.

In other news, there have been some interesting developments regarding what caused me to drop out of uni. Or should I say *who* caused me to quit: that lying pervert Jeff and his nasty wife, Gail. Yeah, they got off scot-free, making me look like a liar. Or so they thought.

Revenge is a dish best served cold, right?

Let me tell you, it tastes even better when it's handed to you on a plate, unexpectedly, by your amazing friend Carmen.

She's off travelling the world now, but before she left, she gave me a cryptic phone call.

'I have a surprise for you. Check the news tomorrow. Maybe focus your search on where we met.'

'What do you mean?' I asked her, confused. 'We met at uni. I don't understand.'

'You will. It's something I've had slow-cooking for a while. I wanted to wait until I was well and truly out of there before flicking the switch, so to speak. It's my going-away gift to you. A small piece of what you deserve, especially after everything you've been through lately. I'll see you when I get back, yeah?'

It was one heck of a gift.

Someone – I couldn't possibly imagine who – had hacked Jeff and Gail's home computer, which contained lots of photos and a couple of video clips of the pair of them in compromising scenarios. We're talking various stages of undress and with numerous other parties – many significantly younger – swinging, dogging... You get the idea. And this nameless hacker had dumped the lot, each captioned #Jeff&Gail #PervsRUs #Jail, all over the university intranet, as well as on the computer systems of various other nearby businesses and institutions, including Gail's employers. The faces of everyone else involved had been blurred out. But there was no mistaking Jeff and Gail.

A university spokesperson said: 'This was a highly sophisticated, targeted attack, most likely involving a team of very skilled hackers.'

It made the national tabloids, where it was announced that a shamed Jeff had quit his university post. Gail had also left her job, it was reported, and the pair planned to retire.

Good riddance, and hopefully an end to their predatory ways.

Carmen – legend – gave me closure on that horrible chapter of my life, which I now hope to put behind me once and for all.

I couldn't wish for better friends than her and Jenna. I'd love for the three of us to hang out when Carmen returns from her travels. Spending time with someone so comfortable in her own skin would be great for Jenna as she moves on with her life.

Hopefully, it should also help to watch the woman who

tried to murder us squirm in the dock as details of all the despicable things she did are finally shared with the general public. I suspect she'll plead not guilty. She's a good liar; I know that as well as anyone. But I can't see any right-minded jury siding with her over me and Jenna. The police assure me that despite the fire at the cottage, there's plenty of evidence to convict.

Fingers crossed.

My intuition is telling me not to worry, and I've learned to listen to it.

Trusting my gut did save my best friend's life, after all. She let out a cry for help that everyone else ignored, but I heard her.

A LETTER FROM S.D. ROBERTSON

Dear reader,

Thank you very much for choosing to read *The Cry*. If you enjoyed it and want to keep up to date with all my latest releases, just sign up at the following link. Your email address will never be shared, and you can unsubscribe at any time.

www.bookouture.com/s-d-robertson

This is my second psychological suspense novel with Bookouture, and again, I've really enjoyed expanding on the darker, grittier side of my writing while staying rooted in the domestic sphere of my earlier novels. I've also enjoyed having a larger cast of key characters than previously, which definitely kept me on my toes when I was writing and editing.

My starting point for this story was the cry that all the neighbours hear at the beginning of the book and from which it takes its title.

It's a concept that had been in the back of my mind for several years before I sat down to write this novel. What if a group of friends at a barbecue heard a terrible scream from somewhere nearby, wrote it off as kids messing around, and then later discovered something really bad had happened?

I often thought about this after jotting the idea down in my notebook, but I couldn't quite decide where to take it. Until now.

I hope you loved *The Cry*; if you did, I would be very grateful if you could write a review. I'd really like to hear what you think, and it makes such a difference in helping new readers discover one of my novels for the first time.

It's always great to hear from my readers – you can get in touch through my website or on social media.

Thanks again,

Stuart

www.sdrobertsonauthor.com

 facebook.com/sdrobertsonauthor

 x.com/sdrauthor

 instagram.com/sdrobertsonauthor

threads.net/@sdrobertsonauthor

ACKNOWLEDGEMENTS

So here we are. My eighth published novel and my second psychological thriller. Cheers to everyone who's helped me get to this point. It's very much appreciated.

Specific thanks, in no particular order, must go to:

My superb literary agent, Pat Lomax, who's always there for me with sage advice whenever I need her.

My excellent editor, Lydia Vassar-Smith, whose insight really helped to shape and focus this story, pushing me to produce my best work.

Jane Selley, Lynne Walker, Mandy Kullar and Jen Shannon for their diligence during the crucial final stages of the editorial process.

Jess Readett, Kim Nash, Sarah Hardy and Noelle Holten, from my publisher's brilliant publicity team, as well as all the other Bookouture staff working hard behind the scenes, dedicated to making this book a success.

My incredibly supportive family and friends, particularly my wonderful wife, daughter, parents, and sister, for always being in my corner with positivity, patience and support. Kirsten was incredibly helpful as the first proofreader of this book and an invaluable adviser when it came to honing the language and behaviour of my younger characters.

My readers, new and old, for investing your time in my work and for helping to spread the word via recommendations and enthusiastic reviews. As always, your support means the world to me.

PUBLISHING TEAM

Turning a manuscript into a book requires the efforts of many people. The publishing team at Bookouture would like to acknowledge everyone who contributed to this publication.

Audio
Alba Proko
Sinead O'Connor
Melissa Tran

Commercial
Lauren Morrissette
Hannah Richmond
Imogen Allport

Cover design
Eileen Carey

Data and analysis
Mark Alder
Mohamed Bussuri

Editorial
Lydia Vassar-Smith
Lizzie Brien

Printed in Great Britain
by Amazon